A REMEDY
FOR ALL THINGS

by
Jan Fortune

Liquorice Fish
Books

L/FB 31

D0260576

70001728329 2

Published by Liquorice Fish Books, an imprint of Cinnamon Press,
Meirion House, Tanygrisiau, Blaenau Ffestiniog, Gwynedd, LL41 3SU
www.cinnamonpress.com/index.php/liquorice-fish-books/about

All rights reserved by the authors. The right of each contributor to be identified
as the author of their work has been asserted by them in accordance with the
Copyright, Designs and Patent Act, 1988.

Copyright © 2018 Jan Fortune.

ISBN: 978-1-911540-04-5

British Library Cataloguing in Publication Data. A CIP record for this book
can be obtained from the British Library.

All rights rese   stored in
a retrieval sy: ectronic,
mechanical, ¡   r written
permission o   t, resold
or otherwise   or cover
other than tl   t of the
publishers.

This is a wo   incidents
are either di   sly. Any
resemblance   ncidental
except when

Book design

Haringey Libraries	
CC	
Askews & Holts	20-Mar-2019
AF	
	3400027082

Printed in Poland.

Cinnamon Press is represented in the UK by Inpress Ltd www.inpressbooks.co.uk
and in Wales by the Welsh Books Council www.cllc.org.uk

The publisher gratefully acknowledges the support of the Welsh Books
Council.

Supported using public funding by
ARTS COUNCIL
ENGLAND
LOTTERY FUNDED

Thanks to the many people who have assisted with the journey of this book:

to my family for their constant support,

to the writing groups who have attended courses I've taught at Ty'n y coed and listened to early drafts,

to Arts Council England for making the research in Budapest possible,

to George Szirtes for his kindness in helping me make connections in Budapest and for help with Hungarian spellings,

to Lászl Kúnos and Gábor Schein for being so generous with their time,

to the staff of the Attila József Memorial Room in Gát utca,

to the staff of Pohárszék Bor & Kávé, Budapest, who kept me supplied with water and coffee through several drafts,

to Anne Clarke for meticulous copy editing,

to Irene Hill of in-words, Greenwich, and Judit of Massolit Books & Café, Budapest, for their assistance with launches,

and to Adam Craig, for listening to drafts, feedback and being endlessly supportive.

To Cottia and Seth
who each have their own ways of seeing life as it should be.

And to Adam, always.

When life itself seems lunatic, who knows where madness lies? Perhaps to be too practical is madness. To surrender dreams — this may be madness. ... — and maddest of all: to see life as it is, and not as it should be.

...

There is a remedy for all things but death.

Miguel de Cervantes, *Don Quixote*

Catherine

In the dream Catherine is not herself.

She enters the yard, walls rising, blind, mute, slabbing out sky, yet its granite light dazzles after the cell's gloom. She has an urge to bolt, run back to the blanketing shadows. Her guts twist. She lurches forward, knotting muscles to hold back piss, shit. Behind her, sharp fingers. She stumbles into a faceless quadrangle, huddles an eyeless wall. Someone is telling her to walk, walk — one foot, the next, right foot, left. Air ices lungs, skin burns cold, muscles tremble in unfamiliar shuffle. Behind her, other feet shamble. Don't look back. Stagger on — one foot, the next, bleak wall grasped for balance. Don't cry. Don't fall. Don't piss. Chant in her head: right foot, left foot, right... Falling — snow — falling, one flake, another, soft, as she sinks onto knees, hands, frozen flakes caressing her neck, hands hauling her out of the yard where women shamble, one foot, the next, women mute as walls, not looking as she is dragged back to the cell, soiled, wet, shivering.

On the wall, a list of dates chalked with a chipping of crumbled stone, the last one — Friday 6 November 1959. She huddles into a threadbare blanket, falls into a fitful sleep where...

on another day in Selene's life —

a train sounds in the distance

Oh!

What is it? You look pale.

I'm fine now. One of those moments when you feel as though someone walked over your grave. Selene laughs. I thought I heard a train and then all the blood in me ran cold.

You need to eat more, Zsófia retorts, you're far too thin. Tell me more about Paris while we finish these sheets. Your parents really knew Brassaï? Why on earth did they ever leave? Isn't your mother French? I can't imagine choosing this miserable place instead of somewhere so romantic.

So many questions! Selene says. Yes, we knew Gyula Halász. I was about nine when my parents met him. He seemed to know everyone. And yes, my mother is from Paris — she met Papa when he was an art student, but we came back when I was thirteen — it got harder to work and Papa thought the Nazis would invade France. Mama has always hated Hungary and I'd known only Paris since I was tiny so I felt the same at first, but Papa thought he'd done the right thing, especially when Paris fell... Not that it's been any easier here in the end...

Zsófia puts a hand on Selene's arm as her words trail away.

Papa didn't survive the Munkaszolgálat. Life as an art-dealer wasn't much of a preparation for forced labour and starvation, but if he'd lived...

He'd probably have been seen as a class enemy?

Selene nods. A middle-class Jew — I suppose he'd have been forced out of Budapest or worse.

Zsófia folds another sheet onto a pile of crisp white linen.

There are only three sorts of Hungarians, she says, those who've been to jail, those in jail and those who will be in jail. So we must be the third sort.

Not everything is so bad, Selene says. The price of bread never changes.

Pah! Don't give me that spiel about how we're all in it together — everyone poor and patriotic. Everyone except the political elite.

All animals are equal, but some are more equal than others, eh?

Pardon?

It's a quote from an English book. *Animal Farm.*

You're far too clever to be stuck here. How do you even get these books?

Mama has family in England. Her sister married there.

It's a good quote. The elite aren't in it with us. They just want to keep us compliant and don't mind using terror to do it.

Maybe it will end, Selene says.

Zsófia looks around the empty linen room, drops her voice to a whisper. Radio Free Europe says there's growing resistance.

I saw that on a leaflet, but Mama wouldn't approve of me 'getting involved'.

How is she?

She talks about going back 'home', but her spirit's gone. She seems so old, Zsófia, but she's barely fifty.

11

Maybe you should have been a psychiatric nurse instead.

Selene smiles weakly. I chose nursing in the hope I'd be able to help, be more understanding and patient, but perhaps I'm too close to her to help. Anyway, I soon realised I wanted to work with cancer patients, not...

Lunatics?

Zsófia, really! She's just depressed. I get low myself sometimes. I feel so responsible for her. You know, this building used to be for psychiatric patients? It was the Siesta Sanatorium. Klaus Mann came here for a heroin cure.

Who?

He wrote *Mephisto* and his father wrote *The Magic Mountain*, about a sanatorium for rich people, and...

You've read everything, haven't you?

Not everything. Selene laughs. But some things — Attila József was here too.

Ah, now him I've heard of.

I should hope so. He was here after his final breakdown — July '37.

And afterwards he went to Balatonszárszó and killed himself?

Yes. So sad.

All Hungarians are sad, Zsófia asserts. Wasn't he in Paris before he got so depressed? Someone else who should have stayed there. Did you know him too?

Silly girl! He left Paris when I was a toddler with very little

12

interest in poetry but apparently he visited my parents' gallery once. There — all done. Selene stands back and surveys their work. Now we can eat.

Good, Zsófia agrees.

I'll meet you downstairs, Selene says, parting from her friend at the crossroads of two long corridors.

Her shoes click on the new green linoleum of the National Institute of Oncology. As she walks, she thinks she hears a train, feels a wave of cold air, rubs her arms and tells herself Zsófia is right. She must stop running out of the house without breakfast in the mornings, it's making her light-headed, but since the pay cuts it's harder to support her mother. She pauses, aware of the faint sweet scent of oranges, blinks as a patch of light floats before her, trailing darkness behind. Not now, she says to herself. You have to work. The citrus aroma intensifies and she feels pressure over her left eye. In the distance a train sounds. She feels gooseflesh rise, turns a corner into another corridor that is not a corridor, but a green path through a meadow running down towards a lake...

Selene walks along a sandy bank. Lake Balaton, she says to no one.

The air is brittle, the lake planished beneath late autumn sun that has torn a hole in the ragged clouds. Selene shivers, folds her arms over the thin cotton of her blue-grey tunic, tugs off the white cap that is useless against the icy air. Not a single boat. No noise but the breeze shushing water. In the distance a train sounds. Selene walks towards clatter and shrill, approaches a bank, draws in a sharp breath as a man turns at the sound of her approach.

Thick brows knit. I startled you?

13

He peers at her and she wonders if she should try to explain her odd dress, a nurse out for a stroll at Lake Balaton, but she is too disoriented to describe her path from the hospital corridor and in any case he looks —

Sorry, you… you look like someone — like Attila József, in fact.

We have met before?

No, I don't think we…

But you know my name?

Sorry?

Attila József.

You're…?

When she comes round he has put his coat under her head in the dust.

So sorry, she whispers. I've only had black coffee today. I was on my way to the canteen for lunch — vegetables and potatoes again no doubt, but… She registers his brows knit in puzzlement, Sorry, I'm babbling. I'm a little light-headed. I was feeling hungry and worrying about my mother and I don't know how I found myself here and I thought you said your name was Attila József.

Please don't faint again, but that is my name. I'm just surprised you knew me.

I've seen photographs of you, read your books… but you… What are you doing near the tracks? You mustn't — I mean…

He wipes a hand across his forehead, lays it on hers. I've liked watching trains since I was a boy, though they make me sad since — I saw someone die once — in Budapest — I was only a child and felt as though that person had died in my place, but I remain fascinated. In dark moments I've even put my hat on the rails…

Oh!

He smiles. But not today, he says, placing a hand on his hat. And your name is?

Selene. Selene Solweig Virág. I'm a nurse at the new National Institute of Oncology. You would have known it as Siesta Sanatorium.

I'm not sure I understand. That place is still there. I was there recently —

Yes, it's still there for you, but for me… I'm not sure how to say this. For me, it's not 1937, or it wasn't only half an hour ago.

He looks bemused, feels her head again.

I'm not mad or ill. I'm just not from… I'm sorry —

Well, you are certainly beautiful and have a beautiful name — moon and sun and flowers in one. It's an unusual name, not Hungarian I think — and unique, he pauses, tilts his head to one side — and yet I can't help thinking I've heard it before… He shakes his head. No, can't quite recall…

Selene smiles. In Paris, perhaps? I was a young child when you visited my parents' art gallery. Sándor Virág and Marie Spire…

Yes, I recall. I swept up a little girl and twirled her in the air.

And you told me to remember you, Selene says, smiling.

Though I think my parents must have told me about the meeting. Even though it feels like a memory. And — as for the rest of the name — Austrian grandmother, Hungarian father, though his father adopted Virág rather than Haas when he arrived in Hungary.

Ah, yes — I too am a mongrel, so much so that my stepfather of a short while said...

that your name didn't exist. He called you Pista, but you ran away, back to your mother in Budapest and discovered you shared your name with King Attila the Hun. You wrote that this made you who you became — someone who would not take the opinions of others for granted, but would always do his own thinking.

Extraordinary, he says quietly.

Selene sits up. I'm fine now; thank you, just rather dusty. Sorry about your jacket. She gets to her feet.

It's nothing, he says, beating it so that dust flies.

I can tell you the name of the poem you will give Flóra when she visits, Selene says. 'You Came With a Stick', and also —

She sees him pale and stops speaking.

So perhaps you are from the future Selene Solweig Virág — or perhaps I am making you up. I've been suffering a lot —

No! You're not imagining me. You mustn't think there's anything wrong with you. It's just hard to understand. For me too.

So you must know the manner of my death? He asks.

Oh!

16

That would be yes, but you are right, it's too cruel to make you tell me. I'm afraid my sisters will be expecting me back. They get anxious if I'm gone too long.

Of course. I'll walk back to the lake and hope I find my way. Selene laughs nervously.

After they've said goodbye, she watches him walk towards the village, retraces her steps, telling herself that she is shaking simply because of the November chill. At the lakeside, she walks across the meadow towards the path, hears a distant train, the click of her feet on new green linoleum...

Selene! You've been nearly ten minutes, Zsófia says. We'll miss lunch.

Only ten minutes?

Pardon? Are you okay? You look pale.

Sorry, it's nothing. A little headache. She links her arm through Zsófia's. I'm so hungry today. Let's hope for fat potatoes and a good sauce on the vegetables.

Budapest: Saturday 6 November 1993

Arrived! Odd to be here alone after two months with Simon, but Margit and András, my contacts at the university, met me at the station and even left me food for the first day: cherry yoghurt and a Kakaós Csiga, a sweet swirl of 'chocolate snail' pastry for breakfast and, for this evening, a pot of lecsó — peppers, onions, tomatoes and eggs, made rich with hot paprika, plus bananas, apples and coffee.

So tired after travelling overnight — bathed and fell asleep before tasting the food. Now I'm ravenous, writing while the water for the coffee boils, trying to clear my head of dreams.

This 'Downtown' area of Budapest has been beautiful — art nouveau and art deco buildings on every street, leaded glass over ornate wooden doors, but so many facades are crumbling or ingrained with dirt, ornate balconies peeled of paint, their metal tarnishing or rusting. The apartment I'm in has a shabby door to the street, tucked between a restaurant and an indoor food market. There's a long hallway with chequered-tiles on the floor and what must once have been shiny blue tiles on the walls, up the staircase that spirals the rim of the building. The tiles are chipped, cracked or missing in places and the banisters are grimy, as though the building is exhaling dust.

Glad I only had one flight to climb and András carried my case. The apartment is at the back of the building, wrought iron grilles over the windows that look into the central courtyard, so there is not much light and the walls rising above me block out the sky. But it's very clean, has a small galley kitchen at one end of the living area and there's a little desk as well as the dining table, so I'll be able to set up a proper writing space. There's also a dressing table in the spare bedroom that will work as a writing room for Simon when he arrives.

The tub in the bathroom is cavernous and the plumbing noisy and slow, but the bath filled eventually and it was wonderful to soak away the dust and the spirits of all the places I'd passed through on the long train journey.

All I want now is to eat, then sleep again, hopefully without dreaming that I'm someone else — Selene Solweig Virág, a prisoner at the end of the Fifties, but in the bizarre illogic of dreams she was also someone who knew Attila József in his final year. I dreamt she was working in a hospital, folding sheets in a linen room, then walking long corridors. I knew, in the way that things are certain in dreams, that it was today's date, first in 1959, then 1952 — a dream within a dream. And she seemed to be experiencing aura — migraine or dissociation? — She turned a corner and was walking towards the lake at Balatonszárszó, the 'Hungarian sea' of the land-locked country. It was the same date still, but fifteen years earlier. I'm sure there is no mention of her in the books or articles I've read about József and, in any case, there is no way a young woman from the Fifties could have been a young woman who knew him in the Thirties. All very odd. But still, I'm glad József's insinuating himself into my unconscious, however strangely. In the dream he reminded me of Simon. I've never noticed a resemblance from photographs, but there was something about the eyes — dark, not blue, but deep-set — questioning, intelligent, but with an uncertainty I've seen at times...

A dense dream, the sort that clings — but looking forward to researching József further. So far this book has been slow. I need to move on with new projects and this one has me fascinated.

I always wonder what Miriam would make of any new place I visit. Four years since she died. I carry her with me, reminded of her daily by the damascene hamsa I found — or was given in a dream of her — in Toledo. I hear her telling me: until death, it's all life, Cassie — there's a remedy for all things, except death. Only my mother calls me Cassie now. And no one will ever call me Casilda again.

So much happens in so little time...

I must eat and sleep. But this afternoon I'll explore the neighbourhood — home for the next month — and then go to meet Margit and András at the university.

Selene Solweig

Falling — snow — falling, one flake, another, soft, as she sinks onto knees, hands, frozen flakes caressing her neck, hands hauling her out of the yard where women shamble, one foot, the next, women mute as walls, not looking as she is dragged back to the cell, soiled, wet, shivering on the bench, where she remembers Zsófia, a day working together when the Institute was new. It was the first day they spoke the word 'resistance' to one another. Zsófia had joked that there are only three sorts of Hungarians, but Zsófia was a fourth sort of Hungarian.

Her mind drifts to Miriam. She tries to picture what her daughter might look like now, says her name out loud, a hoarse supplication to a blank wall. I'm still here, Selene whispers to Miriam or to herself, sinking into a state between sleep and unconsciousness —

slipping into another body that moves through an era that has not yet been, sensing the day as if she is a woman whose name has mutated across thirty-two years: Cassie, Kat, Casilda, Kitty, Catherine; a woman writing a book about Selene's lover, Attila, who died more than twenty years ago in a time that she slips into at unexpected moments. She has not seen Attila for almost a year; December 1 1958, two days before his death in 1937. Was that their last meeting?

In the dream Selene is not herself —

Selene Solweig Virág? Margit asks. Unusual names. No I've certainly never heard of her in connection with Attila József. You've read Flóra Kozmutza's memoirs and letters, of course?

Yes, Catherine agrees. Márta Vágó in the late Twenties, Judit Szántó during his time in the Communist Party and various nurses who treated him before Flóra. I got the impression Selene was another nurse, perhaps someone he knew at the end of his life.

And what did your source say about her? András asks. You read about her in…?

That's the thing, Catherine says, Stupid really — it must have been one of those Internet searches I did and haven't kept the website address. I can't seem to find it again. Maybe I just dreamt her, she says with a nervous laugh.

Maybe you did, Margit agrees, your mind finding a new character for the novel, perhaps? It is fiction after all.

Yes, Catherine assents.

But properly researched, András puts in. After all, József is an important figure and the book should be as true to him as possible.

Oh, András! Really! That's far too literal. Catherine isn't researching a biography. You've read her first novel — people live through centuries, swap souls across time. An invented character to illustrate something in József's life would be a fascinating device.

Well… I don't know…

We have this all the time, Margit says, cutting off her colleague and turning to Catherine. He has the same over-literal approach to poetry translation. Impossible! You've read what Thomas Kabdebo says, András, she says, addressing him again.

Yes, but…

No buts at all. Poetry translation must take account of culture, sociology, semantics, style, but above all it must capture the essence of the poem or the nuance is lost; any irony or humour wiped out. Literal translations are dogmatic, lifeless — there must be association of ideas, my friend. You agree, Catherine?

I'm afraid I do, she replies, smiling at András. It's a discussion I've had many times as an editor, especially working with Italian poets.

See? Margit asks, I knew I was right. And if we need creativity in translation how much more so in fiction?

It's not… András begins tentatively. Not that I don't see your point. I'm just aware of how people might misinterpret the book or react against it if they think it's a historical novel and then it turns out to be something entirely different.

Catherine nods. I hadn't actually thought of including Selene until this conversation. And I see why you're anxious, but it's an interesting idea. There are lots of judgements to be made after all — was the diagnosis of schizophrenia correct or did József suffer borderline personality disorder? Was the death a suicide or a terrible accident? I have to imagine answers to so many unanswerables and Selene might be a device for doing that, though I'm not sure how at the moment.

Well I would only advise caution, András adds, and as for the question of József's death, it was certainly suicide. He…

Pah, to caution! Margit cuts in. Though I agree about his death

— suicide fits the logic of József's life completely. But of course there is doubt in even the most likely things, and in a novel… Anyway, let's show Catherine around the department and then find a good restaurant to continue this discussion in.

Definitely suicide, András insists. I like what you say about logic — yes — his end is absolutely consistent with the life.

Well, it's good to have some agreement. Margit winks at Catherine. A rare event, which we can celebrate with dinner. Our guest needs food and drink.

András chuckles. On that we also agree, dear friend.

Százéves Étterem? Margit asks as they walk through the corridors of Eötvös Loránd University.

Perfect, András says. Piarista utca is just ten minutes if you don't mind walking, he adds, turning to Catherine. We will see the Erzsébet Bridge as we go.

Sounds lovely.

Well, it's the oldest restaurant in the city, Margit says. Rather touristy really, but you are a visitor and should go there once. After this we will eat at real places.

Catherine laughs. Fair enough.

They sit at a table with crisp white linen that reminds Catherine of hospital sheets. There are dark wooden benches with curved backs and table lamps that give an amber glow to the hearty food. Catherine chooses a warming goulash soup while her new friends eat goose liver pate and continue squabbling amiably about the philosophy of translation. The contention continues as András devours a giant steak and Margit attacks a leg of pork. Catherine chooses a baby chicken with vegetables and jasmine rice and hears someone saying, Let's hope for fat potatoes and a good sauce on the vegetables.

Oh, but you must, Margit insists when Catherine declines a dessert. The sweet dumplings here are perfect — or the pancakes.

Catherine chooses a plate of fruit and consents to taste Margit's kecskemeti barack pudding, a sweet apricot concoction, and András's Gundel pancake, all washed down with glasses of tokaji.

Hold utca, 15, Budapest V.
Saturday 6 November 1993.

Dear Simon

My first full day in Budapest has been busy and interesting. The apartment is in an art deco building on Hold utca— I might have been a bit intimidated by it if I'd arrived alone. It's seen grander times, but it's cosy and clean. The university is about a half hour walk away or I can take a bus from Arany János utca if I'm in a hurry. Margit and András are delightful — they bicker like a proverbial old couple and if they have their way I'll put on a stone in dumplings before you even get here — but they know everyone in academic circles and are so eager to help with the research.

I had a bizarre dream last night. It seemed to be about one of Attila József's lovers, except that she couldn't have existed — not only was she a young woman in prison in 1959, as a result of the '56 uprising, but in the dream she appeared to move between time periods and only to meet József in the last month of his life. She's haunted me all day — I don't mean as a memory, but as though she has moved through the day with me, or even in me. I can't shake the feeling that she is real, despite knowing it makes no sense. Margit suggested I use her in the novel, which András objected to — he's worried about historical accuracy — but I think Margit is right — it would add a way of exploring his diagnosis and how his life ended.

I didn't expect any strangeness and mystery in my research here, but perhaps I always make it happen, so it could turn out that both of our novels will deal with the odd — or maybe it is simply the case that life is bizarre and inexplicable. Miriam, as you know, was a fan of Quixote, and never tired of reminding me that the unreason of the world is more insane than any fiction. Surely, that's true. Of course, she also used to tell me that I'm gullible — 'belief is your gift' was her romantic way of phrasing it. Perhaps I'm too suggestible. I often wonder how much of any given day I'm simply making up — I sometimes still think I'm making you up — it seems so unlikely that I could find a soul-mate — but I digress. What I'm trying to write, circuitously, is that this woman I dreamt — Selene Solweig Virág — feels like someone I know and the fact that she seems to slip through time seems eminently reasonable, even quotidian. Does that make sense? Have you ever come across the idea of Tanasukh? It's an Islamic theory of the transmigration of souls, a heretical notion, but one adopted by Sufis, who also believe in bunuz — that one soul can project into another. I can't shake the feeling that Selene is doing just that — sending her soul into mine, or I'm sending mine into hers. You are the only person I could write this to and not be considered certifiable, but I still worry that it must sound ridiculous.

Anyway, I sat down to write how much I'm missing you, how much I'm looking forward to you joining me here, and instead have bombarded you with questions and speculation, so I'll change tack.

How are you? How goes the research in Prague? Did you meet the curator at the Castle archive? I'm expecting photographs of the grimoires and homunculi! Hope you are finding lots of material for your book and that Prague is brimming with secrets, history dissolving into myth at every turn.

Keep safe.

Much love & yours always,
Catherine xx

Catherine

Each night, Catherine dreams the life of Selene; dreams that are nightmares.

On the wall of scratched dates — Thursday 7 November 1959. She huddles beneath a threadbare blanket, falls into a fitful sleep, dreams of life before the *farradalom*, the 'boiling over of the masses' — uprising…

Zsófia makes a slight grimace meant only for Selene to see. They stand in line with the other hospital staff listening to a reading from *Free People*. Finishing the article, the party secretary looks up and scans the lines.

It is a pleasure to see that so many comrades have already subscribed to the peace loans to help our great country, he says. These are hard times for all of us as we resist imperialism, but even in difficult times we are provided for —

Zsófia makes a small snorting sound and István Bálint stops, takes off his wire-rimmed spectacles and peers.

— well provided for and any loyal Hungarian is glad to

contribute to our general welfare. Of course these contributions are voluntary, but if anyone here has so far overlooked the opportunity to make a difference to our national security, let me assure you your donation will be gratefully received. He coughs, replaces his spectacles. You will find new rotas posted. However there are many gaps and no doubt you will be eager to take solidarity shifts, also voluntary, of course.

As Zsófia and Selene line up at the rota board, Zsófia points to a new poster, garish and blocky, a picture of a footballer under the slogan 'Magical Magyars to Strike a Blow for Freedom', advertising the upcoming international match at Wembley between the Mighty Magyars and the English.

Maybe some of them will have the sense not to return, Zsófia whispers, as she and Selene walk towards their ward.

I don't think they're the sort who would defect, Selene says.

Perhaps — but Kovach and Rabovsky did it.

But they were dancers — artists — thinking people, not footballers — and they were lucky — what's the chance of finding a subway under your hotel that will take you to the West?

Very romantic and good luck to them.

Shh, Selene warns as they near the ward. Even saying their names brings suspicion and I don't like the way Boglárka watches you. There are always informers.

Yes, and to think we thought Stalin's death would make a difference, Zsófia agrees.

It's early days, Selene insists. Nagy will make things better. He's already reigning in the ÁVH and dissolving internment camps…

Boglárka walks towards them and they fall silent.

Zsófia, Selene says in her fitful sleep. Miriam!

She half-dreams, half conjures this day two years earlier…

Get up! Filthy Jew! The guard at the door spits. Stinks in here. Get up. Move!

Selene stumbles to her feet.

Quick!

Where?

The rubber truncheon sends her to the floor. She clutches at the pain blazing her kidney.

Get up now! Don't ask questions. He roughly ties her hands behind her back, fastens her feet together with a chain. Walk, he commands.

Selene pulls herself up the wall, staggers ahead of the guard who throws a blanket over her head as she reaches the cell door. She bumps into a wall and he laughs, prods her into the corridor with his baton, roughly guides her with it as she staggers on, or occasionally prods the burning kidney, tittering to himself as she winces and arches forward. She loses track of the turns in corridors.

Stop.

Selene leans against the rough wall as the guard clatters keys into a cell door.

Welcome to hell, the guard says and laughs, goading Selene forward, pulling off the blanket as she stumbles into through the door.

There is no bench, no thin, rough blanket. She thinks of the detention cell at Andrássy út, 60 where she had spent three nights when she was arrested last November. She had planned to join the march of women planned in early December — thirty thousand women who would dress in black to mourn the lost uprising and walk in silent protest, but instead she'd spent the day in a detention cell that was no more than a basement pit, barely a metre across, yet only half a metre from where the elegant boulevard ran, with its neo-renaissance facades, opera house and ordinary life — so close and unreachable — Andrássy út, renamed Stalin út since 1950, and briefly, with so much hope, the Avenue of Hungarian Youth — Magyar Ifjúság út.

The new cell is almost as airless, almost as small, the tiny window high in the wall is covered with bars, roughly painted over like the one in Andrássy út, but without the twin bare light bulbs that had glared at her at eye level, day and night. She slumps against a wall, hugging the pain in her right side while the guard takes off the chain, yanks the rough binding from her wrists.

Well, you wanted a trial and now you will get one — a fair trial from the People's Court.

Catherine wakes sobbing, tangled in sheets and blankets. It is 3 a.m., but she won't sleep until she writes the nightmare away. Simon often teases that she doesn't know her own thoughts until she's written them in her journal. She makes mint tea and sits at the little polished desk in the high-ceilinged living room.

Budapest: Sunday 7 November 1993

Another nightmare that I am Selene Solweig Virág. I dreamt of a conversation with her colleague and friend at the hospital in 1953, the early months of Nagy's presidency, and then was back in 1957, and in prison. I (I mean 'she'!) had been in gaol for a year without trial and was moved to a cramped, dark cell, without even the tiny folding table in the wall or the open metal toilet in one corner, herded there by a bully who struck her with a rubber baton and thought it funny. (Her or me? It felt like me, but I also knew it was happening to Selene)

In her sleep, before the vile guard arrived, she called out for Miriam.

I can't shake the feeling that Selene is a real person, bizarre as that seems. I also can't rid myself of the idea that she is connected with Attila József, despite knowing that she would have been only about ten years old when József died. Her name nags at the corner of my consciousness and I'm sure I've heard it before... Something Miriam once said about former lives...

A large part of me doesn't want to revisit those thoughts. I'm here in this world in the late twentieth century. I'm Catherine Anne McManus, getting on with ordinary life. But something else in me whispers that nothing in this world can ever be commonplace or logical in the face of how ingenious humanity's inhumanity can be or in the face of human suffering.

Selene Solweig

Selene scratches the date onto the wall. Almost three years. She thinks of the grim cell she was taken to — how long ago? two years? — where she awaited trial. All through the first year she had kept hopeful — reciting poetry, clinging to the thought of Miriam, believing that everything that was happening was a terrible mistake. Miriam will be four now, won't know who she is. I'm still here, Selene whispers to her daughter, or to herself. Sinking into the space between sleep and consciousness, she thinks of the woman she has dreamt of being —

No research today, Margit says down the telephone. It's the weekend. I will show you round the city.

Catherine smiles. Clearly Margit, ten years her senior, has decided to make her a project, not only to put some fat on her, but also make her take time off work.

How about this afternoon? Catherine bargains.

Margit sighs theatrically. Very well. I'll take you for lunch and…

Oh, I was just going to have…

No arguments. Proper lunch and then we'll walk it off. All the way to Margit Island.

I was wondering about visiting Andrássy út, Catherine says.

For the shops? Or to see the theatres or opera house?

I was thinking of number 60. The building that was the Arrow Cross headquarters and then the Communist secret police.

There's not much to see, Margit says. The building has had some renovation, but it's not what it was. Terrible history, but not your period. József joined the Communist Party in 1930, when it was illegal, and of course he got prosecuted for sedition for his essay on socialism and literature, but that's a long time before the Soviets took over.

Yes — weren't the charges against him for obscenity and political agitation? Catherine asks. Someone should have warned him not to go looking for trouble, she adds.

Certainly, but he wouldn't have listened. It seemed to be part of his depressive condition to court conflict. He fared no better in the Communist Party — too liberal for them, wanted to unite with the Social Democrats so he was called a Fascist and thrown out. But the Arrow Cross didn't get going properly until after József's death. It did begin in '35, but was banned and started again in '39.

It wasn't so much for József, Catherine says tentatively. I was thinking of Selene Solweig.

Ah, your dreamt-up character. Yes, of course, though I don't think that building will tell you much. It keeps its secrets close. I'll find someone who can talk to you about the Fifties. Someone other than me so you get another perspective.

Thank you. I'm not sure András would approve, but I've got

her fixed in my head.

Pah! He needs more up-to-date ideas about writing. Now we are in the civilised west we have to be modern, Margit adds, chuckling. So? I'll call for you at 12.30. Deal?

Deal, Catherine agrees.

At the little walnut desk, Catherine spreads out copies of photographs and begins making notes as she sorts them chronologically.

The first is of Áron József looking stiff and formal in military clothes, the Romanian father who abandoned his family before Attila was three years old. Another of Attila aged about twelve, thin and mischievous, standing next to his seated mother, Borbála, who would be dead from cancer within two years, and also showing one of his sisters, Etelka or Jolán, who would become his guardian along with her husband Ödön Makai, who in turn later married Etelka as his fourth wife. Makai — the man who saw József's potential and paid for his education. There is no picture of the terrible time at Öcsöd after his almost destitute mother placed him the care of the National Protection League. They sent him to a strict and cruel foster father who told him 'Attila' was not a name, making him doubt his own existence. There are no photographs taken in his late teens when he published his first collection of poetry and, soon after, the poem that got him convicted of blasphemy, facing a fine and a prison sentence. Friends had the verdict overturned, but he was undeterred.

I had a friend like you, Catherine says to the debonair-looking picture of József taken in the late Twenties, I constantly told her not to go looking for trouble. I was always saying 'let's find another road', but she was set on her own path.

By the time this handsome photo of a young man in Vienna was taken, József had been forced out of the University of Szeged, where he was to study Hungarian and French Literature and become a teacher. His rebellious nature had brought him into conflict with one Professor Horger, a lecturer who found one of the poems in József's second collection offensive. 'I have no father, I have no mother, I have no God and no country', began the poem, Nem én kiáltok ('That's Not Me Shouting'). And so he was expelled.

But Vienna and Paris were better places for him. At the Sorbonne Julian Bell was a peer, and in a Parisian coffee house he met his next publisher, Imre Cserépfalvi. His poems appeared often in *L'Esprit Nouveau*, attracting acclaim. He took in French surrealism and it became a major influence on his third collection, published not long after he returned to Hungary.

It might all have worked out, Catherine says to the almost-smiling picture...

But the next image is of Márta Vágó, who he met in 1928. Beautiful, rich, daughter of a famous economist. They shared passions for philosophy and sociology, but when she left for the LSE, the frequent letters dwindled and she ended the affair. After that the poetry was more mature, influenced by unrequited love. Women constantly attempted to save him from himself — Judit Szántó, a fellow Communist, who tried to take care of him, then a series of psychiatric nurses.

So sad, Catherine says to the next picture.

This one was taken only two or three years later, but József, moustached, eyes deep-sunk, looks old, his skin weathered, brows furrowed. From 1931, aged only twenty-six, he regularly received psychiatric treatment, diagnosed, perhaps wrongly, with schizophrenia. He latched onto Freud to find theories that would help explain his torment, but dejection was never far away and he became chronically depressed after being rejected by the Soviet Writers Congress.

He wrote to a friend: My eyes are jumping from my head. If I go crazy, please don't hurt me. Just hold me down with your strong hands.

Until death it's all life, Attila, Catherine says, picking up the next image — a photo of József with Thomas Mann.

By then death was a common theme in József's work and after the meeting in 1937 he wrote 'Welcome to Thomas Mann', but was banned from publicly performing it, another blow to his psyche. Earlier that year he'd met the next nurse who would try, and fail, to save him. Flóra Kozmutza was his final muse.

Catherine pauses. I wonder, she says. She holds the picture of Flóra, writes:

A gifted psychiatric nurse who specialised in treating children, and later married the poet, Gyula Illyés. The affair was once again fervent and brief. She accepted his marriage proposal in April, two months after meeting him, but wrote about the aura of hopelessness that enveloped József and by July he had suffered a complete breakdown and was admitted to Siesta Sanatorium. Flóra visited him at his sister's home near Lake Balaton late in November and he gave her two despairing poems, but then wrote to her that he would be well again, that miracles happen.

Until death it's all life, Catherine repeats.

But on December 3 he crawled onto the railway tack in Balatonszárszó where a salesman, a conductor and the local village 'lunatic' watched, powerless to prevent him being hit by a train. His right arm was severed and his neck broken.

Catherine startles as the apartment buzzer sounds. She presses the intercom to let Margit in and tidies away the notes.

How often were you told not to go looking for trouble? She asks the neat pile of pictures.

Later, after nightmares of a jail, Catherine paces the apartment.

In the early morning — her journal lies open on a small desk, purple handwriting on cream paper, the script small and child-like —

...how ingenious humanity's inhumanity can be.

She goes to the kitchen and pours water into a tall glass, gulps it down in two draughts and returns to the desk, picks up a fountain pen, but doesn't write, sits with the pen hovering over the page until she realises she's cold and exhausted; she must try to sleep again and hope not to dream of Selene.

Catherine

There is no date scratched on the wall of the cell. Catherine wonders if it is the next day for Selene, Friday 8 November 1959 or in 1957 when Selene was remembering the trial?

What did she do yesterday in Budapest? She struggles to remember, but can recall only a guard goading her along, corridor after corridor towards this dank pit, as though Selene's memories are the only one she can bring to mind. She chokes for air, struggles to swim towards night in a comfortable apartment where she is a novelist and editor, has new friends at the university who take her for meals, argue good-naturedly about... but that life feels distant — as though she only dreamt it

Her side aches, a dull, deep pain till she stands up, when agony sears through her and she cries out and someone bangs on her door, muttering obscenities in response to her yells.

Selene slides down the wall, hunches, body crunched, kidney burning. She stays there five minutes, ten, thirty, an hour, two...

till the door swings open and a guard — not the same one,

rough-shaven, squat — pushes a bowl towards her, a scrap of bread, sets down a meagre tumbler of water. When the door closes Selene inches towards the bowl — a few beans float on scum-flecked liquid. The bread is too hard to bite. She flakes it into the greasy fluid, slowly cleans the bowl of every molecule, stopping to dry retch as she eats, sipping the grey water between mouthfuls.

It will end soon, she thinks. The trial will start today. The court will be shocked that a young mother, a nurse from a good family who was hardly involved in the uprising, who returned from Austria believing in the promises of immunity, ready to work, ready to care for her mother and daughter, has been kept in prison for a year without trial, interrogated, mistreated. They will be appalled, will apologise. She will be with Miriam soon.

Her mother's voice in her head tells her not to be so naïve.

Good family? That's what they hate, here, isn't it - the bourgeois, the kulaks, anyone who tries to better themselves. They want us all to be poor together. All biddable like children.

You should have gone to university with your education. Still, they probably wouldn't have let you in. Your cousin Jakov has just been turned down for the third year running. Every time the message comes back 'Perfect exam scores. Currently no spaces.' No spaces! This is a terrible country.

Amnesty? You stupid girl! Look what they did to your papa. And don't tell me it's a different regime. They just swapped uniforms. Fascists. Communists. They're all the same.

No! She cries out loud. She squats on the floor, waiting, believing it will end soon... five minutes, ten, thirty, an hour, two... a day, a week... She will be with her daughter soon.

You'll see, Mama, it's all a terrible mistake…

When the key is turned in the door she inches herself up the wall, standing, ready.

The thickset guard takes the bowl and mug, turns.

The trial? Selene whispers.

The back of his free hand smacks hard into her cheekbone as he turns to face her.

He sneers as she gasps, folding towards the floor.

Fucking sow, he says.

He spits, turns away, leaves humming 'Salt Peanuts', a tune Selene recognises from years ago, played on Radio Free Europe — decadent jazz and anti-Communist propaganda broadcast to inspire freedom.

Selene slumps to the floor, stays there… waiting…

Catherine wakes as though falling from a cliff, arms reaching to catching herself, breath ragged. She is shivering, though the apartment is not cold, feels pain above the small of her back, to the right.

She stands under the shower, turning up the water, hotter, hotter — to erase the cold, the ache.

It's 7 a.m. when she sits down with coffee and yoghurt at the circular kitchen table, plenty of time before she is due at the university to meet Margit and András.

Hold utca, 15, Budapest V
Monday 8 November 1993

Dear Simon

I'm hoping for a letter from you today.

I feel like I am falling and only you might catch me.
Selene Solweig Virág haunts me. In the last nightmare I
knew I was dreaming, but had this sense of sick certainty
that I was becoming her, so entirely that I might never
wake up as myself again. I couldn't remember my days
here or Margit and András's names.

Could she have existed? Could I once have been Selene
Solweig Virág? Her daughter is called Miriam, which
could simply be a co-incidence, but I feel like I'm drowning
in this other life, which is so harsh.

And it's not only the nights that are odd. In the daytime I
feel as though I'm moving through the hours with — I can
only describe it as though someone is on my shoulder —
or as if someone else is moving through me. But neither
of those descriptions is right. I wrote up a set of notes to
photographs of Attila József yesterday, and yet I can't
quite remember writing them. Does any of this make
sense? Of course not — it doesn't make sense to me.

I'm counting down the twelve days till you join me. I wish
it were tomorrow. You are the only person I can write to
like this and having you with me will be so much better.

Despite all this strangeness, I don't want you to worry
about me. I want you to have a wonderful time in Prague,
to come here having completed masses of research for
your book.

If Margit has her way I may be much fatter the next time
you see me!

I love you and miss you,
Your Catherine xxxxx

Selene Solweig

Selene scratches the date onto the wall. Almost three years. She wonders why she persists with this ritual. Will she linger here until she's an old woman, no doubt mad from the years of solitude? Or will she die young, half-starved, her daughter not remembering her? Perhaps there will be another uprising, the regime will change…

She imagines someone telling her, *Until death, it's all life, Selene.* Did someone once say that to her?

She paces the cell, three steps one way, five steps the other. Four steps forward, six steps back. She decides the numbers as she goes. It is a freedom, she tells herself. It is something she decides upon, a sign that she has a will that has not yet broken. She stops in the middle of the small floor, stretches, arms raised, squats. Plié, she murmurs, remembering the ballet classes she attended as a child in the Marais. I am Selene Solweig Virág, she tells no-one but herself and begins reciting poetry.

Later, after a meagre bowl of beans, she huddles onto the bench, pulling the frayed blanket around her, drifts into another life in another time…

Catherine sets out from Szabadság tér with a map marked with sites. She will start at the little apartment on Gát utca 3, where József was born. She heads towards the river to the tram stop near the Parliament buildings, diverts to say good morning to József's statue, solid and sad. She notices how she is constantly comparing this unfamiliar, melancholy city to Paris; there too poets have ended their own lives. Margit has insisted it's too far to walk to Gát utca— more than an hour across the city — and too cold to walk even half so far in November. Even for the short walk to the tram, Margit has instructed her to make sure she has layers of clothing beneath her wool coat. She has dutifully put a cashmere jumper over a vest and long-sleeved shirt, but pulls open the coat as she walks. The air has no bite and there is only a gentle breeze. Despite the clouds, it feels almost spring-like. The yellow tram takes her along the riverfront, past the beautiful Erzsébet Bridge and later under the Szabadság bridge, traffic rumbling overhead, the Corvinus University on her left before the cityscape changes to riverside warehouses. It's a ten minute walk from the stop on Haller utca to Gát utca in District IX, where József was born. With each turn the next street is more dowdy and tired. Lenhossek utcais strewn with litter, the windows of apartments covered in chipboard beneath broken glass, the facades of buildings crumbling. She feels uneasy and conspicuous, wonders how run-down it must have been when József was born here, in poverty, in 1905. She turns left onto Gát utcaand the location is signalled by a wall plaque beside which are bunches of flowers and wreaths, as though someone had recently died. The inscription proclaims, in socialist-realist style, that József was the 'great poet of the Hungarian proletariat'. Catherine smiles, thinking of József expelled from the Communist Party for his liberal views, but he was certainly from an impoverished home. She rings the intercom next to the green door.

Ah, Catherine? The curator asks. I am with you.

Márta Tákacs appears moments later and Catherine holds out her hand to shake. They walk through a small courtyard and into the ground floor two-roomed apartment, Marta tall and elegant, her fair hair held by a blue Alice-band that matches her eyes.

People come from everywhere, Márta says as they enter.

The walls are covered in black and white photographs. Catherine notes the picture of József's father in military uniform that she has a copy of, and one of his mother that she has not seen previously. Borbála is young and pretty, with soft features. Another image shows a house further along the street where the family lived when József was a toddler — Papa disappeared from this flat, Márta tells her, translating the legend.

By the door, a map shows another nineteen apartments that the family lived in after Attila ran back to his mother from the foster family at Öcsöd, who set him to work as a five-year-old swineherd.

They were constantly thrown out for not being able to pay the rent, Márta says. Attila was lucky that his brother-in-law later paid for his education so he didn't have to go on selling newspapers for a living. In his childhood, he'd already known hard work — collecting coal, selling paper whirligigs that he made from scraps to better-off children. In the war he'd queue all night to buy food for the family, only to find that the cooking lard had run out and there was nothing to be had by eight in the morning. He was only fourteen when his mother died and Makai sent him to the Makó boarding school. They tried to send him to a seminary too, but he left after a week, telling them he was Orthodox, not Catholic. He got good grades at school, but he was already suffering with depression and tried to kill himself when he was only sixteen. I will leave you to look, she says finally, but I'm in the next room if you have questions.

There are copies of József's poetry collections on a small table, beginning with *Szépség koldusa, Beauty's Beggar*, written when he was seventeen. Catherine lingers over each picture, each book, but feels no sense of Attila in the rooms.

After a while Márta reappears with another set of pictures. These were his women, she says. This one was the daughter of the director of his boarding school — Márta Gebe. He was very young, but she inspired several poems. Then Maria Esprit, this time his landlord's daughter. And this one is most interesting.

The black and white picture is of a beautiful girl, aquiline features, large eyes, her close-cut bobbed hair under a fashionable cap.

Luca Wallennsz was the daughter of Gitta Genes, a very fine artist and ceramicist. There are beautiful works in the National Gallery. Her husband wrote novels and poetry. Very refined Jewish family. They gave salons and many famous names attended, but Gitta met Attila first in the park. He sat next to her on a bench and declared his love five minutes later. He was only nineteen and she was a mature woman, beautiful, but thirty-six. They became close — not what we would call an affair, but a relationship. He wrote poems for her, of course, like 'It was summertime' and then her daughter, Luca, became interested in the salons and Attila fell in love again. He wrote her many excellent poems, mostly in '28. Very beautiful — 'I bless you with sadness and happiness' is the best known, and often set to music.

He fell in love frequently, Catherine notes.

Indeed. And he loved Gitta and Luca at the same time too.

Ah, Catherine says, thinking of Attila loving Flóra and Selene simultaneously.

You will know this one, of course.

Catherine holds the picture of Márta Vágó. Yes. The first serious love of his life, perhaps.

Márta nods. They wrote every day when she first went to London, but the distance was too much to sustain. I think that's what her parents hoped for. They were wealthy intelligentsia, he was the son of a soap factory worker and a peasant. Márta pauses. And this one —

She hands Catherine an image of Judit Szánto.

I always think her the most sad, Márta finishes. She lived with him for six years, tried to make a place of security for him. He was very broken after the relationship with Márta Vágó ended. But he said it was 'not love, but an alliance'. Particularly harsh from a man who loved easily. He wrote one poem for her, 'Judit', and a few scraps that never became poems. That was all. And while he was with Judit, he met Edit.

Márta hands her the photograph of Edit Gyömröi. She was his doctor and he became... she searches for the word... fixated on her so that another doctor, Robert Bak, had to take over. And then one day he saw this girl — Márta Márton —

Catherine studies the beautiful young face.

He didn't know her. He saw her and decided he was in love. He wrote the poem 'Ode' for her, an exquisite love poem, and when Judit realised that she was not the muse of this poem, she tried to kill herself. They'd already tried to part earlier, but broke apart permanently after this.

And finally —

The last picture is of Flóra Kozmutza. No picture of Selene, Catherine thinks.

They met at Anna Daniels' apartment in February '37 and

were engaged by April, but it was never to be of course.

Catherine nods. Thank you. They're all so beautiful.

Yes, lovely and sad, Márta adds.

She tracks back to Mester utca 67, where József went to school when he returned to his mother aged seven; the plaque there was intended to mark the fiftieth anniversary of his birth, though it was put up in 1957, fifty-two years after he was born.

Catherine sits in a small restaurant on Mester utca. The tabletops are plastic, red laminate beginning to peel, and the menus garish, but the soup is good. She drinks coffee, consults the map — perhaps three-quarters of an hour to walk to Kerepesi Cemetery where József's remains were moved from Balatonszárszó, originally to be near his mother, though he was moved again and again before being allotted his final resting place.

Catherine sets off, musing about how undervalued József was in life compared to death. József's body had been moved twice more before finally being put in an ornamented grave in the Workers' Pantheon at Kerepesi. Finally, in death, he was a working-class hero.

Bones revered, moved, used in a cause. She thinks of Casilda — how a frail Moorish Muslim princess in eleventh century Toledo had been transformed into a Christian saint with healing powers, even within her lifetime, though it was only after death that Casilda was useful as propaganda — buried in the Church of San Vincente near the healing-well that had reputedly cured her, later moved to a shrine near her hermitage-cave at Briviesca. Not a simple anchorite burial place but an ornate altar, complete with an effigy in gold and reds, under a painted domed ceiling, her relics kept in cathedrals at Burgos and Toledo, one even making its way to a chapel in Kansas.

And so too with József — acute sense of injustice had given him a passion for Communism as a means to freedom, along with many Thirties' poets, and yet his independent thought, unbiddable mind and fierce honesty also got him thrown out — but none of this prevented him later being appropriated and put to use when he could no longer voice any objection.

Catherine walks through the main entrance of the cemetery. It's a warm afternoon for late autumn, the grass deep green and the avenues leaf-strewn. She pauses by the arcades, with their Italianate columns and sculptures. There are statues everywhere, mausoleums and ornate memorials. She passes other poets' graves, turns towards the Deák mausoleum and stands before plot thirty-five. There are four names carved into the stone: József Áron, József Attila, József Jolán and his nephew, Makai Péter. His mother, who he seemed to carry with him throughout life, and his sister, Etelka, are not mentioned.

Catherine sits on the grass, takes out her notebook, doesn't look up for another two hours.

She walks back slowly. She will go to the place where he wrote when editing the magazine, *Beautiful Word*, another day, but the statue on the Danube near the Parliament building, where she began this morning, is only a short detour en route to her apartment.

József sits, coat thrown down beside him, hat in his hand, watching the river, the epitome of contemplation and lament. He looks as though he'd spent the day walking across the city, searching for something, Catherine thinks. The lines from 'By the Danube', in raised bronze script across the pavement, are a facsimile of József's handwriting: *Mintha szivemből folyt volna tova Zavaros, bölcs és nagy volt a Duna — As if it flowed straight from my heart / Troubled, wise and great was the Danube.*

How was it that Székely translated those lines? Catherine asks the statue.

> *As if my own heart had opened its gate:*
> *The Danube was turbulent, wise and great.*

She thinks of the conversation with Margit and András, how a thing mutates between languages, but even in one language, how every action, every nuance is open to interpretation.

Catherine sits on the bottom step beneath Attila, looking towards the Danube with him. When she begins to feel stiff with the evening chill, she walks towards the figure, touches his hand.

There is such melancholy here, she tells him. Suicide seems to be everywhere, your language is unlike any neighbouring country's, your borders have changed and shrunk, to say there has been one too many invasions is an understatement and even your national anthem talks of 'pity and sorrow'. So much sadness, and I have endless questions for you that you can't answer. Did you kill yourself? I think I have to agree with Margit and András that you did. Why didn't you take another route, Attila? And the strangest question of all — Did you know a woman called Selene Solweig Virág?

Catherine

Monday 9 November 1959 is scratched on the cell wall. Selene coughs, tries to control the fit as a passing guard hammers the door. She gulps down needling prickles, croaks rasping from her thin frame, but the guard walks further down the corridor and she breathes deeply, drifts towards sleep, towards memories of an earlier time —

Mama, I've brought bread and vegetables, she says, entering the small flat —

Marie looks up from her chair. No meat? She asks.

Sorry, Mama.

I'm too tired to cook, her mother replies. Too tired to eat. Perhaps I'll go to bed.

Mama, it's only 7 o'clock. You need to eat. I'll cook. Let me change out of my uniform.

I thought you would be a great dancer when you were a little girl, or an intellectual with all that reading, not a nurse sluicing out bedpans. Still, they probably wouldn't have let you into university. You know Jakov has just been turned down for the third time? It's always the same — 'Perfect exam scores. Currently no spaces.' This is a terrible country. We should never have come to this blighted place.

Selene sighs, decides not to argue. I can read to you later, after dinner...

After a measly soup of vegetables and bread that doesn't deserve the name. In Paris...

I know, Mama, but it's the same for everyone.

Is it? Nagy eats like this? It's like being in the ghetto.

Mama! You know that's not true. We have food. I have work. In the ghetto thousands starved!

Selene closes her eyes, feels a pulse over her left eye, the scent of oranges that seems to emanate from her skin, sickly...

Papa gone... brave letters telling them how well he is coping, until... The constant hunger gnawing at her, aware her mother is giving her more than her share of the scraps... wondering whether Mama, who is unbearably thin, will be alive the next morning...

She rubs away the pain with a circular motion of her thumb.

It's nothing like that, Mama, she says firmly. Nagy is doing everything he can. It's early days...

Marie waves away the discussion, says instead, That reminds me, what day is it today?

Mama?

Don't look at me like I'm an imbecile, girl. I lose track, that's all...

Monday, Selene says. Monday November 9.

I know what month it is, Marie retorts. And the year is 1953, before you have the impudence to ask me.

Selene sighs, goes into the small bedroom that she shares with her mother, changes into an old skirt and blouse. She picks up her purse and wonders if she should try to find other food, something to cheer her mother, but it is too late now.

She sits on her narrow bed and the smell of oranges returns. A small light moves across her vision bringing a patch of darkness in its wake... she thinks she hears a train sound in the distance —

sits beside the lake, waiting.

Perhaps she will not see Attila again. It's a year since she saw him here and they only exchanged a few sentences, yet she feels a sense of urgency, anticipation...

Selene Solweig Virág, a voice behind her says.

She turns, smiles. You remember my name.

You were here only three days ago.

Of course. It's a year ago for me. So it's November 9 here too?

He nods.

And how are you?

Ah, not so good, but some days…

He inclines his head to one side, makes a closed-mouthed smile, self-deprecating.

I didn't think I'd see you again, he says — or at least I thought… that I'd imagined you, that perhaps I was getting worse…

No, don't think that, she reassures. I can't explain how I'm here, but I am real. I was about to make dinner for my mother. I sat down for a moment and thought I was getting a migraine, but then I heard a train and… I heard a train last time too.

You are still feeling sick?

No, the pain didn't come. I get this phantosmia — of oranges usually — then lights and darkness over half my vision, but both times I've met you… the symptoms have started, but no headache — I hear a train and — here I am.

Phantosmia, Attila repeats, as though savouring the word. You are hungry? There's a taverna on Szoladi utca with good food. I might even have a few worthless pengő with me.

Selene smiles, reaches into a pocket for her small purse. If we eat it will have to be you who pays, she says, holding out coins — forints and fillérs. My currency will be meaningless in 1937.

He pulls a well-fingered, small, square change purse from his pocket. Its stiff brown leather creaks a little as he eases the flap from underneath the cross-strap and peers inside. He nods and smiles. So, I will buy you dinner.

But you… I don't think you can afford…

A special occasion, he insists.

He holds out an arm and she links it as though they are old friends.

The porcini soup is delicious, she says. She looks up to see him watching her intensely. I'm eating too fast, aren't I?

So, 1953 is not a good year?

Oh, it's better. I mean… in the war, that was really hard. Now there is food. We're not hungry, but it's not an easy time. I think it will get better again, though. We have a lot of hope in Nagy…

His eyebrows arch, but he doesn't interrupt, only leans in, gazing more intensely.

After the soup he asks, Pork Mignon or beef stew?

Selene laughs. Oh, I couldn't — I mean…

You are full after that bowl of soup?

But I can't pay for…

A beautiful woman is telling me all about her life and making my day pass without torment. It's a small price.

I'd tell you anyway, Selene says, but beef stew does sound good.

He insists on ordering the only red wine on the menu, a Nagy-burgundi. In honour of your Nagy, he jokes.

Between mouthfuls, Selene tells him about her job, her mother, politics, her friend Zsófia. When she talks about her father, the war, the forced labour of the Jews, Attila holds his head in his hands as though in pain. She stops when tears fill his eyes as

54

she talks about Papa's death, her mother's decline.

This is too much, she says quietly.

No. No, you must go on. We are adept at inhumanity, aren't we?

Yes, but not everyone. And in Paris…

Ah, yes, Paris.

He begins to talk about himself, orders coffee.

And pálinka? Apricot or cherry?

Selene hesitates. I'm not really used to — she pauses — apricot, she says decisively.

Excellent.

It is the first broad smile she has seen from him and something in her melts.

She drinks the pálinka with relish. Maybe he will live, she thinks. Maybe I'll wake up in 1953 and there will be a new poetry collection published by the great Attila József. He will be twenty-two years my senior, will certainly not remember these strange encounters, but he will be alive.

Afterwards, when he walks her back towards the lake, he grasps her hand more tightly, slides an arm around her waist as they near the place where they met.

I hope we will meet again, Selene Solweig Virág, he says. Perhaps in another three days you will be beside the lake again.

And perhaps for me it will be a whole year to wait.

He holds her face between long fingers. His gaze penetrates. The kiss is fierce.

I am already in love, he says. He turns and walks back into Balatonszárszó, his shoulders less hunched.

Selene looks at the night sky. How late is it? She hears a train sound —

Selene! I thought you were going to cook dinner, not sit daydreaming, her mother complains, standing in the doorway of the bedroom.

O! Have I been long? I lost track of… is it very late?

Almost half past seven, her mother says, tetchily.

Only half an hour?

Marie shoots her a withering look. You've become an impertinent young woman with no respect, she says, turning back into the living room.

Selene smiles, hugs herself, follows her mother into the living room with its meagre kitchen corner, begins chopping vegetables and humming a tune she heard on Radio Free Europe, 'Salt Peanuts'.

Hold utca, 15, Budapest V.
Tuesday 9 November 1993

Dear Simon

Thank you for your letter. It's wonderful to hear all

your news and I'm so glad the research is going well. It sounds fascinating. And it sounds as though Nathan had a wonderful time visiting you and getting to know Prague and Eliška, but I'm sure it's easier to research and work alone. Eliška sounds like a great help. I'm eager to see your pictures of the museum, but most of all I can't wait to see you.

Catherine smiles and puts down her pen, picks up Simon's letter. The research is thriving, he says, especially now his brother has left him in peace after being smitten by the woman at the Castle archive who was helping him with archive material and translations. He writes:

Nathan's already asked Eliška to visit him in Nottingham so maybe you'll get to meet her. He was joking that at least our poor parents won't have to put up with another goy in the family, referring to you of course.

Catherine begins to write again:

My research is progressing. Yesterday, I visited lots of sites associated with József and I'm going to see others today. I plan to go to Balatonszárszó soon too. My notebooks are filling up and I feel like I'm getting to know József — someone who felt everything deeply — love, injustice, passion, anxiety — a man of extremes, including intelligence and sensitivity.

But, she wonders, picking up Simon's letter again — is there something manic in the description of the rather kitsch Museum of Alchemists and Magicians? — She shakes her head, continues to write…

A man of extremes, Catherine says out loud.

She scans Simon's letter:

The vaulted ceilings are covered with alchemical texts and symbols, overlaid by a maze of lights like a suspended chemistry set — glass tubes, some long, some arched, or bulbous lamps, glowing eerily, cyan or lime. The laboratories are shadowed, each stranger than the last. Waxwork alchemists, eyes protruding, wild with fear and wonder, inhabit nightmare spaces — a room of manuscripts, paper crumbling to dust from rolled parchments, massive leather volumes on sagging shelves; rooms of shelves crammed with bottles, the vast and the tiny jostling for space and competing in grotesqueness — a foetal pig in amber liquid floating beside eyeballs in puce slime, a human hand in glaucous juice, everywhere distortions. A thin figure sits beside a glowing furnace scribing something dangerous. The atmosphere is fantastical, menacing, and never more so than in one deep catacomb where the rounded indigo walls and floor are alive with sinister runes, inhabiting by hooded figures, one kneels on the floor cackling, one gazes down, looking contemptuous, and a third looks up in glee as the fourth is hauled through the brickwork of the cavern by the devil, hidden from view. When I walked around this nightscape floor of astronomical symbols, I felt myself in a place charged with transformation and dread, a place thrilling to some dark heartbeat.

Kelley allegedly lived and worked here, and the lower rooms are laden with sixteenth century furnishings and tapestries, with velvets and packed shelves of livid potions. The laboratories are in the loft, up a steep, original, spiral staircase — 'the spiral of life' — closer to the angels, whom Kelley and Dee conversed with in Enochian.

I've hardly slept since I visited. I'm writing page after page, words and images tumbling out. I feel myself inhabiting Rudolf's occult Prague. The place is sensationalist, some of it tasteless even, and yet I have fallen under its spell, under the trance of this city of esotericism...

She continues her letter —

I am still dreaming the life of Selene Solweig Virág, but last night, although the dream started in the prison, it went back to 1953 when she was a nurse, and from there to her second meeting with József. Both times she seems to have experienced aura before the 'meeting', the same warning signs I get, though thankfully less and less often these days.

Attila and Selene are rapidly falling in love — people with difficult lives —Selene calmer, more reflective — yet they feel like a good fit for one another. She has an enormous capacity for believing the best, which may be simply gullibility, but I'd rather think of it as a capacity for hope. But I fear that in the prison it is being worn away.

I still can't help feeling there is a truth somewhere in these weird dreams and I continue to have this sense that she haunts my days — perhaps in the same way that I haunt hers? I wonder if she is aware of me? A mad question! Anyway, I feel lighter today, my darling. I've woken up hungry — for food and for more research — so I must get on with my day. More soon.

Yours ever,
Catherine.

Selene Solweig

Selene wakes with a sense of peace she has not felt for... months, years? She rises, scratches the date on the wall. The cough rises in her, but she chokes it back, recalls the dream of Catherine following Attila's trail —

Catherine sets out from Szabadság tér towards the river. There are other statues of József, but the melancholy Attila looking across the Danube calls to her, feels strangely alive, present.

She sits by him in silence for several minutes, takes out her notebook, lets the writing drift from research to journalling —

In some sense we are all deeply connected, share a common humanity, and yet it is not just the past that is foreign. So often we become alien to each other — whether or not Selene existed, people like her were persecuted — many of those who rose up in '56 were imprisoned and tortured, before that Jews were enslaved and treated like animals in the forced Labour Service, while others across Europe were rounded up and slaughtered, as they were eventually in Hungary too — transported to death camps or shot by the Danube so that their bodies would be washed away. The list of human atrocities is endless.

These horrors were in a future that Attila didn't live to experience, but there was increasing political turmoil, plenty of cause for pessimism in his time — the redrawing of Hungary's borders after the First World War left a third of the Hungarian-speaking population outside the much smaller country; at the same time the country was forced to pay punitive war reparations. It lost vast tracts of forests, roads, canals, farm-land... By the time Attila was a young boy, Hungary was impoverished. For anyone like him, for anyone of any sensitivity, it is not hard to imagine such a harsh life becoming unbearable, even without mental illness.

If we had a keen vision and feeling of all ordinary human life, it would be like hearing the grass grow and the squirrel's heart beat, and we should die of that roar which lies on the other side of silence, wrote George Eliot.

And yet if our vision becomes dulled, we fall asleep through life, allow atrocities to go unhindered, participate in them.

Forster advises — *only connect*, but he knew it wasn't simple. He realised the darkness of fascism was rising and had to be stopped. He acknowledged that life is easy to chronicle, but bewildering to practise, yet that somehow we must stop living it in disconnected fragments.

I have felt my mind fragmenting in dreams and nightmares, and yet I feel increasingly connected to Attila, to Simon, to life, and to memories of Miriam. Sitting here beside the statue of a passionate poet, who yearned to connect, I feel more at ease with the notion of connecting across time, connections made between the real and the imagined... Miriam was right — the unreason of the world is more insane than any fiction.

Perhaps I am not unravelling after all, but finding a path between a vision so keen it would overwhelm me and a fragmented dullness that would lull me into uncaring sleep.

When she gets up from the step, Catherine rests a hand on József's right arm, the arm severed when he went under the train in his last few moments, before his neck snapped and...

See you tomorrow, Attila, she says. And thank you.

She walks along Id Antall József rakpart. Lanes of cars thrum beyond the strip of greenery that divides the walkway from the road and the raised tramlines. Red park benches face anonymous boats, moored as expensive restaurants, a new feature of 'modern' Budapest, Margit has told her, full of the new tourists eager to consume all things Bohemian. She continues along the river towards the Széchenyi chain bridge, where Margit is waiting for her.

I'm so grateful for this, Catherine says. Very excited about meeting László.

Nonsense, it's a pleasure, Margit says, hugging her and kissing each cheek.

They continue along Jane Haining rakpart towards the imposing Art Nouveau Vidagó Concert Hall.

Here she is, Margit announces, as they approach the statue of the Little Princess. Tiny, much loved and much copied.

She's exquisite, Catherine agrees, her hand brushing the little girl perched on a chain link, her back to the Danube. She looks so full of life.

So, off to meet her lovely creator.

Mrs Marton brings coffee and pastries.

And pálinka, László Marton insists, winking at Catherine.

Margit translates rapidly as their sixty-eight year old host talks about his work.

The Shepherd Boy came first, László says. I think I got attention because I was only seventeen then and he was a realistic boy. They wanted statues that would reflect human life, real people, not those hulking ideological communist statues that had domineered over us.

We just saw the Little Princess, Catherine says, she's beautiful — a tomboy, I thought.

László chuckles, says the word in English — tomboy. My daughter, Évike. She used to dress up all the time, make a bathrobe into a princess's train, wear a crown made of newspaper. I think I captured her well and I like her location. She feels right there.

And Attila József, Catherine says. I feel as though I know him so much better from sitting with your statue. You make it seem effortless.

László smiles, sips his pálinka. Of course, there is always struggle. Sometimes it goes on for a long time, the idea fighting the material, then there is the moment when inspiration and form are one. I don't care for dogma in art, only for seeing inside the subject. I want essence; the light and dark inside the person, the way everything is changing.

Catherine nods. The sculptures are so vital, that makes sense. They feel personal.

Quite, László agrees, nodding vehemently. This is real existence, complete with imperfections, complexities. Attila

József is one of our greatest poets, an intellectual, but also from poverty with a feeling for ordinary people, someone who thought deeply and spoke out fiercely, a man who knew anguish in love and in his mind, brave enough to choose death rather than a diminished life.

Catherine thinks of Virginia Woolf choosing death when she thought she would not recover from the impending breakdown threatening her sanity.

Yes, she agrees. Margit told me there's an internal logic between József's life and death and I'm sensing that more and more. There's great melancholy in your statue, she adds, but also something solid; something that embodies both his suffering and hope — he radiates comfort to those who sit with him.

You are very kind, László says, smiling broadly. We are all like József in some way or at some point — conflicted, suffering, disillusioned, isolated, raging against injustice, but we also have these inner resources, ways of recognising the depths of one another. Attila carries his predicament in his hunched shoulders, his austere face, but he is connected to others by the clothes he wears — ordinary — and his fellow feeling shows in his expression — meditative, his brow creased in deep thought. László pauses. But you can see all that for yourself. I am talking too much, he says.

Later, dozing while the dinner cooks, Catherine replays the dream of Selene's second meeting with Attila, her mind segueing back to her early meetings with Simon.

It's okay to give up a dream, any dream… There are other things, other dreams.

He says this when she asks him why he gave up a career in music.

64

Is that a quote? No, don't tell me — it's from one of your stories, isn't it? The one about the man searching for something, uncertain of what, snagged on a memory from childhood about meeting with a famous poet who tells him. 'Never close a circle.'

That's amazing memory, he says, smiling.

It's an arresting story.

She believes he's right about there being other dreams. She has a talent for belief, after all. Belief is — or was — her gift. But she also puts store in his opinions because he is someone she thinks about more and more often. And the last two years since Liam left, she muses, have also taught me that there are other dreams.

It's a good thing to know when to let something go, Simon adds.

Yes, she confirms. She spears a piece of crab from the starter they are sharing, smiles across the table.

She's been emailing him daily since their first meeting. She's his editor, so no doubt he expects this. But does he think all editors send five, six, seven emails a day? Does he think all editors find poems their writers would love, send small gifts — books, of course. It's his first publication. Perhaps he imagines… Or perhaps? Perhaps she's been making him up, she thinks. But, no —

She asks him about the CD he brought with him today — a gift to celebrate their second editorial meeting, which she had insisted should be over a proper lunch.

He starts talking about Oliver Nelson, spins from one jazz name to another with unassuming ease —

After Liam left, she would stretch across the king-sized bed at night, savour crisp linen, cool on her skin. On the wall, pictures of Paris that would have made Liam gush hatred of all things French. She'd visited in her first summer as a single woman, spent a week walking the city, lingering in galleries, eating food she no longer had to hear Liam's opinion of, went to a book launch at Shakespeare & Co. She will return the following spring, ride the Batobus, visit Notre Dame, buy a blue painting of the tall apartments that line the Seine.

Have you ever been to Paris? she asks Simon when there is a lull in the conversation.

No. It's somewhere I've always intended to visit.

They will go to Paris together, she thinks, thanking the waitress, who eases plates of sea bass onto their table. They will eat croissants, wander the Marais and buy delicate coffee bowls in a tiny ceramics studio, stand under the Eiffel Tower, walk through Rodin's gardens, pause by 'The Kiss'. He will call her Catherine, not Cassie or Kitty. She will listen to his heart, know there will be no-one else.

Maybe we should both go, she says, pretending not to register his flush of colour, the moment of confusion.

That night, she stretches across the king-sized bed, thinks about falling in love. On the wall, a print from a book she edited last year, Blodeuwedd reflected as an owl, petals for claws and eyes, the legend — *I'm still here*. She falls asleep to the CD of *More Blues and the Abstract Truth* as though she had never known years of insomnia.

The kitchen timer trills and Catherine rouses in the little apartment in Budapest's Downtown district, her mind full of images of Attila and Simon… Later, she drifts into sleep still thinking of how one reminds of her of the other, of Selene…

Catherine

The latest marks on the wall read: Tuesday 10 November 1959. Selene lies on the hard bunk bathed in a film of cold sweat, the cough scouring her emaciated body. Barely conscious, she repeats her daughter's name over and over — a thin-voiced ritual, drifts into memories of a time when she thought she would soon be with Miriam again.

No harm will come to anyone following the great popular movement of the last weeks, Kádár had promised, and so she returned home, believing, relieved, only to be arrested...

I'm going to join with the students, Zsófia whispers as they leave the hospital after their shift. The group I met at The River Room, remember?

I never went, Selene says. It sounded wonderful — an American jazz club, but...

It was shut down in months, Zsófia finishes for her. Anyway Tibor and Luca and the others, they're certain now is the time to act. Since the intellectuals rallied round Nagy demanding freedom of expression, things have been changing, not on the surface maybe, but...

Wasn't that a whole year ago?

Yes, but these things are cumulative, Tibor says. Think of all the signs of protest there've been this year — calls for Rakoski's resignation, Julia Rajk released from prison, that meeting in July to debate change, broadcast to thousands of people, Rakoski disappearing to Russia because he's supposedly ill... and the leaflets we see...

Yes, a lot's happened, Selene agrees.

And that funeral...

Selene nods. I have to admit, getting more than a hundred thousand people to line the streets on a miserable, rain-sodden day in October for Rajk's reburial was something. I wouldn't have imagined Gerö agreeing to that. Perhaps now that Nagy has been re-admitted to the party things might change...

Yes, change is coming, but it won't succeed unless we keep up the pressure, Zsófia puts in. Tibor says the students won't tolerate any more Soviet interference. Hungary is left destitute. Conditions for students are intolerable. We see the same at the hospital...

So what will they do? Selene's voice shakes a little as she asks.

Protest. Tibor says the students plan to break away from the Communist student organisation. DISZ doesn't represent their interests. And they need support. It's not just students suffering.

Selene nods but says nothing.

I didn't have a gun, Selene tells the court again. She tries to stand erect, feels she might collapse at any moment.

Gustáv Tutsek leans forward and sneers.

You intended to fight tanks with your bare hands? Or perhaps you were one of those throwing Molotov cocktails?

It is the third day of the same questions repeated endlessly. Selene rocks slightly on her feet. Her mouth is dry, her head hot.

I was offered a gun, she says, her voice a hoarse rasp. But when they tried to show me how to use it, the... the recoil was too much, and anyway, I didn't think I could shoot someone.

So you did have a gun?

No, I...

You just said the recoil of your gun was a problem. So you must have had a gun.

Not then, not during... Selene trails away, wipes a hand across her forehead.

You would like a break, Miss Virág?

She nods. Yes, yes, please.

Then tell the truth. Tutsek retorts, grinning, triumphant.

I am... I...

You are very argumentative for someone who has committed a grave crime against her country.

Selene falls silent, stares at the floor.

I see you have nothing to say to defend your lies. Tutsek warms to his own voice. You must know, Miss Virág, that the People's Chambers are not here to show leniency. The Supreme Public Prosecutor, Dr. Géza Szénási himself, requires the application of firmness when dealing with violators of the law. It is essential to stability that we liquidate the remnants of counter-revolution. Your intransigence does not serve you well.

He looks up. Take her to her cell. We will continue tomorrow.

Catherine wakes sobbing, cold, her blankets on the floor.

Budapest, Wednesday 10 November 1993

Memories of another life and dreams within dreams. There was no date scratched on the wall of the smaller cell that Selene remembered being taken back to during the trial, but it must have been 1957. I feel so such anger on her behalf, even though she may be entirely my invention. Was she real? Is she still alive? The questions I want answers to are completely different from those I thought I'd come to Budapest to research.

Not least, am I mad?

I feel like I am going about the world with all my senses alert. I feel urgent and alive. I feel awake, especially in my dreams. But none of this is any proof of sanity. All I am certain of is that my dreams are taking my writing in new directions that fascinate and terrify me.

Selene Solweig

Selene huddles onto the bench, hugs her rib cage. She no longer feels the gnawing hunger, only the raw ache from the cough that shakes her frame. She thinks of the statue of Attila she saw in her dream, how strange to go from obscurity to fame beyond this small life. She wonders who will remember her. Catherine? —

They take an early morning bus across the city to the railway station, Catherine pondering how so many of the buildings look run down, some still marked with the scars of battle from the uprising. Margit has told her that no one can afford to renovate, so the already tired apartments become more and more dowdy. Most of the cars are still Soviet Ladas or East German Trabants — cheap and tinny, but András is hopeful —

There are elections next year, he says, and Budapest is cheap to live in. We are the new Paris. Like Paris in the Fifties, bursting with American intellectuals and poets.

Margit seems not so optimistic —

It's all very well having the city full of poets and writers, but publishing here is hardly thriving. I'm not saying I want the old days back, of course, but at least we could get our books published and in good numbers. Now there is no state funding, publishers can't afford to print more than a few thousand or even less of any book and authors never get paid.

András nods. Well, yes, but...

And I'll tell you what else is wrong, Margit cuts in, it's very well if you're a male writer or academic, but if you're a brilliant woman, the best career move you can make is to marry a more brilliant man. Before András can object she adds, A few things are changing, I'll grant you. There are western goods in the shops, fashionable clothes if you want to pay for them, but best of all, we can travel. I took a train around Europe last summer, travelling and camping like a teenager.

András nods enthusiastically. I did a house swap with an academic in France. A whole month in Brittany. He pauses, lost in thought. But we should get back to the present and Catherine's research. July 1937 was Attila's longest period in the institution. When he left, he worked as the co-editor of *Beautiful Word* with Pál Ignotus. He wrote astute articles and reviews, a very nuanced appraisal of Hatvany's *The Soul of Asia*. He was an urbanist, but he saw its limitations. József never wholly threw in his lot with any movement or ideology, always remained critical, which of course made him difficult.

Heretics are always changing their mind, but the orthodox have no mind to change, Catherine says.

Hah! Quite so, I like that.

A university lecturer once said it — Henry Chadwick, when I was studying theology at Cambridge.

József was certainly a heretic. He used to work on the journal in the Japán Coffeehouse that was underneath their offices on Andrássy út. It's a bookshop now, since 1954 in fact — Írók

72

Boltja, The Writers' Bookshop. It did good work there, but it didn't console him. His depression grew worse. His love life was painful, too volatile. His sisters tried to help, but his suffering was too great. It all ended at Balatonszárszó.

I think, like you, I have to accept that he committed suicide, Catherine says.

András nods, but Margit shrugs her shoulders. Yes, it's my opinion too, but, as you said, you're writing a fiction based on his life. Don't let the facts get in the way of your story. She winks at Catherine, but András doesn't take the bait.

Anyway, we must be going, he says.

On the two hour train journey András and Margit bicker amicably about feminism, politics, literature — talking in English to include Catherine as they hop from topic to topic.

She has seen pictures of the lakeside memorial to József and felt puzzled by it. Huge train wheels set on a length of track, stacked with metal rods rising more than sixteen feet high and topped with a huge rock. She has wondered about the thinking behind a sculpture of the thing that killed him, so close to the place he was crushed and mangled. But later, standing by the monumental structure, she sees the letters at the end of each rod and on every side.

The letters make stanzas from his work, Margit says reverently.

Catherine nods. She doesn't need to read Hungarian to feel the enormity of his words crushed beneath the pressure of that stone slab. This is how he wrote, she thinks, under pressure — the work fierce and intense, too bright, too honest.

We should die of that roar which lies on the other side of silence,

73

she says out loud.

András and Margit look at her, quizzical, but waiting for her to go on.

It's something George Eliot said about being someone of keen vision, someone who feels too much. I think, even in my novel, he must kill himself.

Yes, András agrees.

He certainly couldn't switch off the feelings, Margit adds.

They eat lunch at a taverna on Szóládi utca, where the food is hearty and comes in enormous portions. Catherine looks dismayed when the great oval platters arrive, but Margit insists no one will be offended if she doesn't finish it. Relaxing, she finds herself unusually hungry.

I feel as though I know this place, she says, between mouthfuls of rich paprika goulash. Or perhaps I've been here in a dream.

Maybe your imaginary character? Margit encourages, shooting a challenging look towards András, who sighs and rolls his eyes, but says nothing.

Catherine smiles. I think you might be right. I know it sounds insane, but how would I go about finding out if someone of that name existed? She may be from the Fifties rather than the Thirties. I guess she's in her early thirties so I'm not sure of when she would have been born except sometime in the late Twenties.

And you only have a name? András asks. A name from a dream?

Yes. I can't find any reference to her in the research, but I feel like I read it somewhere that I've lost track of.

Perhaps in another context? András asks. She couldn't have known József if she was born at the end of the Twenties, or only as a small child.

Quite, Catherine says quietly, but I'd be interested to know where she might fit. She's so vivid in my dreams and if she were real I'd want to be careful about how I use her in the novel.

András nods more vigorously. Yes, that makes sense.

Catherine feels relieved to have got András on side in this project in a way that doesn't challenge his expectations, but Margit winks at her across the table.

Well, it's possible to look for the anyakönyvi, the official birth certificate, but you would need more information, András muses. You have the name. But Budapest is too vague for the place of birth. There are twenty-three districts. It could take a year and a lot of expense to search them all. You would need a date of birth and family details — her father's name, her mother's maiden name — it would be hard to know where to start otherwise.

Sándor, Catherine says. That was her father's name. And the family name changed when they came from Austria, from Haas to Virág. Her mother was Marie Spire. I don't know how I know all this, but there it is. But it's still not enough, is it?

András and Margit shake their heads together.

There are Jewish records, Margit says, kept by the rabbis, but they are held in their communities, not a central record.

So it's hopeless, Catherine comments.

Unless you dream some more, Margit says.

Or find your reference. She must be there somewhere if you

read all this and remember it, András corrects.

Catherine smiles across at Margit, willing her not to goad András further.

At the train station, Catherine hugs Margit and András. Köszönöm, she says. Thank you — for the trip, the meal, the conversation. You're wonderful, both of you. I think I need a walk after all that time sitting on the train, but I'll see you soon.

She takes a metro under the river, then heads towards Andrássy út where she stands for a long time outside number 60, an elegant building rising four stories on a busy intersection of the tree-lined boulevard. It has a tinge of green and, unlike most buildings, which are faded and tired, this one has been recently refurbished. Selene was brought here briefly, she thinks, others died here, not officially executed but dying 'accidentally' during interrogation.

She shudders, turns away, continues along the street to number 45 where Attila used to work when he was editing *Beautiful Word*. She steps inside Írók Boltja, making her way first to the English book section at the back of the shop. She sits in what was once the Writers' Café, browsing a photo-history of the city by Endre Lábass — vaguely listening to a group of young Americans engaged in energetic literary criticism between exchanging tips on the best night life in Budapest — and wondering about the woman who, each night, she becomes...

Catherine

...in dreams.

Catherine knows herself as Selene.

She enters the yard behind a line of other women, walls rising, blind, mute, slabbing out grey sky that glares after the cell's murk. Her chest aches. She hunches, tries to suppress the cough rising between sore ribs. She inches forward. Behind her more women stagger into the featureless quadrangle, stumble along the perimeter. Walk, walk, the voice in her head says — one foot, the next, right foot, left. Air spikes her lungs, chill pulling the cough upwards, burning her throat, muscles spasming. In front and behind, other feet shuffle — one foot, the next, drab wall grasped for balance. First circuit, second, till someone calls halt and the women are led down corridors, back to cells.

On her bunk, the coughs wrench her innards. She balls herself tight. When the fit is finished with her, she lies still for minutes, hours, gets up and scratches the day's date on the wall of the cell. Next to the list of dates she scratches: Born Monday April 11, 1927, Wesselényi utca, 41, Budapest VI.

She lies back on the bunk, pulls the tattered blanket across her body, falls into a fretful dream —

I was there, Selene. Zsófia's face is flushed with excitement. There were thousands of students. They're going to leave DISZ, set up their own group. I stayed right to the end — Tibor was marvellous. They have a manifesto — sixteen demands. They're going to march to the statue of József Bem tomorrow. This is it, Selene. It's all going to change. You have to come with us.

If something happened to me...

You can't think like that. This is history. This is the most important thing you'll ever do — for your mother, for your children — think of Miriam growing up in a better place.

Selene laughs. Child, not children, she says. It's unlikely I'll ever have another if I have to care for my mother for the next thirty years.

Of course you'll have more children, look at you! But we want children to be born into a different place than this. This is for Miriam and all your unborn children, Selene, and for mine and Tibor's too. Zsófia smiles and pats her flat stomach.

You're pregnant?

Shh. But, yes. She grins. You will come, won't you?

Selene lies wounded by mortar debris, her right arm and leg blood-spattered and fragment-encrusted. She retches from pain, tries to stay conscious, looks round frantically for help. Two young men run towards her, ducking the bullets that fly across the street. One dives to the ground, lies still, then makes his way towards her on his hands and knees.

You'll be okay, someone says.

She feels hands lifting her gently, wonders distantly where Zsófia is... she saw her... when? A bottle of gasoline stuffed with rags clutched in her hands... the fabric alight... Zsófia's face radiant with belief, shouting something wild as the Molotov cocktail hurtled through the air...

Smoke drifts towards them as the men hold her, the distant grating of tank tracks tearing up roads as they move, the awful squeal and clatter of them.

Need to get you out of here, one of the men says, glancing over his shoulder.

They move past Abbazia Coffee House, its facade hanging in broken tatters, glass gone from windows, a hole gouged out of two storeys of the building next door, everywhere the choking smell of burning, acrid, clawing at her eyes and nostrils.

At the hospital on Péterfy Sándor utca, while the doctors remove shards from her arm and leg, Selene drifts in a morphine haze, remembering the brief euphoria and terror of the last week.

Chants fill her head — *This we swear, this we swear, that we will no longer be slaves* — *Send the Red Army home* — *We want free elections.* The crush of bodies, spirits high, outside the Parliament Buildings. She had managed to stay close to Zsófia, but they had lost sight of Tibor and his cousin, Luca, as the crowd swelled. Two hundred thousand demonstrators, someone had said, but Gerö rejected everything they asked for and soon she was being carried forward again, towards the statue of Stalin. She didn't see it fall, far back in the crowd, only heard the roar and cheer.

What should take the place of the statue? Someone asks her.

I…

No, it's a joke, Zsófia tells her. It should be replaced by a fountain to rinse the mouths of those who've been licking Stalin's boots.

Later, when she leaves the hospital, she finds Zsófia and Tibor at a student dorm in Buda, hears about the students who've been shot by the ÁVH as they tried to broadcast their demands from Radio Budapest. Guns, someone said — the soldiers have joined the cause, another added, their red stars torn from uniforms, depots opened to distribute arms. Someone offers her a gun, presses it into her hands when she shakes her head, insists he will teach her how to shoot it — come with me, I'll show you — come with me…

When did Nagy become President again? Days blurring into nights into days — the next day, Soviet tanks on every bridge, but it was the ÁVH doing the shooting, demonstrators returning fire. When had she last been home? Does her mother have food for Miriam?

The chants changing — *Death to ÁVH* — *Death to Communists*.

Király's forces have attacked the Central Committee of the Communist Party building, someone tells her.

Király has negotiated a ceasefire, someone says on another day. The Soviets will leave now.

We've won, someone says the next day, Nagy has just announced the cease-fire on the radio. No one will be prosecuted — he's calling this a great, national and democratic event — complete

80

amnesty — the end of the ÁVH — he's negotiating the withdrawal of the Soviets.

On 1 November, she listens to the radio as Nagy announces Hungary's withdrawal from the Warsaw Pact — Hungary will be neutral — a multi-party democracy.

The roar and cheer.

Only three days later, Free Kossuth Rádiö stops broadcasting. Soviet tanks once more filling the city.

They've arrested Tibor, Zsófia tells Selene when she makes her way back to the ruined student house the next day. Don't go home. We have to get out. Now.

But how? And —

We have to get to the station, get on a train.

Won't they be stopping people?

There's too much chaos. We might not get all the way on one train, but we can get out before the border. There are camps, people showing the way across. The border's too long for them to police all of it.

But I can't leave Miriam, my mother…

They'll be fine, Selene. You're no use to them in prison or dead.

But surely they wouldn't… I mean… I hardly…

They'll associate you with Tibor. He's known as part of the Petöfi Circle and a leader of DISZ. And with me. I set a tank on fire!

Zsófia's face has changed. The glow of zealotry, Selene thinks anxiously.

I'm sorry, Selene, but you really can't stay…

At the border camp everything costs. A litre of milk, a guide to show them across the swamp. Selene's leg burns with pain.

Don't let them think you can't make it, Zsófia hisses, her face pale, eyes puffy and red-rimmed.

Following the flickering torch of the guide as they wade creeks, squelch through marshes that threaten to suck them in, Selene wonders if they are being led astray now that they have no money left. Can we really walk across the border unchecked?

But the next morning they are in Austria, another camp, given food, despite their lack of money. Later that day, a doctor looks at her leg, shakes his head, orders moist bandages to dress the wound.

Danke.

Sprechen Sie Deutsche?

Ja. She explains she is a nurse.

Good, he says. You can make yourself useful once your wounds have been dressed. Do you feel strong enough?

Yes, she says. Yes. And my friend, Zsófia — she's a nurse too…

He shakes his head.

But?

Did you know she was pregnant?

Yes, but...

She lost a lot of blood. I'm afraid...

Selene begins to weep.

I'm sorry for your loss, the doctor says quietly, moving on to the next patient.

Budapest, Thursday 11 November 1993

I have everything needed to find her in the *Motherbook*. In any case I can finally find out if Selene lived. In the last dream she had scraped her date and place of birth onto the wall next to the list of dates marking off her sentence. She and Attila shared a birthdate — April 11 — one in 1927, the other 1905.

It is still possible that this is an elaborate dream conjured by my imagination. Anyone in their right mind would think so, but Miriam taught me to look beyond what appears sane. I believe Selene was real. There are moments when I think we may even be the same person — that she is a previous life. The stories Miriam told me growing up — the stories I believed, and then stopped believing... But now I wonder...

I thought I had come here to write an entirely different sort of novel — a fictionalised history that had nothing to do with my own life. Instead I find myself pulled into a story that is more and more personal.

Will the story and the facts ever match?

Selene Solweig

Selene hunches on the bench staring at the wall, dates scratched to keep track of the years. Next to the dates, beneath where she had written: 'Born Monday April 11 1927, Wesselényi utca, 41, Budapest VII' is a new inscription she has no memory of writing: 'Catherine Anne McManus, born August 15, 1961, Parkside Hospital, Middlesbrough, Teesside.'

She settles into sleep, saying Catherine's name.

He's one of the kindest men I know, Margit tells Catherine as they walk towards the offices of Holló Press.

In the reception, Margit makes the introductions and leaves Catherine with György Kalmár, who ushers her into an office piled with books, clears chairs and asks his secretary to bring water and coffee.

I'm fascinated that you chose a Hungarian poet to write about, he says to Catherine when they are finally seated, the tray of drinks resting on books stacked on the table between them. I think he is more known in Germany, perhaps France.

Yes, Catherine agrees, placing her water glass on the precarious tray. I was working with a Hungarian poet in England and he mentioned Attila József. It wasn't easy finding much in English translation, but I managed to track down a copy of Péter Hargitai's translation of *Perched on Nothing's Branch* through a friend in the States, and Corvina's French translation from the Sixties.

Poèmes choisis?

Yes.

And your other characters?

Well, they are emerging more slowly. I originally envisaged a sort of conversation between a researcher based in the present, loosely based on myself, and Attila József, but while I've been here I've heard so much about the uprising and the years after it and I started to dream another character, a young woman in prison in the late Fifties.

György finishes his coffee and nods. He brushes a hand through wiry curls that spring upright around his round face. It was a strange period. After the turmoil of the Forties and early Fifties, in many ways it felt like a more stable period. There were shortages, but by and large we had food, even if it was basic. There were terrors, but we went on day to day and there we heard constantly that we were all in it together. And, of course, everyone was employed. Publishing was certainly easier under a command economy, even if we had to negotiate the categories of 'approved', 'tolerated' and 'banned' art.

Yet there was an uprising?

Yes. If we'd been convinced — if we'd really believed that everyone was in it together, everyone equally poor, but all working for the same goals… but we could see that wasn't true. The political elites had… not money, they weren't rich necessarily, but they didn't live like the rest of us — there were privileges. And everywhere there were Soviets and the presence of a Soviet system that wasn't our own. It wasn't enough for the price of bread to stay the same in the face of all that.

That makes sense.

And your young woman — she has some connection with József?

Yes. In prison she recites poetry — a way of staying sane, keeping her identity…

Yes. György nods vigorously. I knew people who were in prison who did that. It is a type of resistance, I think.

Yes. And Selene — my character — has previously been through a lot of stressful situations — she's Jewish and lost her father in the war, barely survived the ghetto and supports her depressed mother, who is French and hates Budapest. And she becomes a single mother. She has migraines. experiences aura and begins to have the notion, or the sensation, that she goes back in time and meets Attila. She believes he is the father of her child. It may be dissociative episodes — or it may be real — what's important is not whether we believe her, but how she experiences reality. There's a Quixote theme underpinning the narrative — how some people take on 'giants' not because they can win, but because they see it as the only right thing to do.

I see, yes. Well Attila József could certainly be a Quixote-figure and there were many young women who were something between Sancho and Dulcinea who couldn't save him.

And he killed himself, of course. Quixote always dies. It's the same from Dostoevsky's *The Idiot* to *Madame Bovary.*

Quite so. Suicide was integral to who he was.

Catherine smiles. Margit said the same, that the life and manner of death have an internal logic.

So, to get back to the Fifties — what else can I tell you?

Later, when Catherine arrives back at the apartment, there is a letter for her in the metal pigeon-hole in the grubby hallway.

2 Loretánská, Prague,
Saturday 6 November 1993

Dear Catherine,

I'm hoping for a letter from you soon. Did you get my last? I posted it on Thursday with the mad idea that you'd get it when you arrived in Budapest, though I'm told the mail takes anything from three to five days.

I've been working hard since Nathan left me in peace. It was good to see him, I suppose, but I can concentrate better without him and can talk to Eliška more easily without Nathan at my shoulder, trying to impress her.

I'm eager to hear your news. I've got two full notebooks ready to transcribe, full of strange material — Rudolph, Kelley and Dee are beginning to merge into a single fictitious character in my notes, perhaps in a fictitious city — a nowhere place that is Thatcherite Britain and sixteenth century middle-Europe and neither of those... a place of mists... I had a huge outpouring of notes and prose for a few days, but now find myself feeling exhausted and rather blue. I wish I could explain why, but I never can — it just comes on me and everything appears greyer, more hopeless. I start to feel anxious about meeting people, but desolate if I stay in alone. Perverse, I know. Worst of all, I dither for hours over simple decisions — should I cook an omelette or make a sandwich? And once I've made the decision I am hit by the certainty that it was the wrong choice — If I chose the sandwich, I convince myself that the omelette would have left me feeling less bloated, more optimistic — or the other way round — whatever I choose will be an error and compound my dark mood.

Are you sure you want to put up with me, sweetness?

I have a day with no appointments, which is probably not helpful — nothing to force me to act. So I should be typing up notes, organising thoughts, writing a draft chapter and the fact that I'm doing none of those things makes me despair of myself. Useless! Everything itches — my limbs feel twitchy and unsettled, my skin crawls, my mind hops around from one anxiety to the next and I keep coming back to the thought that I'll never finish this book, that in any case it's a ridiculous subject, that I've published one book that's bound to flop, so why am I thinking about writing another? And what's the point of writing anyway? The world is so uncertain. It seems self-indulgent and insignificant.

I've been listing signs of hope from this year as it gets toward its end — the Maastricht Treaty was a good thing; there seems to be hope in Palestine and South Africa, but there's plenty of violence in other places and the Chinese have begun nuclear tests. Perhaps they will wipe us all out. And meanwhile, we have massive unemployment, even with massaged figures, and are told to go 'back to basics'. And who knows when or where the next IRA attack might be? And now we have BNP councillors in Tower Hamlets, not to mention this new UKIP lot.

Sorry — not much about hope there, just the usual rant, but things seem to fall apart more than they are put together, don't they? I'm here in a country that's less than a year old, formed by breaking apart. I know it was a much more peaceful transition than it might have been — the Velvet Revolution and Velvet Divorce — an easier time than Hungary, which seems to have had more than its share of horror in the past — but it all feels so fragile — and meanwhile the Balkans continues to tear apart bloodily. And here am I, fretting about a novel on occult Prague. Is there really any point?

I visited the Pinkas Synagogue yesterday. The names of

Jewish victims of the Shoah were written on its walls from the late Fifties — name, birthdate, deathdate. The Soviets closed it, but it re-opened in '89 and has taken three years to restore the names — wall after wall after wall. In one room there are pictures drawn by children interned in the ghetto at Theresienstadt, inspired by the artist Friedl Dicker-Brandeis. Most died of the awful conditions or were executed soon after, many in Auschwitz. The sorrow of that room was unbearable. How to make sense of such inhumanity? How dare I write novels in the face of this?

Afterwards I visited the tiny Old-New Synagogue — seven hundred years of worship. It has an extraordinary vaulted ceiling and thin lancet windows, but what's most fascinating is the legend that Rabbi Judah Loew ben Bezalel, the mystic and philosopher who conversed with Emperor Rudolph about Kabbalah and is reputed to have made a Golem to defend the Jews from attack, the body of which is still in the closed attic (the lower stairs have been removed to make it inaccessible). I realise that golem stories may actually be later German tradition, but whatever the case, the Nazis didn't enter that attic and it was one of the few synagogues spared.

So — I have copious material and Prague is endlessly fruitful. Esotericism and mysticism are everywhere and stories insinuate themselves into my senses just walking around the city. Despite which, I am a mess of self-doubt and wonder what right I have to make use of such disparate traditions while the world is full of pain.

But you must be tired of this whining by now. If you haven't already decided to never speak to me again, let me finish by saying, I do love you. Even in my foulest mood, I adore you and can't imagine life without you.

Perhaps I shouldn't send this? But we promised each other honesty and I don't want to hide how awful I really am.

All my love, always,
Simon.

Catherine reads the letter twice. They have agreed on letters since neither of them are talkative on phones — the lack of visual clues, the way silences become awkward — and anyway there is the expense, but she wonders if she should phone him. Would it help? He wrote the letter four days ago and may be feeling better now — caught up in the work again. Or maybe he'll be feeling worse and, if she can't help down a long-distance phone-line, she could do more harm by ringing...

She paces the apartment, makes coffee, walks to the phone and picks it up, puts it down again, thinks of their time together, brief and intense —

They'd met for the second time at the tail end of 1992, after she'd taken on his manuscript. They sat for hours in a restaurant, swapping opinions like earnest teenagers — Béla Tarr's *Werckmeister Harmonies*, Bruno Schulz's *Street of Crocodiles*, the poetry of C D Wright, the jazz of Oliver Nelson — he'd brought her the CD of *More Blues and the Abstract Truth*, played over and over when she got home. At their next editorial meeting, in the museum in Birmingham, they discussed the language of Beckett and Joyce, the untrustworthiness of politicians. When they lunched together a fortnight later they'd raved about the short stories of Jesse Ball, the beauty of *Tree of Codes*. They talked for three hours, neither of them raising the question of what they might be starting to mean to one another or the fact that she might already have inadvertently invited him to go to Paris with her the following spring.

They didn't get to Paris in April, but had found their way to Menton together in May, spent days writing in easy silence, Simon cocooned in headphones while she sat by the window, drinking in the quiet, broken only by the shushing sea and the hourly chiming of bells. On their last evening in Menton, they'd walked along the sea wall, looked out at the picture-book dazzle of moonlight on water, how it spread from the luminous centre and she had wept at the thought of him leaving the next morning while she stayed on for work.

After almost a year she still wonders if she is making him up.

She remembers the story he wrote in Menton and left her with when they parted at Nice airport:

The new day tasted of last night's memories...

Everything she has since read from him has delighted her; his prose tight and distinctive, haunting stories — strange, heart-breaking.

She had been certain for a while that the character in the story he left for her in Menton, Mathieu, was a coded version of himself — blue eyes searching the open window for a sign of the woman he'd built his fantasy around, the shock of meeting her in reality becoming overwhelming so that he decided it was best to leave the relationship on a note of anticipation — looking up at an open window, painting the romance in his head. What could compare with that? After he had made her up, the reality would pale...

...lights go on. It grows dark through the shutter. Through my solitude...

Alone in Menton, she had paced the apartment, wondering why Simon's character had insisted on hugging solitude close, guarding it? She had pulled the shutter tight against the darkness, wondered if Simon was trying to tell her that it was all too much, that she was too much, that he preferred his solitude.

On the train to Nice the next morning she had scanned the passengers' faces, wondering if one of them might be the inspiration for Mathieu.

The sun was high and hot as she followed the line of the railway towards the steps leading to Avenue Docteur Menard. At the top of the second flight, twisted and shaded, she paused to wonder if Mathieu ever walked this route, shook herself. Of course not. Simon made him up.

Had she made Simon up? Was she forcing him to be something he couldn't manage?

In the Chagall museum, the canvasses appeared more powerful, bluer — more overwhelming. She sat in front of 'Moses with the Burning Bush' and felt herself falling, brushed away a stray tear and moved on to 'Noah's Ark', thinking of apocalypse, loved ones lost, God's rainbow promise of no more destruction — a promise no one can make, not even God. She had remembered Miriam, thought of how seldom the story and the facts match, of how much betrayal one life attracts. She remembered her first meetings with Simon, how he had listened, how he had never tried to give her another name...

Your real name is Casilda, but I'll call you Cassie, Miriam had told her.

And later, Liam had insisted on another name — *Kitty* — another identity.

Had she been either of those people? She had believed all of it and none of it; had tried to make the facts and the story match each time. And now? Why had Simon created Mathieu, a character who chose fantasy over the prospect of a relationship? It haunted her as the Chagall haunted her:

...so we fight with being itself to discover who we are; limp on, walking out of a past of victories and defeats and into a future of unimagined losses, fears and hopes; wounded and blessed.

In the room of *Le Cantique des Cantiques* the canvasses were red:

…an intoxication of magenta, cerise; love like myrrh; like honey, milk, wine, herbs, oil, roses; love that lights up the night.

Catherine sat, began to weep.

In art as in life all things are possible, Chagall believed, *if only there is deep love.* But Mathieu had turned his back on love.

Mathieu, but not Simon.

That night, they talked on the phone, despite their dislike of disembodied words. He'd soothed her fears. It's just a story; story and facts are not the same thing, he'd reassured her.

And now he has fallen into depression and she wants to soothe him, feels helpless.

She walks to the telephone, dials the number.

Simon?

Catherine? Oh, it's good to hear your voice…

Catherine

Catherine wakes in the smaller cell, no dates scratched on the wall.

The door slams open.

Get up, lazy sow

She tries not to stumble as she walks ahead of the guard, is goaded into the back of the truck to drive to the court room, his rubber baton searching out the bruise still blooming across her back.

We've established that you had a gun, the prosecutor asserts. Perhaps you would like to tell us who you shot with it. Or what other criminal acts you took part in. I recall you never answered the question about throwing Molotov cocktails.

Selene shakes her head. I gave the gun away, she says. Everything was very confused, I tried to find my friends, but —

We don't want to know about your pitiful 'friends'. You were wounded, yes?

Selene nods. By mortar debris — my right arm and leg. I went to hospital and when I returned everyone was gone.

Gone from the fighting? The fighting you took part in.

I wasn't. I couldn't get involved. I...

Did you witness lynchings? Take part in those? Kick the bodies of fallen heroes killed by your 'friends'?

No! I...

So you did nothing to get injured and then ran away?

I was frightened. Confused. People I knew were being arrested. My friend Zsófia thought we weren't safe and —

That would be Zsófia Široký, née Lenárt, a known agitator and fugitive, the wife of the executed criminal, Tibor Široký?

Yes... Zsófia didn't make it back to Hungary, she...

So, what we have established so far, Miss Virág, is that you lied to the court about having a gun, that you took part in a criminal uprising with convicted revolutionaries, that you were injured fighting the lawful forces of this country and that you fled the country illegally for fear of justice.

That's not...

Enough, Gustáv Tutsek roars from his raised seat beyond the bench. We've heard enough lies and excuses. Thank you, he says to the prosecutor. Does the defence have anything to add?

Nothing at all, says the state appointed defender. I'm sorry to say that this defendant appears to be beyond saving.

Thank you, Tutsek says again. I think we are all agreed that this is a clear case. He glares at Selene. You have had almost a month to make a confession, young woman, and instead you have wasted this court's time with your lies and wheedling. You have shown no remorse.

He scans the court.

We will take a break for lunch before sentencing, gentlemen.

Selene stands to hear the judgment. She can think of nothing but Miriam. How long will it be before she sees Miriam again?

Selene Solweig Virág, this court has heard how you trained in the use of firearms in order to join in an unlawful uprising. We have heard a sickening account of how you took part in open rebellion together with known criminals Zsófia and Tibor Široký. How, having availed yourself of medical services in the country you were seeking to destroy, you fled, crossing the border to Austria illegally and planning to seek refugee status in France, where you had lived as a child. We have heard, moreover that, in your arrogance and with no decent feelings of guilt, you chose to return, believing that your heinous actions would be thought too trifling to subject to justice. Selene Solweig Virág, this court finds you guilty of sedition and insurrection. In the light of your lack of remorse, it is my duty to sentence you to death.

No! Catherine screams, rousing from the dream. No!

She fumbles for the light, shuffles to the kitchen for water, sits down at her desk.

Budapest, Friday 12 November 1993

Woken in the early hours from another horrific dream. I felt so encouraged by finding Selene's birthdate that I'd stopped thinking about how awful her situation is — or was. In the dream I got to the end of the seemingly interminable trial and she was sentenced to death. But that was in 1957 and most of the dreams have been in the other cell with dates from 1959 scratched on the wall.

What happened? Did she appeal? Was the sentence commuted or did they leave her in prison for years before killing her?

Can't sleep after this. I feel desperate to locate some official record of Selene's existence, but everything has its proper channels, forms to be filled — and if I do find information about her, then I may simply be confirming that she lived a wretched life, imprisoned before she was thirty, separated from her daughter, perhaps executed? Maybe it would be better never to have existed, to mangle Dostoevsky, though Miriam wouldn't agree. *Until death, it's all life* — Quixote insists that there's a remedy for all things except death, but is it always worth it? No matter how painful the life? And Attila József seems to be in the camp of those who see death as the remedy, not the incurable harm, when it's all too much. But it's a desperate measure — one there is no coming back from.

Wish I could talk to Simon — preferably right now, at 4 a.m., but after that letter, I don't want to depress him with these thoughts. He did sound better on the phone, but still — he's finding it hard alone in Prague, prey to self-doubt. I can't add to that with stories of injustice and terror.

So what to do?

Work on the novel until I'm so tired I fall asleep and hope there are no more dreams tonight?

Selene Solweig

She paces the cell, six steps one way, four steps the other. Five steps forward, three steps back. It is important to vary the order, not fall into a pattern, it is her only freedom. She stops to stretch, bend, squat, begins to recite poetry as she walks the cell again.

Later, after a meagre bowl of beans, she settles onto the narrow bunk, welcomes sleep, the prospect of another life in another time…

Catherine makes coffee slowly. The dream of Selene's trial and sentencing haunts her. She is meeting Margit today. They will go together to fill in the forms to try to find a record of Selene, before going to meet Attila's sister, a rare privilege. She needs to feel awake, alert, not to look hung-over.

After three cups of coffee, she stands for a long time under the shower, feeling gradually revived. She dresses carefully. It's colder today, the short spell of almost spring-like temperatures suddenly plummeting and she has noticed how women on the street stare at the bright clothes that mark her out as foreign. She chooses a grey sweater and navy skirt to go under her wool coat, which can't hide being purple, but a dark shade at least.

At the university, Margit offers her a journal in Hungarian.

I know you can't read it, but I thought you'd be interested. *Kritika*, it's a liberal journal with very good articles from writers like Konrad, who's championed an alternative artistic culture for years and done a great deal to work for writers persecuted in many countries. There's an excellent article by Károly Makk about his film, *Hungarian Requiem* — of interest because it looks back to the uprising and suggests the authorities knew it was coming. A group of prisoners waiting to be tried — seven men, share a cell and remember their loves, their dreams of freedom — a poetic rhapsody in a deathly place. Reminiscent of what your character is living through, I think. I'll translate it for you if it's useful.

Thank you, yes.

There's also a very depressing piece about the rise of skinheads and violence in Budapest. Shameful. But you don't need to be worried by that, Margit adds.

At the office of Budapest VII's Erzsébetváros district, Margit hands the forms she has helped Catherine compile to a motherly official.

She asks if you are searching for a relative, Margit says.

Perhaps the relative of a close friend, Catherine says, a Jewish friend.

Margit looks quizzical, but translates for the registrar.

She nods and tells Margit they should come back in half an hour, she'll see what she can do.

So Selene might be related to someone you know? Margit asks,

99

when they are sipping hot black coffee at a café on Erzsébet krt.

I'm not sure. Maybe that's how she got into my dreams, Catherine says uncertainly. I thought it might help if there was a link.

Perhaps, though she seems disposed to help.

Back at the office, Hanna Farkas introduces herself properly to Catherine in broken English, shows her a copy she has made of Selene's entry.

You found it?

Catherine feels the world spin.

So she really?…

Margit helps Catherine to a chair, says something in Hungarian to Mrs Farkas, who disappears and returns with water.

Thank you. Köszönöm.

Mrs Farkas takes the water when Catherine has gulped down enough, and hands her the copy. Margit looks over it and translates.

She was registered on April 12, 1927 by her father, Margit says, pointing to two entries. Name: Selene Solweig Virág, female, Jewish. Born Monday April 11, 1927, Wesselényi utca, 41, Budapest VII. Father's name, Sándor Virág, aged twenty-five. Mother's name, Marie Virág née Spire, aged twenty-four. Parents' religion: Jewish. That's Sándor Virág's signature, the other is the signature of the registrar. And that's it. You may be dreaming of her, but you didn't invent her.

Margit insists on what she calls a light lunch before they visit Etelka József. We've got plenty of time and you need to compose yourself, she adds.

When they are seated and have chosen, Margit expressing concern about Catherine ordering a mere bowl of soup, she leans over and puts a hand on Catherine's arm.

Well, she's real, my dear, and she was born only ten years before József died, so she certainly couldn't have had a relationship with him. The dreams about the prison seem more likely, sadly. Maybe the rest is simply because you're researching József, perhaps compounded by Selene and József sharing a birthday.

Catherine nods. Margit has entertained her instincts about Selene being real, but she can't ask her to believe that someone might slip through time.

Still, there's no reason why she can't move through time in your novel, Margit adds. It's fiction after all.

Yes, Catherine says. Maybe that's why I've dreamt her — or remembered her.

The ninety-year-old Etelka József shows Catherine a photograph taken with her younger brother. We were two years apart, Etelka says.

You look so alike, Catherine returns, holding the sepia image delicately.

They have the same dark hair and eyes, the same serious expression, though there is something more rigid, sadder, in Attila's face. Etelka, white-haired, her eyes surrounded by thick-rimmed spectacles, still has that same look of intensity.

I've become the guardian of his poetry, the old lady says

wistfully. A pity I couldn't have been a better guardian to him in life.

Catherine wants to hug her, to tell her she did everything possible, but she is uncertain how it might sound from a stranger.

Etelka takes back the picture and hands Catherine a signed copy of József's first collection.

She holds it reverently, her fingers tracing the loops and strokes of his name.

He was lucky that Jolán married Ödön Makai. He was a rich lawyer, though I'm sure you know all this. We'd lived in so many places — Soroksári Way, Szvetanay Street, Dam Street, Ferenc Square, Peacock Street, Haller utca. We were always running from some landlord. Ödön gave Attila stability, as well as an education, but perhaps it was too late — our father leaving us, mother handing him over to foster care, then dying when he was so young. Attila was already broken, I think, but we did our best.

Etelka pauses and smiles. I married Ödön myself later. We had three children. I think I'm a great-grandmother now. She laughs. But I won't bore you with all those pictures.

I hardly know how to talk about him, Etelka goes on. He's a national hero, but for me he was my little brother, always suffering. I was only two years old when he was born, but I remember it. There was such a commotion in the house. My parents had many other children, but only three of us lived and Attila was the only son to survive. Margaret, my older sister, died very young, and Kalman also. Attila was a delicate boy. The year in Öcsöd was too much for him, having his name taken away from him and being made to look after pigs. I was set to work in the kitchen, but Attila would rather have done that. Pista, they called him…. A terrible year. Our father, who'd abandoned us, turned up when mother was very sick. He sat by her bed and held her hand, but then ran from the room…. I married Ödön Makai in the Thirties, his fourth wife, and we settled in Hódmezővásárhely, had children, stayed together until Ödön died, the same year as Attila. When Attila had no work and no food, he would visit us in Hódmezővásárhely or we'd send food packages to him in Budapest. Ödön had a holiday house at Balatonszárszó, near the lake, a lovely place. Attila often stayed with us and at the end, of course, he was with us there, though not in the same house. I was widowed by then and we'd moved to a cottage — six of us living in two rooms — me and my children, Attila and my sister, Jolán. We were just getting ready for dinner when…

Etelka takes out a lace handkerchief. All so long ago, she says, but still…

Of course, Catherine says, Thank you. Köszönöm.

A key turns in the apartment door and a younger version of Etelka steps into the room.

Visitors, how lovely. Zsuzsanna Makai introduces herself, offers more drinks in good English.

Zsuzsanna finds a photograph of Attila that Catherine has never seen. He's in his early twenties, smiling broadly.

People judge him by his end, Zsuzsanna says, but he was a much richer character than the image of the depressed, tortured poet. With the family he was funny, witty, joked all the time. He was wonderful with me and with Péter and Ádám, my brothers. He always wanted a family of his own. And he could talk on any subject, a brilliant mind. But I'm babbling —

Catherine steels herself. Do you think your Uncle Attila took his own life?

Zsuzsanna pauses. For a long time I tried to convince myself that it was a terrible accident. He'd been depressed, but not that day. He seemed in good spirits, he'd even written to Flóra about their future together. But the day before he was morose when his friends left without him... and of course he'd been suicidal before...

Yes. I'm sorry to ask... Thank you. Catherine hesitates.

I don't mind questions, Zsuzsanna encourages.

It's a slightly odd one, but was there anyone else? I mean any other relationship towards the end of his life?

As far as I know he wanted to marry Flóra, Zsuzsanna says. But I was a little girl, just eight when he died, so I wouldn't have known everything. He certainly fell in love with ease — he was a very open person.

Catherine

Catherine wakes in a cell she does not recognise. Where has Selene been moved? She uncurls from her foetal clench on the floor, a thin blanket tucked around her. On the bench, a woman a little younger sits, watching.

Ludmilla, she offers.

Selene stretches, every muscle wailing. Selene, she returns, Selene Solweig Virág.

Ludmilla Bíró. The young woman stands, holds out her hand formally. They threw you in here last night, barely conscious. I would have given you the bench, but I couldn't wake you. I put the blanket on —

Thank you, Selene says. Thank you.

Did they?... Ludmilla's question trails away.

I was on trial, sentenced to... to death.

Ah, me too, Ludmilla whispers.

Oh! I'm so sorry.

Ludmilla smiles. Well, we can comfort each other while it lasts.

When food arrives there is only one bowl of beans in scum, one spoon.

They want us to fight — entertain them, then they can beat us, not that they need an excuse, Ludmilla says. You eat first.

Spoon at a time, Selene suggests.

Ludmilla nods, dips in the spoon and lifts it to Selene's mouth. Selene takes the spoon, reciprocates.

Best meal I've had in here, Ludmilla says when they have drained the last inadequate morsel, sopped up every drop with the shared lump of stale bread.

Selene staggers when she gets up from the hard floor where they have squatted to share the meal.

You need to sleep, Ludmilla says. Lie down.

Selene collapses onto the bench, the bruise around her kidneys pulsing pain, falls asleep —

Tibor says the New Course is over, Zsófia tells Selene as they walk towards the staff room at the end of a long night shift. There are still shortages and...

At least we can get butter again, Selene points out. My mother was a nightmare when there was no butter.

Yes, there are small differences, a few more traders, even a new cobbler on my street —

… and books, Selene adds, I found the most amazing book of short stories by someone called Carson McCullers — and the title! — *The Ballad of the Sad Café*.

In Hungarian?

No, English. My mother wouldn't approve of the cost, but…

It's your money! Zsófia encourages, and yes — it is better that we can read without fearing for our lives, but it's not enough. The release of prisoners hasn't been anything like as many as it should be and most of the ones let out are former communists, not real opposition.

Shh! Selene cautions, glancing towards the staff room door. But what can we do?

Come to a meeting with me — tomorrow.

Selene hesitates. I'm not sure, I…

You know I'll just keep asking, Zsófia says. I have to run. Tibor will be waiting. She kisses Selene on each cheek and breezes from the room.

In the bathroom, Selene looks at her face in the pitted mirror. Her skin is grey. You're an old twenty-seven, she says to her reflection, peering closer, closer, so the face dissolves into shapes — into forms melting — into reflections on the face of a lake —

Selene! Attila runs towards her as she turns to his voice, scoops her into his arms, lifts her in the air laughing.

I thought I would never see you again. Selene, Selene, Selene, he says, delightedly. He twirls her around, sets her down, dizzy and giggling.

November 13, Selene says, breathless. I was right about it being a whole year of waiting for me, but wrong about it being a pattern of every third date.

Quite. I spent all of yesterday searching the shore, getting more agitated. I frightened my sisters. Etelka tried to prevent me leaving the house after dinner, but I offered to read stories to the children and crept out afterwards while she thought I was still with them. I'd brought you a poem, then tore it up in frustration, he says. Look.

He holds out a ball of paper shreds.

Oh!

I'll copy it out, he promises. We'll go to our restaurant and I'll write it again for you. He strokes her face. You are really here, my moon and sun.

I am. And no sound of trains this time — I think I fell here through a mirror, very disorienting.

But you are real?

Yes.

Of course you are. We ate together in public. Of course you are real.

But I can't keep letting you buy me dinner when I have no way to buy anything, Selene says.

He considers, grins. And money might be a problem today, but no matter — we'll go to my sister's house. It is very small, but she has a gift for providing food even in hard times. Her husband was a lawyer, but he died, leaving her with small children and she has had to move to this tiny place. They are wonderful — the children. The oldest, Zsuzsanna, is only eight, and the boys, Péter and Ádám, just five and two, full of mischief. I would like to be a father, a father who stays with his children.

But the house? I mean, how would you explain me to your family?

Ah, that is easy. They are all out today. I had to work hard not to be dragged along. I was so disconsolate yesterday, thinking you might never appear again, so they didn't want to leave me alone. When I refused to go, they almost cancelled. I had to convince them I was in good spirits by playing with the children, which is no hardship.

Selene thinks how much more talkative Attila seems, how different he is from the images of the fierce depressive proletarian that she has been taught to envision. But there is something of manic high spirits that might be the obverse of his depression, she muses.

Well, if you're sure, she says, and you could write that poem out for me.

Of course.

They set off at a brisk pace, Attila concerned about how cold she must be in her nurse's tunic, no coat in November.

In the cramped cottage, he sits her at the narrow table, begins throwing open cupboards. So — what shall we find?

I can cook, Selene says.

He looks up, grins. I myself am a terrible cook, he admits.

Ah, well, I grew up in France and my mother, when she was well and happy, loved to cook.

French cooking? he teases, I am even more in love than ever, if such a thing were possible.

She cooks slowly, deliberately, while they swap opinions like earnest teenagers — of François Villon's *Le Testament,* how neither have ever met a fan of this mediaeval French poet and thief before; of Balázs, who Attila has met, jovially boasting how well Balázs reviewed his poetry, both wishing they had been part of his Sunday Circles, talking philosophy with György Lukács, another intellectual who has highly reviewed Attila's work, sociology with Karl Mannheim or debating art and Marxism with Arnold Hauser. They discuss Dada; the poetry and plays of Apollinaire; great Hungarian poets like Endre Ady, Gyula Juhász, whom Attila also knows, and Lajos Kassák, whom Attila admires for making no distinction between being an artist and a socially responsible person —

He's been publishing his autobiography in segments since '23, Attila enthuses — *A Man's Life* — bit by bit in *Nyugat* — they will hound him for it eventually — his views are too much his own.

Like you?

Attila smiles. You know me already.

Selene stops cooking for a moment to dip into her bag for a book. Do you speak English?

He shakes his head. Hungarian, German, French, no English.

This is wonderful, Selene tells him — an American, from the south — she has extraordinary style. It was published three years ago in 1951, but English books have just started trickling into the shops.

Attila turns the book over in his hands. I will rewrite that poem for you, he says, but you must not read it until you are home.

She nods, lapses into contented silence as he smoothes out the balled-up shreds, begins reconstructing.

When they make love they are each a surprise to the other.

> *Your eyes are mirrors*
> *of blessed marvels,*
> *for they have seen me...*

Ady? Selene asks.

Yes. It would be far too crass to quote myself at such a moment, he jokes.

He insists on walking her back to the lake, leaves her gazing into the water wondering how she will find herself back in the hospital bathroom gazing into her reflection, peering closer, closer so the face wavering in a lake dissolves into forms melting — into shapes — into a simple reflection of a young woman whose eyes shine with life —

Budapest, Saturday 13 November 1993

Woke this morning refreshed and relaxed. The third meeting of Attila and Selene was extraordinary — a meeting of minds and bodies — they were kindred, whether they met in reality or not, they fit each other — their love of words, their love of France, of art — of each other. The Attila of my dream was not the frowning, suffering person bequeathed to history — even if only for an afternoon, but Zsuzsanna Makai said the same — a 'much richer character' than his image, she said — funny, witty and playful, as well as brilliant. This is the Attila who appears in my dreams with Selene and I want to capture that in the novel. Even if András doesn't approve of varying the portrait of a national figure, perhaps it will please Zsuzsanna and maybe even Etelka. And I think his enthusiasm with women, the rare moments of 'manic high spirits' (something Selene thought) are characteristics that fit with the sudden lows and melancholy bleakness.

It is a relief when the dreams take me further back in Selene's life — November 13, 1954 this time, but I'm acutely aware of what waits ahead for her. Now that I know she existed, will I be able to find out if the dreams bear any relation to the life of the real person? Perhaps it's a name I heard or read somewhere and it's only my imagination giving her this terrible life? Is there a way to find out more about her, to trace whether her life ended tragically in execution? The dream began in a new cell, waiting to die with another condemned young woman, Ludmilla Bíró. Is she also a real person?

Whatever the truth, women like both of them existed and suffered in this way. Why do nations, groups, do this over and over again? Sacrifice their young, the hopes of a different future? *The unreason of the world is more insane than any fiction.* And so I will continue believing in my dreams.

Selene Solweig

She paces the cell, remembering Ludmilla, whom she knew so briefly two years ago, who was…

She shakes herself, stretches, counts steps, settles onto the bench —

The phone trills and Catherine startles, looks up from her journal, comes back to the world.

I hope you don't mind me calling, Zsuzsanna Makai says.

Of course not, no.

We're always thinking about him, of course, always reminiscing — my mother's main occupation these days, though her mind is still sharp — I suppose it's just that, since your visit yesterday, I've been thinking — perhaps we could meet for coffee?

I'd be glad to, Catherine says.

Zsuzsanna gives directions to Central Café on Károlyi utca.

She walks towards the river and takes the line 2 metro from Kossuth Lajos tér, walking the last few minutes from Astoria.

Don't use line 3, Margit has warned her several times. Too many breakdowns. And it's… not so safe.

It's rather upmarket and of course these old cafés attract the new tourists, Zsuzsanna apologises when Catherine locates her. But the coffee is good and it was a great meeting-place for writers and artists., so I thought it might interest you. The staff of *Nyugat* used to work on the magazine up in the gallery here. The Communists shut it down, of course, but it was the first to reopen when the dictatorship fell, and they've done a fine job of recapturing that grand atmosphere again. You must try a café pepperino, she ends, an espresso with chocolate and pepper — perfect for a cold day.

So, Zsuzsanna continues over pepperinos, I've been thinking about your question — the one about whether there was anyone else in his life at the end, apart from Flóra. She hesitates. I think you may have had a name in mind?

Yes, Catherine admits, though it's one that makes no sense. It's a woman who was only a couple of years older than you, who, rationally, I know couldn't have crossed paths with your uncle, but I must have read about her somewhere else and then my mind has mixed them up in dreams. I've wondered about using her in the novel — a way of exploring certain themes rather than suggesting they actually met as young people from different time periods.

An intriguing idea, Zsuzsanna says, and it's fiction. Anything can happen in a story. But may I ask her name?

Selene, Catherine says. I found confirmation of her details yesterday, just before we came to see your mother. She was Selene Solweig Virág, from a Jewish family who'd changed their name from Haas when they originally came from Austria. Selene's mother was French. She was born on the same date as your brother, but in 1927. I've dreamt of her every night

114

since I got here — sad dreams, mostly — I think she may have been imprisoned after the uprising, perhaps even executed, but in some of the dreams I'm seeing her with your uncle, perhaps because I'm spending so much time researching him and thinking about him. If she really lived, I've wondered if her 'meetings' with Attila were in her mind — dissociative episodes — she was under a lot of strain even before being imprisoned — her father died in the forced labour service; she and her mother survived the Jewish ghetto during the war, but were near to starving; her mother suffered bouts of depression and then Selene became a single parent at a time when there was a lot of suspicion of the former middle-classes and Jews.

Zsuzsanna sits still for a while, silent. She reaches into her bag and brings out a book, hands it to Catherine.

The cover is in a beautiful hand-drawn slab serif font — grey and white on the paper dust jacket, the only illustration an illuminated Paris-style street lamp in the top left hand corner. Inside, the publisher's details: Houghton Mifflin and Company, Boston, 1951, and on the half-title page, the owner's name: Selene Solweig Virág.

Catherine looks up, uncertain what to say.

It was under my uncle's pillow, Zsuzsanna says. It was terrible — the night he died. He'd gone out while dinner was getting ready. My mother told him not to go, but he insisted that he had something to do, that he needed a newspaper or cigarettes, I can't recall… Aunt Jolán told him it was nearly evening, he'd be too late, but he went anyway. My mother told him not to be longer than half an hour or he'd miss dinner, and I could see she was anxious about him going. Even though it had been a good day, he'd had a disappointment the day before when his friends had no space in the car to take him back to Budapest. And his mood could change quickly, especially when he'd been in higher spirits. She told him not to shut the door when he left and, after only ten minutes, sent Jolán to look for him.

Jolán came home alone. She'd searched the village, but hadn't been down to the shore. We tried to eat dinner, joking about him missing out, but my mother kept food for him and hardly ate a thing. Not long after the uneasy meal, we heard footsteps, but it wasn't Uncle Attila. It was a worker from the railway. Sit down, he said, you have to be strong, because this is very bad, this is wrong, he said — and then he told us — and the kitchen was full of people crying, children and adults, all wailing — and this poor man, who'd seen it happen, saying over and over — try to be strong.

Zsuzsanna pauses, reaches for her water glass. Perhaps more coffee? she asks, beckoning a waiter, and Catherine nods.

I crawled into Attila's bed later that night. The adults were finally asleep, cried to exhaustion. I sat on my uncle's bed and cried quietly, then curled up and put my hand under the pillow and this was there.

In 1937?

Yes. I didn't take in the date at that age of course. I just thought it was something precious to my uncle so I wanted to keep it. And I did — kept it a secret — even through the war years when we had nothing and were living in one room in Budapest and went without food. I couldn't let it go, never told anyone. And later, when the anomaly of the date occurred to me, I rationalised it away — a misprint — I couldn't read English then, hadn't heard of the author. Even later? I don't know. We're good at repressing whatever doesn't fit, aren't we?

Yes. Catherine passes a hand over the book on the table. I can't explain it any more than you, she says. Or how Selene got into my dreams about Attila. I had a close friend once who was very keen on *Don Quixote* and constantly told me that the unreason of the world is more insane than any fiction. For her, it meant that we could believe the most extraordinary and impossible things. Life was to be lived as it should be, not as

116

it is. Perhaps your uncle and Selene were people living life in a vision of what should have been, at least on those occasional days of high spirits.

Zsuzsanna nods. I don't think I need to make sense of it, not that it's possible in any case, but thank you for talking to me. Attila was an extraordinary person. His voice, especially when he told us stories or read his poems, was so booming, so warm — perhaps he could reach into the future with it. I'm glad you're writing about him.

Catherine

Catherine wakes in the cell shared with Ludmilla. 1957, she thinks. She is on the bench, Ludmilla on the floor, the one blanket underneath her. She stretches cautiously, stands, and Ludmilla turns towards her.

Sorry, I was trying not to wake you.

No, you didn't, Ludmilla says. I was already awake, but I thought I'd stay here until you woke. You looked so shocked last night.

You're very kind, Selene says.

It's something they haven't taken yet, Ludmilla replies, but they will try.

What do you mean?

I had a cellmate before. She asked a lot of questions, fed information to the guards. It was before my trial, so maybe they won't care so much now they've made their decision to kill me official, but that girl wasn't a bad person, or wouldn't have been in other circumstances. They offered her extra food, promised she wouldn't be hurt, that her family would be safe.

What happened to her?

I have no idea. They moved me before the trial and then put me here afterwards. I haven't noticed her when we are taken out to exercise, but this is a big place. I think they take us out in groups.

So, no questions?

We are condemned women, Selene, our secrets don't matter anymore. We can pass the time swapping our stories. Ludmilla smiles. Ah, now you are wondering if I'm the one trying to get information…

No, no, I…

I don't blame you. Why wouldn't you be suspicious? Make up stories if you like, but let's at least help each other's days pass, not always wondering when they will come for us, or worrying how our families are faring.

You're right, it did cross my mind. I suppose they like us to be mistrustful of each other. But I won't make my stories up.

Good. So, tell me about yourself.

Oh, well — where to start?

You have an educated accent — tell me about your family.

Okay — I was born in an apartment on Wesselényi utca to Jewish parents. Papa was an art dealer. He studied art at the École des Beaux-Arts in Paris, which is where he met Mama. They came back to Budapest, but Mama didn't like it so they returned to Paris when I was a baby, about six-months old. We left in '39 before the Nazi invasion, but things were already getting difficult for Jews. There were Nazi supporters, especially amongst students and Papa thought we would be safer in Hungary.

When we got back, it was soon obvious that life for Jews would be difficult here too. But Papa was wealthy and for a while we believed we could live quietly, not attract attention. But more and more Jews were called up to serve in the Munkaszolgálat. It was the young at first, but then they started to target 'privileged' Jews. Papa worked for six months in a stone quarry in the Ukraine. He came home like a skeleton, depressed and withdrawn. Mama rallied though, fed him, didn't complain about moving to a smaller apartment so that we could manage. He started to improve, but then was called up again. That time it was to the Eastern front, men were used to search for mines. He didn't return home from there...

I'm so sorry, Ludmilla says quietly. This country has been at war with its own people for so long.

Yes. I was sixteen when Papa died. My mother had aspirations for me to become a great dancer — she loves ballet — but that was never going to happen. I loved to dance, but I was never gifted or disciplined enough to do it for a living. I wanted to study in France or England, but I could see that wasn't going to happen for a young Jewish girl. We were lucky to survive with our lives — we were moved to a ghetto and then another. We heard of people being taken away in trains, told to take just one suitcase. It was a rumour at first, then it was people we knew. In the Dohany ghetto people helped each other, but there was so little to share. Every day more people died of cold or starvation. My mother would insist I had more of our food than was my fair share, and refused to eat anything unless I agreed. She was very strong then, not in body, but... But afterwards it was like all the air had drained from her. By the time we were liberated, we were destitute, like many others. I trained as a nurse. I thought the Soviets were our liberators in those days, especially when the coalition government rescinded the anti-Jewish laws. There were even trials of those who had terrorised Jews and religious freedom for a few years, but all that stopped in '49, of course. We were lucky not to be expelled from Budapest in '51, but there was a lot of anti-Semitic feeling and we lived in terror, like so many, afraid we might be branded class-enemies or religious aliens at any moment. My mother shrivelled inside herself. She hardly ever leaves the apartment now…. Selene swallows a sob… I mean, the last time I saw her. She'd stopped cooking or reading or seeing friends. I don't know how she'll be coping, especially looking after Miriam alone.

Miriam?

My daughter. She was born in 1955 — July 7.

You have a child? A husband?

No husband, just Miriam.

But you're a mother!

Yes, I…

They won't execute you if you're a mother.

I don't understand.

The bastards didn't tell you?

No, I'm…

Condemned mothers have their sentences commuted to life imprisonment. I'm sure of it.

How?

The girl in my cell. She'd had her trial already. She was sentenced to death and then informed that due to being a mother she would spend life in prison, a great kindness!

121

Selene begins to shake, weeps. Oh! I'm sorry, I'm so…

Ludmilla folds herself around Selene. Don't apologise. There's hope for one of us, that's something. But I want to know more of your story — about Miriam!

Selene breathes deeply, lets the last sob shudder through her. There's not much to tell. I had a strange and brief affair with a wonderful poet. He suffered from terrible depression — but with me he was… kind and witty and intelligent. I met him in 1952, but we met seldom. When we were together it was as though we'd always known one another — or were always meant to know one another.

Ah, so romantic! My only affairs were with students — it was all politics, drink and sex, nothing romantic, but I suppose it was what I wanted then. Now I wish one of them had got me pregnant. Ironic, eh?

Maybe they won't…

No, don't say that. They'll come for me one day and that will be that. Won't your marvellous poet look after your daughter? Or help your mother?

He died, Selene says quietly.

Oh, that's awful. I'm so sorry.

An accident, Selene says, seeing the longing to ask how he died on Ludmilla's face. It was a terrible accident, she says, thinking, I'm sorry Attila, I know you decided to take your own life, but I can't tell her that, not in here.

Perhaps having to care for Miriam will be good for your mother, Ludmilla offers. It will force her into the world again, give her purpose.

I hope so. They sit in silence for a few minutes until Selene says, And you? What's your story, Ludmilla?

Rather dull compared to yours. I was born in Debrecen, the youngest of four children and the only girl. Horrible brothers, who I adored, of course. My parents belonged to the Reformed Church and my father worked as a journalist. An ordinary family. I grew up a tomboy, always trying to keep up with my brothers, always trying to prove I could make a den or a raft as good as theirs and so I got interested in how things work. I was studying structural design at the University of Technology and Economics. Lots of boys, of course, and student politics — so here I am. Not a great story, I'm afraid — no Parisian childhood or poets, but it was the life I wanted.

Selene nods. Quite — and you shouldn't be so modest — a woman in a man's world.

There were others, but not many, and it did feel good, Ludmilla agrees. So that's us. We'll have to spin out these stories a whole lot more, or make up wild adventures we never had, if we're going to keep this up.

Budapest, Sunday 14 November 1993

I am still reeling from my meeting with Zsuzsanna. To have someone else who believes, or at least does not disbelieve, that Selene and Attila met is extraordinary, inspiring, but also somewhat disorienting.

Meanwhile, it seems that Ludmilla is a good cellmate and I now understand why Selene was still alive in 1959, two years after her trial. Ludmilla told her that mothers were not executed, but kept in prison. If this was the case, then perhaps Selene was re-united with her daughter. Could she still be alive? She would be only sixty-six, a little older than Zsuzsanna. And yet I can't help thinking that this can't be the case — that I am not simply dreaming about her life, rather that it is a life I lived — that I was Selene Solweig Virág. Everything rational in me says this is a preposterous idea. I don't believe in re-incarnation. And yet I grew up believing in Miriam — my Miriam, and amongst all this strangeness, this notion persists.

Selene Solweig

Selene paces the cell, remembering Ludmilla, who she knew so briefly, the stories they told each other, the...

She shakes herself, stretches, counts steps, sits on the bench reciting verses from Ady, and József —

She traces the roughly scratched name on the wall — Catherine Anne McManus — there is only the past and the future, she thinks — these things are real, visions of life not as it is, but as it should be — where did she read that? Her mind drifts, thinking of Ludmilla, of Miriam, of Catherine, of life as Catherine...

who pauses over her journal, lets the pen hover mid-air for a moment —

I feel my world imploding and yet I feel lighter than I have since I arrived. I have to know what became of Miriam Virág. If she survived, then she will be only thirty-eight, just a few years older than me. I have the birthdate, but I need to find out where she was born if I'm to have any hope of tracking her down. Perhaps I could leave questions for Selene on the wall of her cell? Or —

pauses over her journal, lets the pen dangle in mid-air once more, feels a pulse of pain in her temple, the faint aroma of citrus... writes —

Miriam Marie Virág, born July 7, 1955, Népszinház utca, 19, Budapest VIII.

Selene shifts on the bench, feels a wave of something between euphoria and nausea, huddles onto her side, half-drowsing, imagining or dreaming that she is —

Catherine staring at the journal page, confounded.

She rouses, walks to the phone, hesitates, holding the receiver. For a moment she thinks she will ring Zsuzsanna, but despite Zsuzsanna's willingness to live with the inexplicable book she'd found under her uncle's pillow, this might be too much — to ask her to help find her uncle's daughter, born twenty-eight years after he died is... Is what? She begins to punch the numbers for Margit, but wavers. Margit has indulged her 'dreams' as creative inspiration for a more inventive book about Attila than she had ever imagined writing, but this? She steels herself. She must stop vacillating. Carefully, Catherine picks out the sequence of numbers, listens for the unfamiliar dial tone.

Hello?

The voice is sallow. She almost replaces the receiver.

Simon?

Catherine?

His tone is warmer. She exhales. Yes, it's me, she says. How are you?

Oh, you know —

She tenses.

But what about you? Simon asks. Are you okay?

I'm fine, just more of those dreams...

Ah, yes, but you seemed... better... when we last spoke... more...

I know. I'm fine really or more hopeful at least. I think Selene might not have been executed and I think her daughter might be alive, or at least it's possible — she'd only be thirty-eight. I was journalling just now, thinking about ways to discover her birthplace so I could look her up, or at least start to search for her, and I found myself writing her name, then her birthdate and birthplace — as though, well as though I knew it. I felt dizzy looking at what I'd written, as though I might be about to get a migraine, but only for a few seconds. It reminded me of Miriam's free writing when we were at school — my friend Miriam, I mean, not Selene's Miriam and...

Catherine...

Sorry, I'm gabbling. I was going to ring Zsuzsanna — have I told you about her? — but then I thought it may be better to ring Margit, but this is all so strange so it had to be...

The strangest person you know.

No, that's not what I meant, at least not in a bad way, just...

Catherine...

Sorry, I'm a million to the dozen again. What is it?

I don't think I can carry on.

Sorry? What do you mean? Carry on with what?

Everything. Anything.

The writing?

Partly. The research has — I don't know... I can't concentrate on it — I'm not sure I see the point of it in any case, of anything really. I'm just... It's futile, isn't it?

What's futile? I don't understand. When we last talked...

I was probably deluding myself. The whole idea of this book seems idiotic. Too grandiose for a start. And self-indulgent — all the awful things that are happening in the world and I'm wandering around Prague writing notes for a novel. And who's going to want to read it?

But what changed? I mean, I know you'd been down, but when we talked on Wednesday I thought you felt better again — more positive.

Nothing changed. I simply woke up and realised it's rubbish — the novel, trying to convince myself I'm a writer, thinking I can make a difference, imagining you'll go on putting up with me.

There is silence. A choking sound.

Catherine? Oh, shit! I'm such an idiot. Don't cry, sweetness.

I'm not. I mean, I'm confused. Your book is going to be wonderful — and you don't need me to tell you how powerful fiction can be — politically, aesthetically. You know art isn't pointless or decadent, but that's not what this is about, Simon.

It's not?

Don't be obtuse. You're a good writer. You have important things to say, but not if you keep undermining yourself, not if you won't give yourself permission to write. And more than that — we don't stand a chance if we just go round and round the same circles. I don't 'put up' with you, I love you, but if you want to drive me away, just tell me, don't do it like this.

There is a longer silence.

Right.

Right? What does that mean? Simon?

So it's finished then? Between us?

For fuck's sake, that's not what I said.

It isn't?

Simon, I'm unravelling here. I thought I'd got my life together — no more imagining past lives that someone else told me I'd had, no husband telling me what to call myself and who to be. But now I'm having nightmares of someone else's life. And then I find out she actually lived at exactly the period I'm dreaming. And, even crazier, I can't throw off the certainty that she had an affair with another real person who lived in another time, someone who died while she was a child, yet who she believed was the father of her child. And then Zsuzsanna comes along with a book she found in 1937 under Attila's pillow, even though it wasn't published till 1951, and it has Selene's name in it. I don't know which way is up anymore, Simon, and you are the only person I can tell this to. On what planet does that make you think I don't want you in my life?

Sorry. There is a long pause. I get everything wrong, don't I?

No, she shouts down the phone. No, you don't, but right now you're driving me mad and I need you.

I'm always a letdown.

Please! I'm not saying that. I...

The phone line makes the burr of dead air.

Simon?

Catherine dials, hits the wrong buttons, dials again. The sound is of an engaged line. She replaces the receiver, tries again. The same tone. And the next time. And the next.

Later, Catherine rouses from her slumped position by the wall. She tries the line again, willing the dial tone to return, willing Simon to pick up the phone, but there is no change. She replaces the receiver, picks it up again, dials.

Margit? I'm so sorry to bother you, I...

Catherine, you sound... are you all right?

Catherine sniffs, sobs.

I'll come and get you...

No, I...

Don't argue. I'll be half an hour. We'll go somewhere for dinner and you can tell me...

I don't think I can face a restaurant, I —

Okay, we'll come back here. Get yourself into warm clothes — this cold snap is vicious, even by our standards. I'll cook. We'll drink wine, put the world to rights and you can stay here tonight.

Okay, Catherine whispers.

In her apartment later, the phone will ring, fall silent, ring again, pleading, insistent, unanswered...

Catherine

Catherine wakes in the cell that Selene shares with Ludmilla. She is on the floor, the one blanket underneath her, Ludmilla on the bench, gingerly stretching.

Tell me more about your poet, Ludmilla says, bending to touch her toes, then reaching towards the sky.

He was... she hesitates. He was an extraordinary person. He had the warmest voice, and when he read poetry it was like entering another world. I met him only a few times, she pauses again — and each time it was like we had always known one another.

Selene takes a deep breath.

Ludmilla leans towards her, waiting.

I'm waiting to meet him again, Selene whispers.

But you said he died. Ludmilla looks puzzled, but leans closer.

If I tell you this story, you'll think I'm insane.

What's insanity in a place like this? And anyway, if it's a good story, I'm happy.

You know of the poet Attila József?

Of course. You recite his work all the time.

Selene smiles. He's my daughter's father.

But… Ludmilla frowns, calculates with her fingers. But he died in '37. Your daughter is only two-and-a-half. How…?

I don't know how. The first time I met him I was working at the National Institute of Oncology. I'd been talking about writers with my friend Zsófia and then, walking down a corridor, I found myself walking a track beside a lake. The Institute had once been the Siesta Sanatorium. Attila had stayed there during a breakdown, but that was the only link I could think of. It was November 6, 1952 and it was the same day for him, but in 1937, near Lake Balaton. We talked as though we were friends. The next time was November 9, a year later for me, but the same year for him — his last month alive. I was at home with my mother that time. She was fractious and I sat on the bed, summoning the energy to make dinner after a long shift and there I was, by the lake again. He took me for a meal at a taverna, though I'm sure he couldn't afford it, and we talked and talked. After that we both imagined it would be November 12 the next time we met — three days wait for him, but over a year for me. But the day passed and I went to sleep thinking I'd never see him again. The next day I bought a copy of Carson McCullers' *The Ballad of the Sad Café*. English books were just starting to be available and it felt like treasure to get a book that had been published only three years earlier in America. I was in the bathroom at work gazing into the mirror, then found myself staring into my reflection in the lake. He was overjoyed to see me. He'd walked by the lake the day before and brought one of his poems for me — he showed me the torn-up bits of it, shredded when he'd given up hope of seeing

133

me again. He wanted to take me to the taverna again, but I had no coins from his time and I knew his family had so little, so we went back to the tiny cottage he shared with his sisters and nephews and niece. They were out for the day and I cooked for him and... and then we made love. That was the day Miriam was conceived. Afterwards, he recited Ady:

> *Your eyes are mirrors*
> *of blessed marvels,*
> *for they have seen me...*

Later, he wrote out one of his own poems — 'Only You Should Read My Poems'. I still have it.

Here?

Selene nods. I've carried it with me always.

And you managed to hide it? How?

It's been in an unsanitary place more than once, Selene says.

Ah. And now?

Selene reaches into thin underwear and brings out a tiny roll of flimsy paper, the outside soiled. Inside the tube is another sheet of paper and a tiny talisman, a silver and gold hand the size of a finger nail, but more delicate. She hands Ludmilla the paper.

Is this his signature?

Yes.

I suppose anyone could have written it. And I can't make sense of how you could meet someone years after their death, but...

Selene waits.

134

But you're not making this up, are you?

No.

And you met him again?

Yes, the next year was when Miriam was four months old and then we met again last year after the uprising. I'm convinced I'll go on meeting him until...

What day did he die?

December 3, 1937.

But you haven't met this year?

No.

So it will happen soon?

I think so. I hope so.

And that...

The hamsa?

The what?

It's a hand of Miriam. A protective amulet, I suppose. Mama gave it to me when Miriam was born. It's damascene, a kind of inlay done with thin silver and gold wires onto black enamel. It came from Toledo.

Ludmilla nods. You're amazing, Selene.

She glances down at the poem that she is holding by the corners of the fragile paper.

'... like a prophet, can foretell the future', Ludmilla reads. That's you — because you came from the future to meet him.

It was written for Flóra Kozmutza, but perhaps it was for both of us in different ways.

'the silence in your dreams...' Ludmilla reads, as the door to the cell slams open.

What is that? The squat guard grabs the poem, spittle gathering on his rough-shaven chin as he spits on it, tears and crumples the shreds. Behind him, a taller guard grins, flashing misshapen yellow teeth.

Something else to punish you for, the tall guard says.

No. Selene moves forward. It was mine. She hasn't done...

The back of the tall guard's hand cracks across her jaw, sends her spinning towards the bunk.

We'll get to you, later, whore, he says. She's the one we've come for.

No, Selene says again, bracing herself against the wall, but he only glares at her.

She's the one, he repeats. She had her chance to co-operate. Now she pays the price. Bring her, he commands the squat man, who grabs Ludmilla by the hair, pulling her towards the door.

Oh God, Selene says, kneeling beside Ludmilla on the floor of their cell hours later.

Ludmilla moans, tries to lift her head, but lets it fall to the concrete.

136

I want to help you to the bench, Selene says softly. Can you move?

Selene has no idea how long it takes. The few steps from the floor to the bench stretch before them.

Good bit of cunt that, the thickset guard had proclaimed as he'd flung open the door again, chest puffed, tossing Ludmilla into the cell.

At last Ludmilla is on the bench, blood caking on the bruises that cover her emaciated thighs, more blooming along stick-arms and across her back, where the torn fabric of her inadequate tunic exposes flesh.

Oh God, I wish I had water, Selene says, tucking the threadbare blanket around her friend, feeling the heat of her forehead as she brushes a hand gently across.

She squats next to the bench, back to the wall, holds her head in her hands.

Budapest, Monday 15 November 1993

Woke at Margit's apartment with a headache from too much wine, anxious about Simon and haunted by another dream of Selene's life. Her cellmate was taken and raped. The guards found a poem that Selene had from Attila and destroyed it, but it was Ludmilla they were there for. They accused her of not co-operating so I suspect she was told to collect information on Selene, perhaps as an enticement to have her sentence commuted, but refused. No doubt they wouldn't have honoured any 'promise' anyway, but it's still extraordinarily brave of her. She told Selene that they were both condemned women so what they said didn't matter, but perhaps it did. Why do the guards want more information on Selene? If she can't be executed because she's a mother, what's the point of them finding out more about her? Or is it just a game they play to pit people against each other or a way to fabricate excuses to 'punish' those who don't do what they tell them? It's all so senseless.

In the midst of this, Selene managed to conceal her other treasure — something much stranger than the poem — a hamsa identical to mine, like the one Miriam gave me (or I dreamt Miriam gave me) in Toledo.

I am at a loss to make sense of any of it and I hardly know how to face today. I'm worried about Simon. I tried calling again last night from Margit's apartment and again when I woke, but still nothing. If I write to him it will take four or five days to get there, but perhaps I should write anyway, perhaps all I can do is send a message that might reassure him in the hope that he will contact me when he's feeling less desolate.

Selene Solweig

Selene wakes in the cell, her mind crowded with dreams — of Ludmilla — of Catherine. She is beginning to think that she and Catherine are the same person, but if that's the case then her life, this life as Selene, must end before Catherine is born. No, that can't be right. She will not be executed — she's a mother. She will not die here of injuries or rape or starvation or...

She scratches the date on the wall, the chip of stone becoming...

...Catherine's pen poised over her notes.

She shakes herself, stands and paces, returns to her notebooks, to the books of poetry and biographies ranged around her desk, but she can't find the next sentence, can't concentrate.

Outside, the cold is almost unbearable, even through many layers of clothing. It's the fourth day of extreme cold and Margit has told her it's set to continue. On the street, people walk with their heads down, huddle into thick grey coats, hands gloved, faces muffled by scarves.

Catherine sets off at a brisk pace.

Hanna Farkas seems delighted to see her.

In the drab office with its scratched desk and high windows looking onto grey clouds, Catherine explains slowly, trying different words to tell Hanna that she's searching for Selene's daughter this time.

Hanna nods. I make coffee, she offers. You drink while I search. Don't go in the cold again.

Thank you. Köszönöm, Catherine adds, wishing she knew more Hungarian.

You write his details here, Hanna says.

Catherine looks puzzled, but remembers the translated articles with confused gender pronouns. It must be something to do with how pronouns work in Hungarian, she thinks.

She writes the details on a blank sheet and Hanna checks each one.

Ah, Hanna pauses. His details... they are. She points to the district.

Oh! I forgot, Catherine says. Each district has its own records?

Hanna nods. No matter, she says suddenly. I fill in the form and take to my...

Colleague?

Colleague, yes.

That's very kind, but... I don't want to put you to so much trouble... I...

No trouble, but I will have to do... later. You can come back?

Catherine walks in the cold, not noticing where she is going, head down against the biting air. Eventually she stops in a small café, orders hot chocolate and peers at the map she carries in her bag. She's walked for an hour, but there's a tram stop nearby. She will back-track after another hot drink. She gets out her notebook and begins journalling, loses another hour before suddenly emerging back to the café.

When she arrives back at the office, it feels like a long time before Hanna emerges into the little front area, smiling broadly.

You've found her?

Hanna nods. See — Registered on July 13 1955 by her mother.

Name: Miriam Marie Virág, female, Jewish. Born July 7, 1955, Népszinház utca, 19, Budapest VIII.

And look — there is a father's name, Hanna says, and quite a name too — I was thinking he must have been named for the poet, though József wasn't really so — what would the word be? — revered perhaps? — until after his death and this young man would have been born in the twenties. Hanna pauses and points —

Father's name, Attila József, aged, thirty-two. Mother's name, Selene Solweig Virág, aged twenty-eight. Parents' religion: Christian Orthodox & Jewish.

Thank you. Köszönöm. Thank you so much. Do you know?...

I mean... Where could I find listings for addresses? A phone book? Or records of people in Budapest now. Does the library have that? Or are they in areas too?

Hanna laughs. My English is not so fast, she says.

Sorry. I'm hoping to find Miriam.

Ah. Hanna pauses. She might not be in Budapest any longer. A lot of people left. There are many possibilities.

Yes, Catherine agrees. But is there somewhere I could start?

Your friend is helping you?

Margit? I'm sure she will.

Good. I think you will need help. He's a big task.

At the apartment, the phone is ringing as Catherine enters. She runs to answer it.

Simon?

Catherine, you're back. I kept ringing. I...

I went to Margit's. I didn't want to be alone last night. I phoned you too — last night and this morning.

I was walking, he says, voice flat and small.

At night?

Yes. When I couldn't reach you again I just set out and walked. I walked all night.

Oh, Simon...

No, it helped. Prague is extraordinary at night. I had breakfast at a tiny little café near the Charles Bridge this morning — I was ravenous — ate two croissants, a galette and hot chocolate and then I started writing in my notebook. I didn't want to stop.

For your novel?

Yes. I've finally found my character — a wanderer, an alchemist, though she doesn't realise it for a long time. Obvious really — I've written about her before — a short story, and always wanted to revisit it.

So it's not all futile? Catherine says warily, feeling her neck muscles tense.

There is a pause. I was just being a self-indulgent prick last night, wasn't I?

No. You were feeling depressed. I was really anxious about you, and I was worried you didn't want to go on with — well, with us — I wanted someone to pour out all this weird stuff about Selene to and...

I wasn't exactly there for you, though, was I?

You are now.

Yes, he says quietly, and Catherine feels the tension drain from her body. Yes, so tell me about this book József's niece found.

Well the amazing thing about it is that it was published in 1951 and has Selene Solweig Virág's name inside, but was found by Zsuzsanna under Attila's pillow the evening her uncle died.

Pretty weird. So you know she lived and you know her name is in a book that couldn't have existed in 1937 and you know she had a daughter?

Yes — I went back to the office for Erzsébetváros district today and found her birth record. I stupidly forgot that each district keeps its own records so I was in the wrong place, but Hanna Farkas took it to a colleague for me so that I wouldn't have to go through all the bureaucracy myself. She was so kind. Anyway, Selene listed József as the father with the age he was when he died. I'm amazed they didn't think she was insane, claiming the father was Attila József, but I suppose it's possible someone could have had the same name, even if Attila wasn't very usual. And it proves that Miriam's real too. I want to find her, Simon.

Is that possible? I mean, she could be anywhere. And if she got married or left…

Hanna said the same. I know it's a big task, but I have to try. I'm going to ask Margit for help.

How will you explain it?

I'm going to tell her Zsuzsanna mentioned that Attila had a friend with the surname Virág, someone he met in Paris. So that made me think my dreams about Selene might have been sparked by reading about this connection somewhere after all. So I decided to do more research on the Virágs and the wonderful Hanna not only found Selene, who would be the daughter of the man Attila met in Paris, but also Selene's daughter, who might be able to help us trace the connection between the men.

Brilliant thinking. OK. That could work. Although how would Hanna have found Miriam without a birthdate and place? Especially when she had to go to another office to find it.

I may have to fudge that, Catherine admits. I can hardly tell Margit Selene wrote the details in my journal while she was dreaming my life. But I've got time to think about it. I won't have time for a proper conversation with Margit until after my

144

visit to Paris.

Quite.

I keep thinking of bunuz, Catherine says.

Pardon?

It's something Miriam talked about — my Miriam, not Selene's — bunuz is a Sufi theory of how one soul can pass into another. I'm sure I've mentioned it before.

Ah, yes, Simon assents.

I feel like that's what me and Selene are doing. Am I insane?

No, Simon says emphatically. I believe all of it. Maybe belief is becoming my gift too — you're rubbing off on me. Or maybe it doesn't matter how you know this or what is real. What's the Quixote quote? The unreason of the world is more insane than any fiction?

Yes. Thank you, Simon. A million thank yous. And you're really feeling better?

Feeling foolish mostly. Simon sighs.

Don't. I'm glad you've got the impetus back for the work. It's important. And...

Catherine hesitates.

And I love you.

The sound of a choked back sob makes Catherine tense again.

God, I don't deserve you, Simon says. I love you, Catherine.

She relaxes.

Thank you. And not long now, she adds, smiling into the blind receiver.

Catherine

In her dream of Selene's life, Catherine dreams about Ludmilla, wakes tearful in the cell that is scratched with dates: November 16, 1959, drifts into a feverish sleep, whispering Ludmilla's name.

I'm here, Ludmilla whispers.

Selene stretches slowly. She aches from sleeping on the floor, but she has insisted Ludmilla must have both bench and blanket. She has nothing else to offer, a nurse without even the gift of water to bathe the crusted blood away.

Tell me another story, Ludmilla says.

Selene walks the few steps to her friend, lays a hand on her forehead — fever, she thinks.

She crouches beside the bench, back to the wall.

This is the story of my dreams, Selene begins. In my dreams I see myself in different lives. I am no longer Selene Solweig Virág, and yet I'm still myself — as though these dreams are of lives I have lived or will live in the future.

Ludmilla turns towards her. Do you believe they're true?

You decide, Selene says.

Ludmilla nods.

Once there was a Moorish princess, Casilda. She was the daughter of Alamun, the king of Toledo and a Berber girl, who died in childbirth. She had long golden hair, green eyes, pale skin. She wore only white or the palest blue, almost white, like the halo of sky around the sun. She had a half sister, Zoraida, a beautiful and tempestuous girl who longed for romance, and a brother, Ahmed, who filled their father's dungeons with captive Christian knights, but Casilda hated to think of their suffering and each night she visited them, took them food and learnt the stories of their religion.

You were Casilda?

Selene notices how ragged Ludmilla's breath is and winces.

Yes, but I was very ill. When I started to menstruate, the blood would go on and on and I was getting weak, but a prince named Ben Haddaj came to the Alcazar and cured me, or at least he gave me respite to seek a lasting cure. He was in love with me, but my brother betrothed my sister to him and he was everything Zoraida wanted, except that he didn't love her. He told my brother that he must first make a pilgrimage and Ahmed, who was a devout man, approved, not knowing that Ben Haddaj wanted to return to the religion of his ancestors, Judaism. And so he set off and never returned. He died making his way across the sea to find his roots.

Ludmilla exhales and moans, curls tightly on the narrow bench and Selene jumps up, stoking her friend's clammy forehead.

Let me look, Selene says, gently easing Ludmilla's knees from her chest, revealing the bruised thighs, the fresh trickle of blood.

Oh. The guards, I'll shout for the guards...

Ludmilla clutches her arm.

No, Selene. There's no point...

But the blood. What if it gets worse?

Ludmilla spasms into her foetal ball.

It will pass, Ludmilla whispers. Tell me about Casilda.

Casilda travelled to the north of Spain, became a Christian hermit and saint, died young, and yet I have... this feeling... that she lives on, like Ben Haddaj — each of them born generation after generation in search of each other. Or sometimes born a generation apart, but finding each other even across time...

You and Attila?

Yes.

And in the future?

Sometimes it's only vague dreams, Selene answers. I have a recurring image of a long beach with white sand. A hot summer day, listening to the rub of grains that sing as we walk, me and another girl, Miriam — the same name as my daughter. Something happens, something that makes me panic and then I see Miriam as though she is surrounded by light. Her arm judders, such an odd movement, and she looks so sad except for one moment when her face changes as though lit from within, and she is smiling and calm. But then that uneven jerk again, this time through her whole body, and the strangest sound, a single keening note. And she collapses, not dead, but no longer there.

And you?

I'm not sure. It's just fragments of images, yet always the same. My name is Cassie, like a pet-name for Casilda.

Ludmilla nods, then moans, moans again louder.

From the corridor someone bangs on the door and curses.

Selene stands over her. I need to see if there is more blood, Ludmilla.

Her friend shakes her head feebly.

If I can unwind the blanket I could use it to —

Save — the bl-ank-et — for your-self, Ludmilla insists. Colour drains from her, she shakes, pulls her knees hard against her bruised skeleton.

When Selene finally eases Ludmilla's legs apart the blood is slowing again, some of it crusting onto her skin, but the shaking continues until Ludmilla falls into a state between unconsciousness and sleep. Selene stays by the side of the bench, rehearsing what she might say when the guard brings bread and beans, how she might speak so that he will listen, let Ludmilla see a doctor — at least bring water.

When the door opens, her body is almost too stiff to rise from beside the bench. The squat guard sneers, sets down two bowls.

Thank you, Selene says quietly, looking at the beans on the floor. She's very sick. If she could see a doctor…

She flinches as he moves forward, inspects Ludmilla on the
150

bench.

His smirk widens. Lucky for you, eh? You can eat her beans as well as your own, put some fat on those bones.

He leaves, sniggering.

She cannot wake Ludmilla to eat the beans. Selene slowly forces down one bowl, one scrap of bread for herself.

She doesn't remember falling asleep, wakes crying, saying a name —

Ludmilla, Ludmilla — dry sobs heaving.

Selene looks around the cell she shares with no one. Two years since she last saw Ludmilla, and still she is haunted by her. She settles to sleep again, hopes she will dream of being Catherine —

Budapest, Tuesday 16 November 1993

There is no Ludmilla in 1959, except in Selene's dreams or when she (or I?) dream of that other cell that they shared. Perhaps they were separated, but I fear Ludmilla died in that awful place. Some of the dreams are so vivid, so appalling, that I find it hard to eat, to go about my day, and yet somehow I do. Other dreams fill me with optimism and I find myself longing for the next time Selene will meet Attila. But whether my days are sluggish from dread or inspired by hope, they are all becoming hazy. It is my nights, my dreams, that are real and intense, while the days blur, hard to reconstruct as my own. I want to know more of Selene's life, but I fear losing the thread of my own.

Selene Solweig

Selene scratches the date onto the wall, rises from the bench and begins to pace. Outside, a train sounds. She pauses — it is not the sound she hears before meeting Attila… and anyway it's too far away, she thinks, hearing it again —

Catherine steps onto the train heading towards St-Rémy-lès-Chevreuse. She takes a seat, pulling her small red suitcase towards her, and glances at her watch. It's only 9.30 and she's been travelling for five hours. She smiles, thinking of Margit insisting on taking her to Budapest Ferihegy Airport at 4.00 that morning for her 6.25 flight. When she steps onto the concourse at St Michel, it is not the usual sense of familiarity that she has come to associate with visiting Paris, but a feeling of coming home, almost elation. Her hotel is a short walk from the station and she hopes to sleep for an hour and shower before meeting Monsieur Deschanel, yet she feels an urge to keep walking, towards the École des Beaux-Arts. She resists, turns into Rue Git Le Coeur, enters the Hotel Résidence Des Arts.

Monsieur Deschanel is waiting for her in the Café Latin when she walks in at 12.30. He stands and kisses her formally, encourages her to choose the full formule.

It gives me an excuse to indulge in tarte tatine, he says, winking.

I think two courses for me, Catherine says, but I wouldn't refuse a glass of Chablis.

He smiles. Now, our mutual friend, he says, when the waiter has taken their orders. Shall we speak about him in English?

French, Catherine says confidently before her usual self-consciousness over her accent makes her choose English.

Excellent. Monsieur Deschanel holds his wine glass up to her in salute.

Catherine gulps, but finds her accent changed, her pace sure. You met József I believe?

He nods. I was fifteen. My father taught art history at École des Beaux-Arts and my uncle taught at the Sorbonne, where József studied. You can see I am a very unoriginal person, becoming an academic like everyone else in my family. He chuckles, closes his dark eyes for a moment. He was full of vigour, he adds, opening his eyes. A man of strong opinions, but charming.

Not depressed?

I think he had that darkness in him even then. Such a difficult childhood and then that miserable affair with Professor Horger, who threatened him for his so-called irreligious, unpatriotic poetry. But I think he liked Paris and this was before he'd met Márta Vágó, his first major experience of rejection in love. And, of course, I met him only two or three times amongst my father's and uncle's colleagues and other students. There was wine and talk of politics and of how poetry and art could change the world and I was in awe of all of them.

Catherine pauses. The École des Beaux-Arts in the Twenties?

Monsieur Deschanel nods. I met József in 1927 — he was in Paris a little less than two years.

But you met other Hungarians?

Like Brassaï? Everyone seems to have known him. Everyone in any way connected to art that is.

I was thinking of an art dealer. He studied at the École in the early Twenties, married a Parisian student. They had a little girl, Selene.

Monsieur Deschanel screws his face into a mask of concentration. Yes, he says, now what was the name? My father taught him, both of them in fact. They returned to Budapest not long after they were married, but came back to Paris again soon after.

Yes, Virág. Sándor Virág. She was Marie Spire.

Of course, Sándor and Marie. I was very young, only ten or eleven when they went back to Hungary, but I met them again later. They opened a gallery in Montmartre, I remember. It did very well for a time, but...

The Nazis?

Quite. Paris became impossible for Jews. Are they alive? They'd be in their nineties...

Catherine shakes her head. He died in the Labour Service, she says quietly.

Terrible times. And the daughter?

She was — a relative of a friend, but they've lost track of her
154

— she had her own daughter and I've been trying to trace her… She trails away, takes a sip of wine. The gallery. Would it still be there?

The building undoubtedly. I'm not sure if it is still a gallery, though.

But you might know the address?

Monsieur Deschanel closes his eyes for a few moments. I am a hoarder of anything written, my dear. I may have something in an archive of my father's, but it could take some time to locate.

Ah, Catherine says. I'm only here for one night.

He smiles. Maybe another visit?

She nods, returns his smile. Anyway, back to József. I have a million questions…

Two hours later she is in Montmartre without an address, walking to where she knows she — or Selene — once lived. On Rue Saint-Vincent, she stops in front of a narrow shop, Galerie Delval painted on the blue sign, looks at the André Renoux paintings in the window and hesitates. Inside, a man in his early fifties looks up and smiles.

Bonne après-midi, Catherine says, entering. The Renoux are lovely.

You are a collector?

I'm afraid not, I'm actually looking for some information about a couple that might have lived here before the War.

Ah. She notices his colour drain, then rise.

Virág. Sándor and Marie.

He nods, sits on a stool behind the counter.

I'm sorry. I — it's nothing bad, just...

He looks up. My father's waited for this moment for over fifty years.

Sorry?

Are they alive?

No. No, Sándor died in the Labour Service. Marie became very depressed. Sándor was my father. Catherine stops, inhales deeply. Sorry, my French... Sándor was the father of a friend of my family — their daughter, Selene.

And she wants the gallery?

No, oh no, I'm not even sure she's still alive; I fear not, but her daughter — Miriam — she's the relative of my friends — I think she would simply like to piece the past together. No one wants — I mean, why would they take the gallery?

Marcel Delval, he says rising and holding out a hand.

Catherine McManus, she returns.

I will make us some mint tea?

That would be lovely, thank you.

He is gone longer than Catherine imagines it takes to make tea, but returns bearing a tray with a heavy iron pot, two lapis coloured ceramic bowls and a small package. He pours the tea slowly and hands Catherine a tiny bowl, indicating a chair in front of a rack of prints. He pulls up his own stool from behind the counter.

My father worked for Sándor and Marie Virág. Marie was Parisian, they both knew good art when they saw it and had met at school. Sándor had a particularly good eye. He could draw too — a very good sense of line, but he was a gregarious man, they were good with people, good at finding homes for art works and good at spotting whose work would sell. They lived above the shop here with their daughter. All was going well, but then...

The Nazis?

It was before they arrived, before their foul ordinances and the even fouler Vichy Statut des juifs, but by the late Thirties even so-called liberals were denouncing Jews, blaming them for luring us into a war with Germany that was nothing to do with 'real' French people. The rhetoric was more and more violent. Sándor decided they should leave. He could see what was coming. My father, Charles, wanted to buy the gallery, but he didn't have the savings. They hoped to return and they liked him, wanted to make him a partner. So my father paid what he could, nothing like the worth of the gallery, but they drew up their own agreement — when they came back he would use the profits from the intervening time to make it a full partnership.

But they never returned.

My father tried to find them, but in Hungary...

Jews were forced to move into ghettos, it would have been hard.

Yes, and then Communism — but it's preyed on him all these years.

He's still alive?

157

Yes, eighty-eight and in failing health, but his mind is sharp.

I can't imagine they'd think anything other than what good hands they left the gallery in.

The granddaughter — Miriam you said? — if she could write to my father, even visit. I know he'd want to compensate her, there is still a clause in his will...

She's another missing person at the moment, my friends are trying to locate her, but if we find her...

Thank you. Marcel hesitates, lifts the package from the tray. If you find her, could you give her this or pass it on to relatives?

Catherine unfolds the carefully layered brown paper around a sketchbook, dark brown card covers, a taped binding in burgundy. Inside, thick sketch paper, each page a study of a person —

They are all of Marie or his daughter, Marcel offers. He leans over, stares at the open page. You look like you could be Selene as an adult, he says. You are also related?

Catherine shivers. No, she says quietly, just... a coincidence, I suppose. They're beautiful, very delicate.

Yes — so few lines, so much expression. You will take the book for Miriam?

Well, I —

For my father to know they are on their way to Sándor's family — even if you don't find her for some time — it would give him great peace.

Catherine nods. Thank you.

Catherine

Blood drying on flesh... bowl of beans, scum forming on the thin liquid as it cools... once there was a Moorish princess with a flow of blood that wouldn't stop... sound of gunshot... whistle of a train... mud in fields as they walk towards the border... once there was blood, beans, a hard bench, trains, the concourse at Gare du Nord... blood drying in Galerie Marie... once there was...

... there are no dates on the wall of this cell —

Catherine surfaces from a fog of images. The body she moves in is thin and stiff, she rolls into a sitting position on the hard floor and, despite the pain, stands with the grace of the girl who once walked from the metro to a little ballet studio in the Marais two nights a week, then onto line A and back to the flat above Galerie Marie, just as her father and Marcel, his assistant, were shutting up shop.

She looks across at the bench, where a crumpled figure huddles in the one blanket.

Good morning, Selene, Ludmilla whispers.

You're awake! How? Oh god, you must be starving? How's — I

159

mean — are you...

It hurts. Everything hurts, but I don't feel hungry, just dry, terribly dry, Ludmilla manages.

What can I do?

Ludmilla smiles slightly. Help me stay awake, distract me from the pain. Tell me another dream.

I dreamt of Paris last night, Selene says. I was talking with a scholar about the work of Attila József, but he was someone I'd met before, when I was a young child and he was in his teens. His father knew my parents and they had met Attila too. And there I was again, or at least there Catherine was, asking him questions to help with writing her book about Attila. Strange connections...

Are they real?

I don't know. Catherine's life feels more real than my own, but perhaps I'm just going insane in here.

It's a good form of insanity, if that's what it is.

Selene smiles. Yes, *too much sanity may be madness. And maddest of all, to see life as it is and not as it should be.*

Tell me more, Ludmilla says.

About Quixote?

No, about Paris, about Catherine, about your dreams.

All I know is that while I'm asleep, I'm never afraid — another Quixote quote, but true. Anyway, this scholar, Monsieur Deschanel, who I'd known as Jean-Louis when he was a teenager, showed me a facsimile of a letter Attila had sent to

160

his sister about his first room in Paris — a tiny attic that he shared with an Austrian student — it had a single bed that they took turns using.

Ah, like our beloved bench?

Absolutely. It was in a place called Hotel du Vatican, near Saint Sulpice, but he soon moved to a room near Place Saint Michel, 10 Rue de la Huchette. He shared that room too, but it was bigger, freezing cold, but it had two beds. His brother-in-law sent him money and he spent lots of time in the Café de la Gare with other students, but within a couple of months his depression was taking hold again. He stopped being able to sleep, stopped answering letters to his fiancée in Vienna, Hertha Böhm, stopped writing. He lost weight, had stomach pains and couldn't get out of bed in the mornings. A Hungarian friend, who'd helped him find his first room, got him medicine and insisted on naps after lunch. He rallied for a while, but what he wrote about Paris changed constantly — Parisians were boorish and charming, he loved oysters and snails, but preferred pommes frites, which were cheap and reminded him of home. He learnt French, ten pages of the dictionary a day, and was soon fluent. He went to lectures that interested him, became fascinated by surrealism and wanted to know everything about the medieval poet-turned-outlaw, François Villon. And of course, he fell in love — one poem suggests a brief affair with a girl named Jeanette, but one day, walking out of a café in Montparnasse with his arm around a dancer, a young woman from Hungary, a man appeared, blocked their way and shot himself.

Ludmilla exhales loudly. How awful.

Attila gave evidence at the inquest. He said he and the girl were just friends. The man was the girl's fiancé and he obviously thought differently. Attila never spoke about it again, but there is one poem, 'Transparent lion', written for a surrealist journal that says —

I mustn't think of you, I have my
own work to do,
you are dancing.

He has quite a past, your poet.

Yes, Selene agrees. He is very intense. He wanted to be the Magyar version of Villon in Paris and I think he succeeded. And he was so happy at times, there and in Cagnes-sur-Mer, where he went for the summer. Jean-Louis said there is a house in Cagnes-sur-Mer with a plaque to say that Attila stayed there. His friend, the artist Vince Korda, painted the house.

The art director?

Yes, the same.

The one who designed sets for *The Third Man*?

He did.

Wow, your poet hung around with some interesting people. But then, so have you.

Mostly as a child for me. Vince and Attila had a summer of swimming in the sea, wine and conversation. He wanted his sisters to visit him and Etelka did.

Did he write many poems in Paris?

He writes slowly, Selene replies, thinking of the man she knows as her daughter's father. He writes notes, lets them incubate, often for months, so he brought back lots of… seeds for poetry, I suppose, but he wrote only a few in France — the greatest Hungarian surrealist poem of all time was written there, though.

Modest too.

Attila wouldn't call it the greatest, but Jean-Louis did, and other scholars agree.

Ludmilla turns, makes a bark of pain.

Selene rushes the short distance to her side.

It's just moving that hurts, Ludmilla pants. Go on.

No, Selene says, you tell me a story. Maybe it will take your mind from the pain.

I don't have such good stories, only my own little life.

Tell me about that, about what you did in the uprising.

Well, as I told you, I was studying structural design.

Lots of boys, Selene says, recalling Ludmilla's introductions.

Well, potentially, but I wasn't — well there were one or two at first, but then just one. He was older, a graduate engineering student, from a family of intellectuals, part of the Petőfi Circle. Péter was there the day Julia Rajk made her speech against Rakoski, and, of course, we both heard the meeting in July broadcast over loudspeakers to six thousand people, demanding a free press, and we both stood in the street the day Rajk was reburied — a hundred thousand of us that day, cold, wet, but fired up at the thought of opposition figures, even Nagy, standing together with Julia Rajik and her little boy. It was intoxicating — I was living an independent life in the capital, a girl on a mostly male course at university, immersed in politics, sex, perhaps love even. I was one of the five thousand students who decided to leave DISZ to form our own youth movement. We argued all day, drew up the Sixteen Points, dizzy with exhaustion, drunk on notions of change and sure that we'd get support from the people we admired, ignorant that Nagy had left Budapest that day to go to a wine festival in Badacsony. We marched to the statue of József Bem the next day, waving our manifesto, full of confidence.

Ludmilla takes a sharp breath, closes her eyes. I think I should sleep, she says.

Of course, Selene agrees. But there will be food soon. Can I wake you…

The cell door slams open, but the guard who enters has no tray.

Get up, whore, he snarls, marching towards the bench.

But she can't, she…

Selene steps in front of the bench, crosses his path — there is the sight of a hand parting air, the sound of knuckles on soft flesh before she reels backwards, head slamming into wall, hand at throat, head to wall, falling… head to…

Paris, Wednesday 17 November 1993

Dear Simon

I hope you are feeling better and better. It was so good to talk to you and I adore you for not thinking I'm going insane, even if it means we're both mad.

The sense of any boundary between Selene and myself is more and more blurred. I went through my day in Paris as though only half myself, or less than half. Normally when I meet French academics, I always ask to speak in English, if possible. My French is fine for reading and I can speak conversationally, but I always worry about my accent or losing the thread in more technical discussions, but with Monsieur Deschanel I talked for two hours without a second thought. Yet it wasn't my French, it
164

was Selene's — he said I spoke like a Parisian, which was true, but not of me.

And it wasn't just the French. I saw Paris as though I knew it, not from visits over the last few years, but from living there. I couldn't resist going to Montmartre and once there I knew my way home, Selene's way home. What was really exciting was that it's still a gallery and the owner, the son of the man who worked with Selene's parents, gave me Sándor's sketchbook. He wanted Miriam to have it, which makes me all the more determined to find her, and it will help enormously with the conversation with Margit — to have met people who knew the family and to have a real object to give to someone who I know was born in Budapest.

When I introduced myself to Marcel Delval, I said something very odd before I could stop myself — I said Sándor was my father, and then had to cover up what I'd said — or rather what Selene had just said.

When the dreams started, I still went about my days fully myself, sometimes sensing her presence, but now it's as though I'm immersed in her life in prison so fully that it's more real than my waking days, which I seem to drift through only half-conscious, or less. And when I am conscious of being myself, I find I have taken her pains into my body and it scares me. I don't want to be lost in that cell in 1959. Is that horribly selfish? That I'd wish that on Selene rather than me — or is it that I am wishing it on my former self rather than my present one? I want this life in 1993 with you and yet I also can't let her go.

But oh, I wish you were going to be with me sooner — even though it's not long now, I'm counting the days, the hours.

Hoping you get this before you leave Prague (perhaps the post will be quicker from Paris?)

All my love,
Catherine

Selene Solweig

Selene opens her eyes, feels the side of her head, thin crust of blood across her temple, pain pulsing, crushing her skull, she lifts her shoulders cautiously, feels nausea as she sits on the floor of the cell. She tells herself the date — she must do this daily to keep track — Sunday 17 November 1957, she whispers, scanning the cell for Ludmilla, but the bench is empty. She hunches over her pain, weeps, chokes back the sobs as a guard hammers the cell door, cursing. Outside a train sounds. She pauses — not the sound of any train that she knows, but she hears it again —

On the train to the airport, Catherine takes the sketchbook from her bag, fingers the board covers, the taped binding. She stares at a drawing of Selene aged twelve — graceful, none of the gaucheness she'd known in herself at twelve, but just as thin — birdlike wrists emerging from a woollen ballet cardigan over a dark skirt. Selene has a poise she had craved at that age, but otherwise it could be her own face — the same wide, dark eyes, Selene's hair darker, but pulled back in the same wispy plait, a serious little mouth.

We are one and the same, she says out loud to no one —

and Selene strokes the lines of the sketch her father made of her one afternoon after she returned from her dance class, flushed with energy, proclaiming she had a real part in the end of term show.

Sit down a moment, Selene, her father had said.

I'm too excited to sit. She pirouetted across the small room.

Her mother shook her head and walked into her parents' bedroom, closed the door.

Is Mama alright?

She's worried, she... Her father looked at her and smiled. I'm so sorry, Selene.

Sorry? For what?

I'll explain, but first let me sketch you — I don't have a sketch of you as a dancer — I'd like to remember this moment.

She smiled. Yes. She pirouetted again while her father fetched his sketchbook.

It's the last page, he said. Now, stand still a moment.

Catherine closes the sketchbook and wraps it carefully in the brown paper, slides it into her bag and closes her eyes.

Dozing, she sees herself walking across Paris, not streets she has known, but as Selene knew them. Selene, walking through her memories, Catherine in search of traces of Attila. She walks past Servandoni's façade, Église Saint Sulpice regal and dominant, along Rue Saint-Sulpice, small hotels dotted between cafés, shops, turns onto Rue de Condé — more shops, hotels more expensive, inducements to buy increasing as she nears the richer artery of Boulevard Saint-Germain, tacks along Rue Danton, past Place Saint-André-des-Arts, Fontaine Saint-Michel, turns right into Rue de l'Hirondelle, left along Boulevard Saint-Michel, pink marble pillars, black winged angel, right into Rue de la Huchette, narrow-streeted buildings rising five floors and the invisible attics above, gazes towards those hidden roof rooms. Up there, she says. Attila lived up there. She walks to the street's end, turns onto Rue Saint-Jacques, pausing to take in the Sorbonne where József, like most students, took no exams, attended few lectures, heard Wallon lecture on psychology, Huguet on lexicography and Cohen on literary history. At Rue Gay-Lussac she turns towards Café André, where József met Cserépfalvi — Hungarian, working as a publisher at Huchette, who would become his own publisher in Hungary. She takes in the black and white awning, the tables inside and those perched along the pavement, the swell of voices, scent of coffee and buttery pastries, turns in search of his favourite Café de la Gare, heavy with smoke, sweat, cheap round tables, loud conversation. Conjures him there, at that table — blue shirt, high forehead, uneven smile, dark hair swept back, a glass of red wine in his hand. She turns back towards the river, zigzagging through Attila's life in Paris, crosses Pont Saint-Michel, Île de la Cité, broad conduit of Boulevard de Sébastopol, on and on to Café Les Halles, where Ferenc Hont introduced him to the Hungarian Workers' Club. She stands outside, imagines she hears the choir of manual labourers singing *And we searched for the truth, And we searched for the truth*, cheering, then groans, a voice shout above the crowd — None of that avant-garde stuff here — a raucous cheer, another voice calling — We want more like the Poor Man ballads. She watches Attila leave the building, head held in his hands, Hont coming after him. I'm fine, Attila says, I'll walk alone. Hont looks questioning. Really, I need to mull over what they said.

Catherine rouses as the train pulls into her station.

168

Catherine!

Margit, I wasn't expecting anyone to meet me.

I hate arriving alone at airports, don't you? You must be tired.
And anyway, this cold — the worst for years — they say it
will get to minus thirteen before the spell breaks. I've got a car
waiting.

You're amazing. Catherine hugs Margit. And I've got so much
news — lots of notes about József's time in Paris — Monsieur
Deschanel was wonderful. But also news about Selene — I
found the gallery her parents had in Montmartre — Monsieur
Deschanel again — his father knew her parents when they
were students and he remembered meeting them when he was
a boy and this…

She rummages in her bag —

Let's get to the car — I don't want it to be damaged, it's such
a find. Catherine hesitates. And I need to talk to you about
finding Selene's daughter — Miriam…

Catherine

Catherine wakes on the bench, feels the side of her head, trickle of dried blood, scent of iron, temple beating pain, vice of her skull. The bench holds Selene's emaciated body; the rest is emptiness. No dates scratched on the wall. No Ludmilla. Above the stench of piss and blood and sweat, the sticky whiff of oranges... A train sounds —

Selene stands on a platform, a train pulling away in front of her.

Zsófia leans out of the window, Tibor behind her. I wish you could come with us, Zsófia says.

I'll see you soon. I hope it's wonderful — it will be wonderful!

Tibor grins and nods. My family will love her — they've always wanted a daughter — six sons is too much noise, my mother says, and mess — so much mess. They will adore her.

Tibor tugs Zsófia further into the train as it pulls out and they run along the corridor waving to Selene until they run out of train and she stands, waving into the smoke...

on the platform, another train pulls away in front of her, the mingled scents of citrus and smoke... clearing...

Selene! Attila runs towards her and she turns to face his voice. He holds her tightly, lifts her in the air laughing, twirls her back onto the platform, dizzy, grinning.

Five days, he says. How long five days can seem.

A year and five days seems even longer.

Of course. 1955? He holds her at arms' length and smiles broadly, a smile that rises higher on the right of his face. And how are you?

It's not a good time for Hungary, Selene begins. We had such hope for Nagy, but he had no room to manoeuvre with Rákosi constantly undermining him. Political detainees were released, but so slowly, and too many are still in prison. The New Course was doomed from the start, I suppose — but we were taken in by small things — we had butter for a while, farmers could leave collectives, private businesses were allowed — small ventures like selling vegetables grown in gardens or lángos — but it was not enough...

Selene looks up. Am I rambling?

He shakes his head. It's terrible, the future of our country, but I want to hear.

She breathes deeply. The Kremlin lost patience, told Nagy he was unpatriotic, incompetent, even bourgeois. He had a heart attack and was out of office by April. But that wasn't sufficient for them — he wasn't only out of power, but expelled from the Party. There are writers and intellectuals who've gone on supporting him, even though he insists he is still a Communist.

171

Fifty-nine of them signed a protest manifesto in October, objecting to the treatment of intellectuals and demanding freedom of expression, but no-one knows how Rákosi is going to respond to that.

Attila nods patiently. Seeing into the future is disturbing and fascinating, he says, and I could rant all day about the unsocialist ways of communism, but you — what I most want to know is, how are you?

I'm well. My mother struggles, but small things help and she's done better since…

She had butter? He laughs.

Yes. And my friend Zsófia, who I work with, has gone off to the countryside to be married to Tibor. He's a student in Budapest, but his family come from…

And you, my dear Selene, you who are concerned with so many things and people, how are you?

Okay, I'll tell you, but…

He looks anxious. You are not ill?

No, no far from it, I just don't want you to be — I'm not really sure, it's just that it involves you — my news — it's not really the butter that's helped my mother, but another small thing. Selene closes here eyes, gulps I had a baby. Miriam. She was born on July 27, nine months after we…

Attila blinks, moves his head to one side and studies her seriously before his smile widens. He scoops Selene into the air, throws her upwards as though she is a toddler, catches and spins her, sets her down, the two of them falling in a giggling heap on the platform.

Such news! Such news! His face stills, a frown wiping the smile away. Oh, but I will never meet her. I will never meet my daughter born so far in the future.

I know, Selene says quietly, putting a hand on his arm.

He grins again. Still, she is there — out there in time I have a child.

The change of expression is rapid.

I'm so lonely here, he says. I love my nephews and niece, but my sisters — they mean well, of course, they think they will cure my depression by isolating me here, but my head fills with despair and there is nothing to distract me from it. I need the journal to work on, I need to talk with people brimming with ideas, good ideas, bad ideas, anything I can fence with to ward off the darkness. I live from one visit to the next. In fact — he hesitates — I just sent a postcard… to…

Flóra?

Quite. It's impossible for me to have secrets from the future, I expect. And she is…

Here, in your own time.

But you are more faithful than me. I'm a bastard.

No — this is — well, what we have is so strange, but I'm glad of it anyway.

You are a generous person, which only makes me adore you more. I worship you, but I love Flóra and we'll be married — soon, I think. I asked her to come this Sunday, but I suppose it will not be so soon.

He seems suddenly drained, Selene thinks. I have a picture of

Miriam, she offers. It's a little blurred, but… She rummages in her pocket for a small envelope.

My daughter! He proclaims, and begins to march up and down the platform, declaiming poetry to the tiny image, his voice sonorous, lyrical cadences tumbling into the cold November day. After the third poem he stops, kisses the photograph, returns it to the envelope and kneels on the platform, sobbing.

Attila, oh god, I'm sorry, I shouldn't have told you, I…

Selene stands on an empty platform, a train pulling away in front of her, smoke clearing, a deep well of pain pulsing over her left temple, a glare of light dancing before her so that she feels the ground swaying, a wave of nausea and…

She wakes on the bench, puts a hand to the side of her head. There is no blood. The scratched outlines on the wall tells her it is 18 November, 1959, two years since Ludmilla was wrenched from that other cell, four years since her fourth meeting with Attila, the day he had collapsed on the station platform, weeping. There is a scent of iron over the syrupy odour of oranges, her temple beats with pain, the vice of her skull throbs…

Thursday 18 November 1993

Another meeting between Selene and Attila. Until today these encounters have provided a respite between the more traumatic dreams, if 'dreams' is the right word, but today was heart-rending. Attila seemed — is manic the right word? His mood was up and down so quickly it was dizzying. One moment he was thrilled at the idea of Miriam, the next desolate that he would never meet her. He was torn between his love for Selene and his love for Flóra, and still hoping for marriage. And there was no resolution. They didn't have a meal or make love or even walk by the lake. And the constant presence of trains — knowing what is to come — seems horrible.

Selene was, at least, still alive four years after that meeting, but she is so weak, skeletal.

Is it possible to find Miriam? I felt so optimistic yesterday, and now so uncertain and drained.

Selene Solweig

Selene opens her eyes, rises slowly, scratches the date onto the wall. Keep track, you must keep track, she tells herself. The ancients didn't start their stories any way they wanted, she says to no-one, closing her eyes, hoping to doze, to dream another life, Catherine's life...

Catherine sits at her desk, notebooks spread in front of her, the sketchbook propped facing her, gazing into the eyes of a girl who might have been her at the age of twelve. She thinks of Miriam, of being with her when...

She reaches for her journal, begins to write —

I saw Miriam again three years ago this month — and watched her die. I went home, went to bed, and stayed there, but it was another year before Liam left. Yet spring came and I decided to listen to Miriam — until death, it's all life.

Catherine fingers the blue silk cord strung with the tiny hamsa: the hand of Miriam in damascene black, silver, gold that she had found by her bedside in Toledo when she had gone looking for... for whom? For Casilda, the Moorish princess that Miriam had insisted she had been in a former life — or for herself, freed from the stories others told her she must fit into? She had found so little, but, in pain and feverish from a flow of menstrual blood that had overwhelmed her, she had dreamt of Miriam, woken to this tiny charm on its bit of silk and to a bowl of mint tea cooling by the bed in the empty apartment.

I retold and retold the story until it was mine again. I wrote the story I'd made safe. And now?

Transmigration of souls — Gilgul Neshamot in Kabbalah — Miriam had told her, when they were about the age of the girl in the sketchbook standing open on Catherine's desk. What had Miriam told her when they first met? Keep track, you must keep track, she thinks, struggling to recall Miriam's words ...and begins to write:

We've been numerous people through the ages... I think we were most truly ourselves as Ben Haddaj and Casilda... We've even crossed through time to find each other — in Hungary when you were Selene Solweig Virág...

Oh God! Catherine says out loud. I knew I'd heard the name before. She is me. Or I was her. Miriam told me all that time ago... we even have the same hamsa...

When the phone rings, she startles, looks at the clock, wonders how more than an hour has passed.

Hello?

Catherine?

Simon, it's so good to hear you. I'm...

You sound strange, are you —?

I'm not sure what I am, or who — I...

Catherine?

Simon, do you believe in the transmigration of souls?

I — I don't know. I mean I can't see how — there's a million reasons why not — and — are you okay?

I'm sorry, it's these dreams, these weird dreams. I'm losing all rationality. It's just — I thought I remembered something Miriam told me — when I was about eleven, the first time we met — she said we'd been other people in earlier lives — Casilda and Ben Haddaj in Toledo, but I'm sure she also mentioned Selene Solweig Virág. Do you think I've imagined that? Imagined she told me that, I mean? I'm losing my grip here, Simon.

In the pause there is only silence.

Simon?

I...

You think I'm going mad?

No, no, of course not — I just don't know — I'm mean it's hard to make sense of, but there might be other explanations...

Silence.

Catherine? I don't mean to doubt you, I'm only...

Silence.

I'll be there soon, Simon soothes. Maybe you need — have you talked to Margit?

No, Catherine murmurs. No. I told her I wanted to find Miriam — Selene's daughter Miriam. We're going to meet in a day or so to talk about which newspapers might help with it. I'll see her later today, but there won't be time to plan much — we'd already scheduled a meeting with a young academic who's going to talk to me about growing up in the Sixties and Seventies here and what the transition from Communism was like for young people — it's not part of the novel exactly, but I feel I need to understand the place more deeply — he's a graduate student of András's and apparently already on his way to being an interesting poet and novelist.

Good. That's good. Try not to worry. I mean…

You rang me, Catherine says, shifting direction. Was it…

To tell you my train time, mainly. I get to the station on Saturday morning, a bit before ten.

How many hours?

Nearly sixteen, but most of it overnight and your wonderful employers have paid for a private compartment for me.

Catherine laughs. Hmm, must think you're a real rising star.

Tax deductible more like, Simon retorts, his voice lightening.

I'll come and meet you.

You don't have to, I could…

No, Margit will insist anyway. And thank you.

For what? Making you think I distrusted your sanity, which I don't by the way.

For listening. For not turning me into the loony bin. Whatever's going on here, I do want to find Miriam. Elle devrait avoir le carnet de croquis de son grand-père. C'est beau. J'étais un bel enfant.

Catherine?

Yes?

You do know you spoke in French a moment ago, and referred to the pictures as being of you?

I did?

Yes.

Silence.

Simon — Catherine begins to speak at the same moment as he says — Don't worry —

I'll be fine, she says. I've got to get ready for this meeting at the university. Speak again tomorrow?

Yes. Yes, of course. Take care.

I will.

Viktor Kovács is tall and softly spoken. His sandy hair flops into his face as he leans in to talk across the table at the café Margit has chosen. Too formal to talk at the department, she had insisted, ushering Catherine and Viktor out of the university and along the street, leaving them to talk once they were seated in the warmth of a tiny café.

Your character from the Fifties sounds fascinating, Viktor says when he has taken a sip of scalding coffee. Margit tells me you dreamt of her, but she was a real person.

180

Catherine nods. I think I must have heard about her somewhere, or read something, but she resurfaced in a dream, yes. Her family had been Haas in Austria, but changed their name here.

Viktor nods, Yes, the 'Golden Age of name changes'. My family changed their name from Klein to Kovács. There are endless jokes about Hungarian Jews changing their names. He pauses. Like: How do two Jews introduce themselves? My name was Klein, what was yours? — Or — What do they call *Who is Who* in Israel? *Who was Who*. It didn't really help. We were still Jews.

Even in the late Sixties and Seventies?

Yes. I grew up in Budapest, but I felt I was a stranger to all but my own small area of a few streets. I was very aware of being 'other' at university. But otherwise, life was much more relaxed then than it had been a decade earlier. Viktor pauses, flushed. I'm sorry, he says, Am I talking too much?

Not at all, Catherine reassures him.

He smiles. A Jew is always a stranger, even when he has a Hungarian name. But it's not only in Hungary. I spent a year in Austria after my degree and I was a stranger there too. Vienna looks like a bourgeois version of Budapest — they were the same empire, after all, but the similarities are only on the surface. My German is good, no-one could tell I was a foreigner from my accent, and yet I was still… Viktor brushes his hair from his forehead, leans further forward. In Austria people believe in security, that a man can be king of his own house. It's a myth, of course, and in Hungary it's a broken myth. It's what makes politics here so strident, there is always the fear of the one who will take something from us, the one we can't protect ourselves from. Both are bad thinking. I suppose both make me feel out of place in different ways.

Catherine nods. Tell me about the change from Communism, she says.

It was like... Well, it meant I could travel, meet my grandparents for the first time, but otherwise... He shrugs. People got up, went to work, cooked dinner, argued with each other, drank too much under Communism. Then there was Capitalism and people got up, went to work, cooked dinner, argued with each other, drank too much.

Yes, Catherine says. You know the novel, *The Leopard*? In it Lampedusa says something like 'we change so that we can remain the same'.

Quite, Viktor agrees. There's a sculpture by György Galántai from the time of the change. It's called 'Changing Step' — a set of footprints cut from iron, one row of striding in iron footprints, the other in negative, where the prints are cut out. So there is a change, but the striding goes on just the same.

Catherine

Catherine wakes on the bench, feels the side of her head, no blood. Selene is alone in the cell. The date scratched on the wall must be yesterday's, she thinks, Wednesday 18 November, 1959. Two years since Ludmilla was taken away —

Selene drowses, remembering her friend being dragged from the cell, the woman who came afterwards, the years alone, her mind wanders through the tedium of days broken only by small rituals — how she rises daily, stretches, reaches for the memory of a body that could once dance, poised, graceful; how she scratches the date on the wall, thin line of chipped stone against stone; how she carefully folds the tattered blanket before pacing the cell, a different route each day, reciting poetry under her breath, breathing in the recollection of her daughter, recalling the scent of plump limbs, the shape of her mouth, giggling, the sweet taste of her milky breath. Miriam. The reverie broken each day by a bowl of gruel, scum-flecked, sour, never enough. The slow drip of afternoon, dusk signalled by a meal of beans filmed by grease — thin broth and hard, dark bread. The shuffle towards sleep that only ever held nightmares until this month... until she began to dream another life...

Catherine, she says out loud, and feels the answering resonance of a shadow that is her own, yet unfamiliar.

Selene wakes from half sleep, forces her aching limbs to rise, to unbend, straighten, reach. She delves for a body that once seemed hers by right — supple, at ease. She scratches the date on the wall, Thursday 19 November, 1959, the uneven strokes of chalky stone barely scraping its mark. She turns to gather the threadbare cover, smoothes frayed fabric into a neat parcel and begins to walk the cell, counting steps, varying the numbers, segueing into whispered lines of Ady:

> *This is why I sing and I torment myself.*
> *I should love to be loved.*
> *I wish to be of someone, I wish to be of someone.*

She thinks of her daughter, pink and chuckling, fresh from the bath, dark hair in damp curls smelling of soap, her butter-soft skin in cotton flannel, eyes straining to stay awake.

Miriam, I wish you knew me. I wish I knew you as you are now.

There is a graunch of keys, the scrape of the uneven door against concrete as it is pushed open. The scowling guard says nothing, deposits the gruel on a rickety stool, leaves. Selene squats, lifts the cracked bowl, cradles it, sniffs the grey porridge as though it might be fine oatmeal floating with honey and cream. She spoons it into her body slowly, savours every bland lump, swallows carefully, scrapes out the last remnants before placing the bowl back on the stool.

She stretches again, counts steps, plays memories through her mind's eye as she walks...

pacing her bedroom with Miriam cradled in her arms, a tiny consciousness fighting to stay awake, exhausted, red-faced, then suddenly heavy with sleep... pacing briskly towards the studio in the Marais for dance lessons, ten-year-old arms swinging, sun on the fountains in the Place de Vosges... her

The gloomy light of the cell fades to twilight, the murk telling her famished body that food will come soon. She sits on the bench, remembering meals with Attila, at the restaurant, at his sister's house the day that...

A fat, scarlet-nosed guard makes a noisy entrance, tosses the bowl of beans onto the stool so that the rancid juice spills over. He grins at his effort. Filthy bitch, he offers, leaving Selene alone with the chipped bowl of grey fluid, no spoon today, no bread. She wipes the residue from the stool with her hands, licks them meticulously before lifting the bowl, tipping it to her lips in measured mouthfuls.

Afterwards she walks more slowly, reciting the poem that Attila had given her, another of his, another of Ady's, an evening liturgy to see her into night, hoping to dream of Catherine as she feels Catherine dreaming of her now...

Budapest, Friday 19 November 1993

Seeing Margit later today and will make a time to see her alone soon, to talk about which of the newspapers we should advertise in to try to find Miriam. We have plenty of information — Miriam Marie Virág, female, Jewish. Born July 7, 1955, Népszinház utca, 19, Budapest VIII. The wonderful Hanna not only found Selene in the Motherbook, but also Selene's daughter, but I realise that gives us no idea of where she might be today.

When Zsuzsanna mentioned that Attila had a friend with the surname Virág, someone he'd met in Paris, it made me wonder if my dreams about Selene might have been

185

sparked by reading about this connection somewhere. For myself, I can't doubt the dreams any longer, but finding the link with Paris gives me an explanation that I can pass on to Margit about how I've come up with the connection between Sándor Virág & Attila. And having the sketchbook is a good reason to search for Miriam. I only hope we can find her and that I get the chance to hand her the book that belonged to her grandfather.

So much happening at once — the sketchbook, the search for Miriam, and Simon arriving tomorrow. Overwhelmed with anticipation and feeling restless, but I have a pile of notes about Attila's last month and it might distract me to write, to do something methodical.

Is that why Selene orders her empty days so carefully? No, it's something deeper than that. There is a graciousness in her that I admire, that makes me think we must be separate people after all. In that awful place, with food that makes me retch just thinking of it, she persists in dignifying her life. She lives as if there are possibilities, as if everything matters. And she's right. She has to be right, but I have no idea how she sustains it.

Selene Solweig

Selene wakes feeling light-headed, eases away from the bench, more difficult today. She lifts a chipping of stone to begin to write the date, pauses. Keep track, you must keep track, she tells herself. Slipping…

Catherine sits at her desk surrounded by notebooks and papers, the sketchbook propped to one side, a sheaf of poetry collections open or stuffed with bookmarks.

After his death, the fragments of poetry, over a hundred of them, though perhaps more were lost, were gathered together at the Petofi Literary Museum. He often wrote from snippets of notes, though some might arguably be finished pieces, despite their brevity. Others are certainly fragments, but they fascinate nonetheless.

> *My heart has wandered far and lonely,*
> *to learn that all may live to see*
> *that who is mortal, may only*
> *love a mortal immortality*

His poems were collected and published, his body moved to a 'better' grave; an act of national guilt that came too late. He is beginning to be more widely translated and compared to great names in poetry. And yet his sister, Etelka, told another researcher that she thought Attila might have lived if he hadn't been a poet. But then — if he hadn't been a poet, he wouldn't have been Attila.

For all his connectedness and political engagement, he lived largely in an inner landscape. And that line 'may only / love a mortal immortality'. I can't help but read my own dreams of Selene and Attila into that vivid inner life with its mountains and valleys and strange terrain and its passion for life that goes on, yet also dies, and is made all the more intense and vital for that dying.

Whether some of us live one life and others a hundred, what matters is this life, now. And if some of us return, find our loves again, still, there will come an end at some point. Miriam taught me to 'love a mortal immortality', though I didn't realise it at the time.

Until death, it's all life, Cassie, she would say. *There's a remedy for all things except death.*

More and more, I want to write a novel that brings to life the Attila that Selene knew or dreamt, the Attila Zsuzsanna described: funny and witty and tender; the passionate Attila whose mood might change like the wind, but whose genius and integrity burned bright. Kabdebo mentions that George Klein suggested that Attila maintained a child's worldview over against an adult one, refusing to conform or adjust, resisting giving up playfulness. In the face of rejection and anguish he kept on tilting at windmills. He did so despite extreme existential doubt, *perched on nothing's branch*, and in spite of mental anguish, a mind that could descend into delusion and which too often was *measured out in coffee spoons*. His propensity for fighting battles that could not be won reminds me so much of Miriam, which is perhaps why I want to write about his life as though it had Selene Solweig Virág in it — even if only for brief segments of eight days — and even if I may be writing nothing more than my own inner landscape's wild imaginings. I want, more than anything, to say something about the truth of this awesome man that is not shown merely in facts, but in spirit.

Catherine puts down her pen and picks up the sketchbook. She leafs slowly through the pages of thick soft paper to the drawing of Selene, looks into her eyes.

You lived a life not even meted out in coffee spoons. Did you really believe that Attila was the father of your child? Did you ever see her again?

Outside, Catherine pulls a thick wool scarf across her mouth and nose. She is swathed in layers, silk thermals beneath her trousers and shirt, a cashmere sweater under a fleece, a coat that Margit has insisted she borrow for the cold weather, two sizes too big for her, yet it only just fits over the layers. She would like to walk, but the cold air bites and stings and she heads for the tram, head down, nose and mouth covered.

When she arrives at the café, Margit waves from a window seat well away from the draughts of the door.

Pastries, Margit insists, and chocolate. You need more than coffee in this cold.

Catherine nods for once, takes off the bulky coat, but remains huddled into her zipped fleece while Margit orders thick chocolate and cherry rétes.

It's horrific, Margit says, over a week of this terrible cold and no sign of it getting any better. And it's predicted to be even colder tomorrow.

Catherine eyes the sticky strudels on the tray the waiter brings. I'll never get used to how huge they are, she says, but I have an appetite for one today.

Good, Margit says. Now, about your search.

Catherine nods, wiping cherry and pastry crumbs from her lips before cradling the mug of chocolate, letting the warmth seep through her hands.

The family were Jewish, left-wing, so if Miriam is still in Budapest most of the weeklies will appal her with all their populist rhetoric. There's *Népszava,* Communist mouthpiece in the bad old days, but it's revived itself as a paper of the people, or of the trade unions at least. Circulation is going down every year as the country moves to the right, but still big enough to be worth a go. Most importantly, Attila József wrote for them in his time, and Endre Ady before that and you said the grandparents knew József in Paris, so there's at least a tenuous link.

Is it the only one we should try?

There's *168 Óra* — left, liberal, a weekly magazine that was an offshoot of a radio programme — it's only been around for three or four years, but it's got a good readership — political, intellectual, comes out every Thursday.

So two then?

Margit purses her lips. There's also Mancs — an abbreviation of *Magyar Narancs*, the Hungarian Orange — a long story, but basically a satirical swipe at attempts to grow oranges in Hungary during the Communist regime. It's a bit more, Margit pauses, informal, a sort of gonzo libertarian style. Might be more to the right than your family might appreciate, but some people like its irreverence.

Okay, let's go for it.

More chocolate first, Margit says, fishing a notepad from her bag before signalling to the waiter.

Coffee for me, Catherine says. I don't think my body will take any more sugar.

It sounds really positive, Simon says from Prague when Catherine telephones him.

It's a pity two of them don't come out till next Thursday. It only gives us the last week to find her, Catherine points out. But I'm glad we're going to try.

Yes, Simon assents.

You don't sound… Catherine pauses. Are you okay?

Just nervous about the journey, Simon admits. I know I won't sleep on the train. I've been pacing for the last hour, just thinking about it and the taxi doesn't arrive for another hour. I'm not sure the overnight train was a good idea now.

You'll be fine, Catherine urges. It's an adventure and you might sleep through some of it at least.

Feeling nauseous already, Simon offers.

Oh, darling. Just think, in about twelve hours time you'll be here. I'm so excited to see you again.

Yes, Simon says softly. Yes. I want to see you too. I just wish I could magically be there.

Catherine laughs. You'll have to brush up on more occult powers for that. But not long now and we'll be together.

191

Catherine

Catherine wakes on the bench in the cell Selene had shared with Ludmilla. Her vision blurs as she lifts her head. She puts a hand on her skull and feels the sticky smear of caking blood. There is no date on the wall. No Ludmilla.

The cell door is pushed open and a fat guard deposits a bowl of gruel, spits to the side of it, turns.

Ludmilla, Selene says, her voice catching, barely audible.

The guard turns back. What was that, bitch?

Ludmilla, she says, trying to steady her voice.

What about the whore?

I wondered… I mean…

Well don't. No need to wonder about her. Put out of her stinking misery.

Selene chokes down a sob.

So eat up, bitch. Eat and be merry, eh? You never know when

it might be your turn. He chortles, turns, slams the door as he goes, whistles as he walks the corridor.

Selene drowses, remembering the days after Miriam's birth...

The strangeness of days broken by the small rituals of changing and feeding, walking the flat with this new life cradled in her arms — how she would rise, stretch, reach for the memory of a body that had not always been dazed by half-sleep, nights spent breast-feeding this tiny voracious child, days inventing new routes from one room to the next, reciting poetry under her breath, telling her small daughter, Your papa wrote this, breathing in the infant's milky breath, the scent of plump limbs. Miriam.

She wakes from half sleep, forces her aching limbs to rise, to unbend, straighten, reach. She delves for a body that once seemed hers by right — supple, at ease — turns to gather the threadbare cover, smoothes frayed fabric into a neat parcel. She begins to walk the cell, counting steps, varying the numbers, segueing into whispered lines of Ady:

> *This is why I sing and I torment myself.*
> *I should love to be loved.*
> *I wish to be of someone, I wish to be of someone.*

Miriam, will they let me live to see you again? She asks the empty cell. Will they come for me today, even if I am your mother?

She thinks of Miriam's dark hair, damp curls smelling of soap, butter-soft skin in cotton flannel, large eyes in a tiny face straining to stay awake.

There is a grinding of keys on metal, scrape of door against the concrete floor as it is pushed open. The guard says nothing, deposits the gruel, leaves. Selene squats, lifts the chipped bowl, hugs it to her, breathes in porridge as though it might be fine oatmeal lavished with syrup and cream. She spoons it into her mouth carefully, savours, swallows slowly, scrapes the dregs.

Stretching, she stands, walks counting steps, replays again memories of walking her bedroom...

Miriam cradled in her arms, a tiny consciousness fighting sleep, fatigued, scarlet-faced, before drooping, leaden with sleep, face clear.

With every noise in the prison corridor, distant or near, she tenses, imagines the guards throwing open the door, dragging her away.

The dim light of the cell fades to dusk, the gloom telling her famished body that food should come soon and if not food... She sits on the bench, remembering meals with Ludmilla, sharing single bowls of beans floating in a froth of grit...

A flabby guard enters, roughly shoves a bowl onto the floor, oily liquid sloshing onto the concrete. She eats, wondering if they might come in the night, tomorrow.

Afterwards she forces herself to walk, thinks of Miriam, the day she said her first word. *More.* Flinging chubby arms in the air to be picked up. *More.* Waiting to be spun and twirled. She remembers reciting the poem that Attila had given her, sailing her giggling daughter through the air.

Drifting into sleep she dreams of Miriam, of the days before the uprising...

Zsófia drops her voice to a whisper. Radio Free Europe says there's a growing resistance, the regime is weaker than we think.... I'm going to join with the students... Tibor and Luca... They're certain now is the time... You must join us, Selene, for Miriam, for your unborn children...

Selene stands on a platform, a train pulling away in front of her, Zsófia leaning out of the window, Tibor behind her, both of them grinning, flushed, train pulling out and they run along the corridor waving to Selene while she stands, waving into the smoke...

sound of a train, another platform, counting every second of the journey, hardly daring to breath as they near the last stop before the border...

Zsófia pale-faced eyes puffy... Selene telling the young doctor... My friend. Zsófia — she's a nurse too... The shake of his head telling her too much...

Zsófia Široký, née Lenárt, a known agitator and fugitive, the wife of the executed criminal, Tibor Široký...

Budapest, Saturday 20 November 1993

Awake insanely early — 6.30 and I've been up for hours already. Dreamt of Selene remembering times with her baby and with her friend Zsófia, who died in Austria. She has known too many separations. I muse over the child Simon and I will have together. I can't imagine what it might be like to give birth and then be separated from the life that has grown inside you.

Today Simon arrives by train. Another reason for not being able to sleep. We have known each other such a little time, not quite a full year, and yet I feel more 'known' than I have ever been. Of course, I didn't mention

Casilda when we first knew each other, but now he knows the whole strange history, memories that I might have made up and yet he seems unfazed.

I poured out so much in Menton in May... And the night before he left, I cried so many tears, I thought the ocean would overflow. He held me, made up stories, shushed the tears... Sometimes I still wonder if I am making him up but no — I have not invented him — we talk across the miles, write letters, spooling in distance, stand beneath the same moon, planning... and today he will be with me. We will return to Menton next summer, but for now, Budapest, this place that is haunting me with another woman's life, one that makes me wonder who I am, or might have been, but does not make me doubt Simon, just as Selene never doubted Attila.

There are so many trains in these 'dreams'. Almost every time Selene slips into Attila's time there is a train, and there's a train coming in Attila's future that neither of them can stop. Zsófia and Tibor left on a train, flushed with hope, yet the next train was the last one Zsófia took. A train brought Selene back to Budapest, believing in amnesty when she was travelling towards prison. I feel uneasy going to a station to meet Simon, much as I'm excited to see him. These liminal spaces are charged — powerful and dangerous, yet all human life is there. Stations are alive with memory, loss and love; the wicks of desire and disappointment burn there. I suddenly feel that trains are strange vehicles, profound and terrible, carrying their freight of unbearable hope and overwhelming fear across the mindscapes of countries; cargos of sentiment gliding by farms and cities, leaving residues of emotion, so that people wake bathed in the invisible remnants of longing or distress, unaccountably restless with expectation or presentiments.

The train will arrive and I will be dizzy with anticipation, my stomach churning with optimism and all the possibilities of a future with Simon, whilst my heart drums a warning that he will not alight, that doom has already come, unseen. I will hear the carriages on the tracks, see the coaches coming to a halt, the people pouring out, being met and held as though they might disappear if not grasped firmly; others, searching for faces that are not there, walking away alone... And I will be nauseous with anticipation. afraid that when the crowd clears, I'll be left on the platform, solitary and forlorn, wondering if — after all — I made him up.

It is treacherous to be in love. Always, the chance of misunderstanding, of betrayal. Always the prospect that the train will arrive empty; might crush us under cold metal wheels. And yet I am still longing for a train which will bring the future, arriving with the promise of all I desire and more...

Selene Solweig

Selene wakes dizzy and stiff, crawls from the bench, each day the movement more strenuous. She lifts a fragment of stone and wills herself to know the date, to write it... to write... slips...

...longing for a train will bring the future, arriving with the promise of all I desire and more...

I will make coffee, do yoga, shower, wrap up in layer on layer to brave the cold, be ready for the car that Margit has so kindly arranged, ready to meet Simon at the station, that threshold where fear and anticipation collide like weather fronts.

Catherine moves through each ritual deliberately, preparing. Before she leaves the apartment she soaks oatmeal in milk in a little copper pan, leaves it on the unlit stove ready to cook when she returns. It will be the first treat — buttery oats, dark chestnut honey, blueberries, blackberries, swirl of thick, rich cream.

In the car, Margit is motherly and excited.

You know we really could have taken the trolley bus from the station or got the metro, Catherine says, not for the first time. It's only twenty minutes away.

Far too cold, Margit says, They're predicting it will be as low as minus thirteen today. And Simon will have luggage, she flutters objections away with her articulate hands.

At the station, Margit tells Catherine she will wait in the car, give them time to greet each other alone after such a long parting.

You want some privacy, Margit insists.

On a train platform?

You know what I mean, Margit says, smiling.

Catherine nods, skips into Keleti station through the grand Thököly Avenue entrance to Lotz Hall, stomach fluttering the way it might have on Christmas Eve at the age of seven. She makes her way through the Saturday crowds towards the entrance to platform nine, craning to see if a train has recently arrived beneath the imposing arc of glass and steel ceiling supported by stone pillars. A throng of newly arrived travellers surges towards her and she scans faces, hopping from one foot to the other, muscles taut.

A gap in the crowd, another wave of passengers, some scanning the concourse for familiar faces, searching for the recognition that will signal they have arrived, will not be left in this indeterminate portal where no one belongs. Catherine watches the masks of anxiety transformed by relief and glee, keeps scouring the figures moving towards her. The next tide of bodies passes her, some finding solace, holding on to those they know, others wearily lugging bags towards the enormous doorway and the taxis and trams beyond. The throng thins, the last arrivals streaming from the train in ones and twos and

Simon is there, almost in front of her, his pinched grey face dawning pink with delight. He throws his arms around her and she cannot remember ever being held so tightly, both of them shaking, laughing, kissing.

I hope you'll be warm enough, Catherine says eventually, holding Simon at arm's length. Margit is waiting with a car so we only have to run that far.

She kisses him again, skips on the spot, twirls, laughs and pulls him towards the exit.

At the apartment, Catherine waves a hand around the large living area with its desk tucked into one corner and kitchen area at the other end.

I've got oats soaking ready for breakfast, or brunch at least. Lots of berries and the local honey is wonderful. I'll make hot chocolate or do you want coffee — or something now and another drink with food?

Sshh, Simon says. He walks towards her and puts his hands on her shoulders, moves closer.. Sshh, Catherine can feel his body shaking like her own. He takes her hand, leads her to the bedroom.

Over a lunch of oatmeal, berries, hot chocolate, Simon talks about his research into alchemy during the reign of Rudolph II at the Castle archives.

Eliška was such a help, he says, after finishing a long description of esoteric manuscripts, especially when Nathan wasn't there making googly eyes at her like a teenager.

Poor Nathan. Catherine laughs. And they've stayed in touch?

They have actually. In fact, she's taken up on his offer to visit him in Nottingham. I hope he doesn't mess it up.

I hope I get to meet her. Do you think Nathan would move to Prague?

Czech isn't one of his languages, but he learns them so quickly, he could definitely survive there. And programming skills seem to be in demand everywhere, boring as they are.

Tell me about the Kafka research.

A lot of the places he lived in have been rebuilt, but what struck me is how attitudes have changed — his aficionados used to have to make samizdat copies of his stories under the Communists, now his face is on T-shirts and mugs all over the place, yet I met a Czech guy who thought Kafka was a famous American. He's everywhere and he's on sale, but people haven't a clue who he is. Well, that's probably not fair, but the masses… Simon swallows a spoon of sweet porridge. Ironic, eh?

Kafkaesque joke, Catherine agrees.

I want to invest my writing with the idea of an existential space. For Kafka, context is anthropomorphic, Prague makes him who he is — its possibilities and its limitations mould his character.

That's fascinating. Go on.

Prague is a myth of itself, full of hidden magic, a place of uncertainty and it marks him. It's also a place that won't let him go — the mother with claws. He sees its surface, but he also sees beneath it; a strange warped interior vision. His description of place is fact and fiction all at once.

Catherine laughs. I'm beginning to think the two elide constantly.

Simon nods, lifts an empty cup.

I'll make coffee, Catherine says, rising. Go on.

So the landscape of the city is both topography and mindscape, both real and imagined. The city is mysterious, transmuted. Real places are not as they appear to the eye, so trying to pinpoint the 'actual' buildings he wrote about misses the point. Every location is a metaphor for what might be, for how we might be changed by interactions with place; psychogeography working at the deepest level.

You make me want to re-read him, Catherine says. She places fresh cups and a pot of coffee on the table. There are pastries too, courtesy of Margit.

I don't think I could, Simon says, pouring coffee.

Me neither.

So what about your writing?

I hardly know where to begin. Catherine cradles her mug, sips. I certainly didn't expect to be tussling with ideas of reincarnation or questioning notions of identity...

Simon waits.

This book is changing who I am. Or maybe I'm just unhinged.

Reincarnation's a pervasive belief, even in religions that officially reject it or persecute those who cling to it. And it's not only an 'eastern' idea', there are elements even in Norse mythology and perhaps Druidism, what little we know of it.

I know... Miriam used to talk about the soul-cycle, Gilgul Neshamot, and Kabbalah. I just thought I'd...

You'd what?

Grown out of it, I suppose. Or learnt to be myself.

We're never static, are we? And would you be less yourself if…

I don't want to think that I'm only here to complete some task or get something right. The thought of determinism…

Freewill isn't a given though, whether we have souls or past lives or not. Do you think?

Catherine shakes herself, stands. You've only been here a couple of hours and we're already talking philosophy. She smiles. Margit says it's going to be too cold to live today, but would you like to walk anyway — just for a short while maybe?

Simon nods. Of course.

It's only twenty minutes to Kazinczy Street and the Erzsébetváros district. I want to show you the synagogues there — the Orthodox one is so bright and alive, full of folk design — and the windows are painted glass — Art Nouveau — Secessionist I think. I don't think Selene would have known it. Or not inside, anyway. Her family don't seem to have been Orthodox — I think they'd more likely have belonged to the Dohány Street congregation, the Tabakgasse Synagogue — a distinctly Hungarian branch of Judaism — Neolog — not exactly liberal, but not so strict either. It's the biggest synagogue in Europe and looks more like a cathedral — even has an organ and choir — staffed by non-Jews in a wonderful bit of theological casuistry. And the bimah isn't in the centre, which is very unusual.

Sounds fascinating, even though I don't understand all of what you just said, Simon assents. Can I take the camera?

Catherine laughs. Sorry, the theology degree will out. But, yes — you have to cover your head, but they're fine with photos. It's quite low light — Moorish ochres, and deep pinks, lovely dark wood polished like mirrors and the glass is gorgeous — mustard and cobalt with flashes of scarlet around the opaque stars of David. It feels sombre, but then, it's seen a lot of tragedy.

Simon rubs his forehead. I can never take in the sheer scale of inhumanity, he says glumly. Makes me feel hopeless.

Yes. I try to tell myself the human capacity for love is even larger, but it's hard when you're looking at evidence to the contrary. It was bombed by the Arrow Cross in the war and when the ghetto was liberated afterwards, the garden was piled with bodies. Thousands died of starvation and cold. Selene must have been a child or young teen there — just her and her mother after her father was taken into the forced labour service and died. The Jewish community managed to keep the synagogue going as a prayer house right through the Communist era, but it wasn't renovated till a couple of years ago.

Bloody hell!

Sorry. Too much?

Simon's smile is wan, but he pulls her to him. We have to make the best of this scrap of life, don't we?

I think so. There's an exquisite memorial in the garden — erected during the renovations. A silver weeping tree — and every leaf has a name inscribed on it. A tree of life in the face of death.

I think I'll need a drink after all that.

There are lots of cafés in the area.

Even today?

It's not Shabbat till sunset and some are open anyway, but if we're too late we can walk ten minutes to the next district.

Fair enough. We'd better wrap up.

Do you think Selene will meet Attila again? Simon asks, his voice muffled by a thick scarf, dark green wool quivering between the wind and his breath.

Yes. Catherine snuggles into him as they walk, cold air clawing at any exposed skin. It seems to be only once each year for her, and so far she's seen him on a day in November from 1952 to '56. I dream of her in 1959, often with flashbacks to earlier periods, but '59 is the constant, so that's at least three more years when she should meet him.

And in 1937, Attila only has thirteen more days to live, so he will meet with her three more times in those last days?

Yes, if we assume Selene didn't meet him after 1959, but if she survives maybe there's more in the future — there are thirteen possibilities, after all. Are we mad walking in this cold?

Better than walking in belting sun, Simon says.

Ooh sun, wouldn't that be lovely. South of France in June.

Nope — woolly jumpers and hot chocolate for me. Walk faster, we'll warm up. He puts an arm around her and scoops her along the almost deserted street.

It must be terrible for Selene, knowing Attila's future, Simon says as they stride.

Yes — awful. And he knows that she must know his end, of

course. So strange. They both know there's no future in the relationship — Attila is still pursuing Flóra, even though he loves Selene, and she seems to understand that. They have something heartbreakingly limited and yet...

It's still love, Simon offers.

Yes.

We're lucky to have been born at the same time, aren't we? Think of it — the chances of us meeting, the chances of being born in the same time, the same culture, into lives that coincided — across all the possible lives that could have been...

But it's not really like that, is it? Catherine queries, breathing hard to talk and keep up.

It isn't?

I suppose if you think there is one other soul, whatever that means, out there in all the universe and all time, but do we really find 'the one' or do we find someone who, for various reasons, we feel at ease with, feel able to love. And sharing time and culture or other coincidences is part of making that happen, surely?

The facts and the story must fit, eh? Simon laughs. But what if they don't? What if the story won't bend to what the facts require? What if a woman falls in love with a man in another era?

Miriam used to say belief was my gift. I think I've got more sceptical with age — or at least more questioning, but do you really believe all this?

I believe you. Whatever else these 'dreams' are, they are meaningful.

206

Catherine stops on the cold, empty street and throws her arms around him.

Walking back, the air chilling further so that that they scurry, heads down, the hot chocolate of five minutes ago seeming a dream, Catherine stops.

Blast!

What?

We've taken a wrong turn, I think we've gone in completely the wrong direction. She looks up, scanning for street signs.

Oh, Simon.

Catherine?

Wesselényi utca. This is where Selene was born. Number 41.

Across the road I think.

Catherine peers across the strip of greenery and trees lining the centre of the wide street.

Next corner if the numbers go up from here, Simon offers.

She nods and they set off.

Handsome building, Simon says, looking up at the large windows on the floors above street level.

They were well off when Selene was born.

A door opens and a woman in a smart black coat and thick fur hat exits.

Excuse me, Simon ventures.

The woman shakes her head.

Sprechen Sie Deutsche?

She nods. Ich spreche ein bisschen Deutsch.

We're looking for a place where... Simon begins in German. A friend of ours, her mother was born here. We said we'd try to get a picture for her. He reaches into his battered satchel for the compact camera that always accompanies him. Wesselényi utca, 41.

Yes, she says. Yes, that's where I live. Do you know which apartment?

29, Catherine says and Simon translates.

How strange. That's my number, as it happens.

My... Simon looks at Catherine, searching for the word. My... Er... Fiancée... she's here doing research on Attila József, working with the university...

She looks less suspicious. Well, I'm on my way... I mean... She hesitates. Perhaps tomorrow. My son will be home tomorrow. Perhaps you would like to see the apartment, though it may have changed. How long ago was it?

A long time. They moved to Paris in the late Twenties, Sándor and Marie Virág, a long time ago, but still...

Tomorrow then. 11 o'clock?

That's so kind. Very kind. I'm Simon, by the way. Simon Garrett and this is Catherine McManus.

Catherine smiles, holds out her hand.

Róza Frankel, the woman says. Until tomorrow.

Fiancée?

I was trying to think of a word — girl-friend didn't seem quite right. You speak German?

No. Just a few words remembered from school. Like 'Verlobte'.

Simon pulls her to him. Till tomorrow, he echoes. But for now — you must be freezing. Any more hot chocolate in the flat?

Catherine

Catherine dozes on the bench, Saturday 21 November, 1959, etched into the cell wall, the tedium of another of Selene's days aching before her… alone, cold, hungry. She dozes…

…Selene half remembering, half dreaming an image of the ironically-named 'exercise yard'…

a day not long after Ludmilla was taken away two years ago…. She enters the yard behind a ragged column of emaciated women, walls rearing, sightless, dumb. Her gut twists. She lurches forward. Behind her, fingers prod. She stumbles into a featureless quadrangle, edges along the wall. Someone is telling her to walk, walk — one foot, the next, right foot, left. Air ices lungs, skin burns cold, muscles tremble. In front and behind, other feet shamble. Falling — rain — thick globules of icy rain — falling, one hailstone, another, hard, piercing her skin. She glances upwards, sees…

…I don't like the way Boglárka watches you. There are informers everywhere, she'd said.

Yes, and to think we thought Stalin's death would make a difference, Zsófia had agreed.

210

It's early days, Selene insisted. Nagy will make things better, I'm sure of it. He's already reigning in the ÁVH and the decree to dissolve the internment camps will —

Boglárka walked towards them and they'd fallen silent.

…sees… Boglárka?

Did she say the name out loud? Hands hauling her out of the yard where women shamble, one foot, the next, women mute as walls, not looking as she is dragged back to the cell.

Selene wakes, head muzzy with images from years gone by, images of cellmates, of her daughter, her mother.

I have only a past, she says to the empty cell, no future. She forces herself to rise, walk, stretch, wait for the gruel that arrives each day…

When food arrives, the guard reaches into his pocket, brandishes an envelope.

A letter for you, he says.

For me? Selene moves towards him.

He raises his arm, waves the letter high in the air, grinning. Now, let me see…

He pulls the letter from the already opened envelope and begins to scan it. Hmm.

Please…

His look silences her. He reads on. Interesting… but no, no, perhaps dull really. You wouldn't want to be bothered with all this whining and complaining, surely?

I... If I could...

No, I think you wouldn't. Just your mother moaning as usual, eh? He smirks, rips the letter into two, then four pieces, quickly.

No! I mean... please... if I...

But you already decided not to be bothered with all this moaning... too late now. His sneer widens as he rips the pieces smaller. Maybe just a little, he taunts, sprinkling a meagre handful into Selene's food, balling the rest in his fist. Savour it, he says smugly, turning to leave. Savour every word.

Budapest, Sunday 21 November 1993

There are days when Selene is resilient, determined to look forward, still hopeful of seeing Miriam again, and days when she is overwhelmed, on the verge of giving up. 'I have only a past,' she said today. I feel desolate for her and can do nothing except hope to find Miriam, perhaps find out what happened to Selene.

We returned to Wesselényi utca, 41 today, the apartment where Selene was born. Róza Frankel's son, Vilmos, spoke good English, making me aware of how poor we English are at languages, though Simon's German impresses me, especially compared to my limited French and passable Italian. There is so much I don't know about Simon still. Sometimes I look at him and wonder who he is, not in a hostile way, but as though I've been taken by surprise to find him in my life, which I suppose I have.

The apartment was lovely, high-ceilings, long windows,

polished parquet floors, an art nouveau door of two curved walnut panels leading into the sitting room. Vilmos told us that his mother, Róza, had lived there all her life, that his grandparents took the flat over from Sándor and Marie Virág in 1929 and Róza was born in 1933. Apparently, it was when Simon had said the Virágs' name on the street yesterday that she decided we were genuine, so invited us back.

I took Sándor's sketchbook and told them we were searching for Miriam on behalf of another family member and Róza left the sitting room and returned with photographs. Vilmos explained that his grandmother had found them in the back of a drawer not long after they moved in.

Most likely taken with a Box Brownie, Vilmos said. Not bad for the optics they were using.

There was Selene, not quite two-years-old, but recognisably the same person as the lithe ten year old in Sándor's sketchbook — dark eyes and a frame of dark curls around her serious little face; Marie, beautiful, smiling, effortlessly elegant as she held her daughter towards the camera, looked towards her husband, and Sándor, Selene got her eyes and colouring from him, her bird-like delicacy from Marie. Three pictures of the three of them. Another three of Selene, staring into the camera with the confidence of a child who is loved.

How do we get from that adored child of artist-parents to the degradation of a cell? The capacity for cruelty, for hatred... that guard with his glee at destroying Marie's letter... taunting Selene...

And yet, there is an extraordinary capacity for generosity in so many people too. Róza cried when she heard about Selene ending up in prison after the uprising, then insisted we take the photos to give to Miriam when we find her.

A terrible time, Vilmos kept repeating. And Róza quietly told Simon that she'd lost her husband during that awful time. He was twenty-three, a post graduate student fervent for change... Vilmos was born two months after his father died.

This evening Margit and András came for supper with us. András is more relaxed about the search for Miriam now that there is some kind of connection between Attila and the Virágs, and we talked about the newspaper advert, about Simon's next novel, which I think seems very fanciful to András, though he remained polite, despite Margit's goading.

Simon only arrived yesterday, but he already feels part of this place with me. He has a quiet way of merging into a space, an ease that is in striking contrast to his anxiety and self-doubt. It is good to have him here.

Selene Solweig

Selene wakes feeling nauseous, wishes she had something in her stomach to vomit, to relieve the hollow ache, but not even bile rises. She shifts on the bench, lifts a chipping, puts it down. She will write the date later... she curls into herself, drifts, dreams she is...

Catherine saying, I don't suppose we'll be lucky enough to get into the building, but I'd like to see it anyway. I don't know why I haven't already visited.

They must have lived somewhere else when they came back from Paris, Simon says. And maybe somewhere else again when her father was sent into the forced labour service.

Yes, the Jews were increasingly ghettoised. Those that weren't transported and killed in death camps.

An hour later they stand before the once-imposing doors of Népszinház utca, 19, the dark wood parched, peeling and cracked, the windows to either side protected by iron grilles, the stone facade of the first floor crumbling away from the brick-work beneath. The narrow street is gloomy.

I can see why it would have been difficult for Marie to move here, Catherine says.

Simon pushes against the heavy door, but it remains shut.

They step away as a woman in a grey coat too thin for the biting cold emerges, knots a mud-coloured headscarf under her chin and glares at them.

Think we'd better go, Catherine says, retreating.

A café beckons with steamy warmth as they walk back towards their apartment. Inside, Simon orders hot chocolates, and they sit nursing the cups to thaw their hands.

Bit dire, eh? Simon offers.

Yes, but not as bad as Selene having to run away and then being imprisoned when she returned.

So that was the last address you have for Miriam?

Yes, twenty-four years ago. I'm not feeling optimistic between visiting that squalid place and waiting for the newspapers to advertise.

Wasn't one of them yesterday?

Yes, but the other two don't come out till next Thursday and one of those is a long shot. Catherine pauses, sips chocolate. I suppose they're all a long shot actually and I feel like I'm in limbo, waiting and…

And?

It's stupid, but I've got this sense of foreboding.

Might just be the cold.

Catherine smiles. Tell me about Prague, she says.

I had a favourite café there, very similar to this one. Right on the river, full of shelves of old books and an odd assortment of tables and chairs. They did really good chocolate too. Excellent carrot cake. I used to pass a shop on the way there that made me think of you.

Catherine leans forward. Full of woolly jumpers? She teases.

No, guess again.

Hmm — ceramics?

No. More Czech than that.

Not glass?

Still cold. It took me ages to go inside. It always looked so quiet and exclusive, but eventually I went in and the woman running it was really welcoming, even though she didn't speak much English. We discovered we could get by in German after a while. They had these amazing dolls. I remembered you telling me you collected rag dolls when you were young. These were moulded, but so lifelike — not toys — more works of art, some with rag bodies or fabric parts. I knew they'd be mad amounts of money, well, maybe not for the work that goes into them, but unaffordable anyway...

Catherine nods.

But they also had this case of silver work. I thought they would be expensive, especially when she told me in a mix of English and German that each piece was a one-off, but...

He reaches into his pocket.

I thought today might be the right time, especially if it proved hard going — something to cheer it, perhaps…

Catherine takes a tiny cardboard box decorated with stylised brown leaves and flowers. Inside, purple tissue paper cradles a silver pendant, a tulip with a row of diminutive garnets trailing from its fine stem.

It's beautiful, Simon. Really gorgeous.

He smiles. I'll get one of those dolls one day, he says, or a Prague marionette, they're amazing too.

This is better, Catherine says, clasping the silver tulip around her neck.

I'm glad. It's not, he hesitates, it's not a ring, but…

Simon?

Well, I did tell Róza Frankel that you're my fiancée. I mean, if…

Yes, Catherine says. Yes. She moves around the table and pulls him to his feet, throwing her arms around him.

Walking back to the apartment, Simon winds his fingers into Catherine's and she leans into him. They're almost home when a beggar looms across their path.

I've got no change, mate, Simon says.

The man blocks their path, animal breath on their faces, eyes glazed, hands gesturing. Simon tries something in German and the man leans in further, spits out wet words, raises a hand.

Fuck off, Simon screams. Fucking get away from us. Go on,

fuck off, you filthy bastard.

Simon!

The man startles, shambles away throwing curses over his shoulder as he goes.

Catherine looks at Simon.

He is trembling. I've messed up everything now, haven't I?

No, Catherine puts a hand on his arm, but he moves away.

I have. I always bloody do.

No, it's just…

It's alright, I wouldn't blame you for dumping me. I'd dump myself if I could.

He hunches into himself as Catherine moves towards him.

Let's get to the flat.

They walk in silence, not holding hands.

Sorry, Simon says, when they get indoors.

It's fine, I was just…

But Simon has begun walking from the living room and she hears the bedroom door click shut.

Catherine

Sunday 22 November is barely visible in a thin line across the wall. Catherine tries to sit, but Selene's body slumps back onto the bench, weak.

Half-conscious, she recalls seeing Tibor and Zsófia off, as they left for their wedding. One train becoming another — Attila on the platform. She dreams of Miriam, of taking a tiny photograph from her pocket to show him…

My daughter! Attila marching along the platform, declaiming poetry; his voice — so sonorous, so uplifted, until he kneels on the platform, sobbing because he will never meet his daughter.

And then she was on an empty platform once more, Tibor and Zsófia's train pulling away, smoke clearing.

Selene wakes on the bench, murmuring, Miriam, Attila, Miriam… falls into a deeper sleep, a train pulling into a station…

Crowds throng between the soaring archways as Selene alights onto platform six at Keleti station. It is barely a month since the uprising, since Zsófia...

Don't let them think you can't make it, Zsófia had warned, her face glistening, pallid, eyes blood-shot.

They had followed the guide's unsteady torch, wading streams, feet sinking into bog... but the next morning they were in Austria, given food... a young doctor ordering moist bandages to dress the wound on her leg, telling her with a shake of his head... she was pregnant... she lost a lot of blood... I'm afraid —

She remembers him asking her if she is sure, over and over, when she decides to return to Budapest.

I have a daughter and we've been promised amnesty.

I understand, but perhaps your daughter would be able to join you here. You have skills, good German...

I've signed to say I agree to return, she tells him finally. I'm leaving tomorrow.

He nods. I hope you can trust those people, he adds, turning away.

She wishes she had gone to find him before she left, said goodbye, but the leaving was swift. She walks past a line of guards, moves out of the file of people who have returned with her, thinking of Miriam, not seeing the gun swing across her path...

Back in line.

I'm...

Back in line.

But…

He stands in front of her so she can smell his breath — tobacco and bacon fat, something rancid. You will be taken to Andrássy út to be processed. He spits. Then you'll be tried with the rest of these dogs.

But the amnesty…

He grins. Spits again. Dogs and bitches. Keep in line. He pushes her back towards the plodding row of people who have each signed to say they are returning of their own volition, that they wish to return home. But she is not going home. Her stomach lurches. She wants to run, but can hardly walk, can hardly stay upright. Her vision blurs, lights dancing before her eyes, a black cloud blotting out the sight on her left, the scent of oranges mingling with smoke as a train sounds behind her… And she turns, dizzy… falls into the arms of —

Attila, who catches her on the platform, smiles.

Selene. His eyebrows meet and he bends over her. You are so pale…

Oh, Attila, I've been so stupid. I believed them. How could I have believed them? Gerhard warned me not to come back, but I… I had to come back to Miriam… I…

Shh, shh, you must slow down, tell me what is wrong.

Sorry… She looks around at the quiet platform in Balatonszárszó. Can we go to the lake?

Attila nods, winds an arm around her as they begin to walk.

Miriam is safe, she says, as they find a place to sit, looking out at the water. But things are very bad and I think I've just been arrested.

Attila startles. Arrested?

A lot has happened since last year.

His brows knit. It's only been four days for me, though it feels like an age since I last saw you — it was so brief and I did not behave well — but tell me...

When she finishes the breathless monologue of a year's events, each month more fateful than the last, she looks up to see his face covered in tears.

Oh, Attila, I'm so sorry — I...

This country! How can this country become so debased?

He begins to pace, to rant.

Attila, she tries to break into the rapid fulmination, takes his face in her hands and turns it towards her. He stops, kneels by her and weeps.

Oh — no, I mean... I'm sure it will be alright — that it's a mistake — they promised amnesty, maybe they just want to scare us, keep us quelled...

He looks up and gets to his feet. And I can do nothing to help you, to help my child — I...

A train sounds far off... and the guard spits at her feet. Keep moving, bitch, and keep in line.

Budapest, Monday 22 November 1993

I dreamt about the next encounter between Selene and Attila. Trains again — mechanical beasts freighted with human stories. There is so much longing as a train moves towards a destination or as a lover waits on a platform, and so much fear as an overcrowded car hurtles those trapped inside towards unwanted, brutal futures or as someone stands, watching the crowds disperse with no trace of the beloved they'd anticipated would be there to meet them.

A train sounds and my body resonates with *the uncertainty of the hope and fear of all the world...*

And Simon. He came by train only two days ago and so much has happened in such a short time. It is treacherous to be in love. I learnt that from Liam, and even from Miriam, but this has felt... 'different' is too weak a word — 'other'?

In two days he has tramped all over Budapest with me and listened to what most people would think is lunacy — ironic given my dream-persona's name — moon-goddess Selene, bathing in the sea before riding across the night, showering her lovers in moon-rays in order to become pregnant with her daughters... None of this seems to unsettle Simon, yet a beggar on the street can throw him into complete turmoil and depression. Nothing I can do or say today seems able to shift the darkness from him. We have spent the day in different rooms, me writing a journal into which Selene breaks constantly, so that I have revisited, trance-like, her memories of Zsófia and relived not only the day Selene and Attila met on the platform on November 18 1955, but also their next meeting on November 22, 1956, another platform — Selene dizzy with trauma, arrested as she returned to Hungary, where she had expected amnesty. Her last moments of freedom were spent with Attila in some dislocated mindscape that might have been more 'real' to her than anything else in her life.

And Attila — his mood-swings, from rapture to desolation — reminds me so much of Simon. Yesterday, I think he proposed to me, not with a ring, but — with characteristic eccentricity — a silver and garnet pendant shaped into a tulip. Yet today he is withdrawn and depressed and will not believe that I want him in my life.

Selene Solweig

Selene wakes with the sound of trains reverberating through her thin body, images of the day she was arrested soaking her mind, images of Attila — a man she has met only seven times over the last seven years and who she loves more than anyone — anyone since her father — except Miriam…

She closes her eyes against the pain and monotony of the day beginning…

Please, Simon…

No one will want me there. It's you they've invited…

They invited us both and it's just a few people. You've met Margit and András, but I'd really like you to meet the others. You'll like Zsuzsanna Makai, she's helped me believe strange things can happen and György Kalmár and András's student, Viktor Kovács, will be there too. You'll like him, he's very earnest and intelligent.

I'll just be in the way.

No, you won't. I want them to meet you. They've become friends. They've been so generous and I don't want to go to dinner with them and have to make excuses for you.

He looks up, startled. I'm a burden either way, aren't I?

No, that's not what I meant. I just…

She turns to leave the bedroom —

OK. I'll get ready. Is there something I should wear?

She turns back and smiles. Thank you. Wear something warm for scurrying between buildings and layers so you can take them off when we're inside.

I didn't do very well, did I? Simon asks as they return to the apartment a few minutes before midnight.

I don't know what you mean, Catherine reassures. They loved you.

They tolerate me because they love you — everyone does.

I don't think that's true, but really —— it was a good evening.

I think András is in love with you.

Catherine laughs. András thinks I'm a very unorthodox researcher who he can't quite make sense of.

Perhaps both are true, Simon adds. He's got good taste at least.

And anyway, what matters is who I'm in love with, and that's definitely you.

Simon puts his arms around her and pulls her close. You're amazing. He stands back, still encircling her with his arms. It

227

wasn't really the guy begging that unsettled me — it was more the timing — I was thinking about…

She tilts her head to one side, waits.

I've been having my own dreams… Do we have any brandy? Let's pour a drink and I'll tell you about them.

In bed, cradling balloons of caramel-soft liquid, Simon begins:

On Saturday it was a nightmare about drowning. I was on a ship, well — tiny thing really — maybe fifty or sixty feet end to end — one mast, one square sail and enormous waves. In my head I had this litany — *myrrh, pepper, cinnamon, saffron, cardamom, silk… myrrh, pepper, cinnamon, saffron…* as though these riches that the Spanish traded for would act like a charm to ward off the sea. I was afraid, but calm. *Myrrh, pepper, cinnamon, saffron, cardamom, silk.* And then the chant changed — *Shir hama-alos,… Out of the depths I call to You, O Lord…* There were people running across the deck, trying to steer against the wind with only that one unbiddable sail. But I felt distant from it all. I could hear sailors cursing the winds. I could hear the crew shouting about the changes from westerly to north-westerlies to southerly to violent north-easterly, hollering about how it was sending us off-course and into the pull of waves swelling and swelling. *Out of the depths I call to You, O Lord…* as a wave broke over our heads and the ship dipped and another crashed around us and… *Hear, O Israel! The LORD is our God, the LORD is one! You shall love the LORD your God with all your heart and with all your soul and with all your might…* and a wave battered us into the deck… and another… and a crack louder than thunder… There was only sea and cold, so intense, yet I was numb and calm. But when I inhaled, water filled me and my body began to fight. I panicked, exhaling water, inhaling water and my lungs burned, my insides tearing, on fire… *Out of the depths I call to You…*
228

And then a sense deep peace, tranquillity… *out of the depths*… such serenity… and I surrendered… And woke pushing the blankets from my face, disoriented to be dry and alive…

Ben Haddaj? Catherine asks.

Yes. He died leaving Spain to return to his Jewish roots didn't he?

Yes, but you know the story. I mean, you read it my novel and in *Casilda of the Rising Moon* and I've been thinking about Casilda again since these dreams of Selene, so perhaps that set off your dreams?

Could be, certainly — but it felt… personal. It felt like… I *was* Ben Haddaj and then, last night, it was Attila I dreamt of… dreamt of his…

His death?

Yes. And I know there are plenty of accounts of it, but there was something else —

Catherine leans forward, takes his hands.

In the dream I was on the tracks and I knew I wanted to die. But then I thought I saw Selene and ran towards her, calling her name, and she was shouting at me. She looked so afraid and was screaming and waving her arms, but all I could think of was running towards her. I heard a noise like the world fracturing, but I didn't want to move out of the way of what I knew was coming. I only wanted to make her leave the track and I turned for a moment and the wagon was almost upon me…

Simon takes a deep breath and Catherine squeezes his hand. It doesn't mean it was you. It was a dream, just…

Like your dreams of Selene are 'just dreams'?

She says nothing.

Of course, I know how Ben Haddaj and how Attila died. I'm not saying it proves anything. But I can also tell you the next date that Selene and Attila will meet, and I don't mean on his last day.

Catherine leans further forward, tense, listening.

They will be together on… Simon pauses. I'll write it down, but not say it, he says. If I tell you then I might be influencing you to dream them together on that date. You can look at what I've written after the date. And she'll have had a new cellmate before then too. I'll write down the name.

Catherine

The date is on the wall — Tuesday 23 November. Catherine looks at the list of dates, the uneven marks charting Selene's ragged attempts to keep track. How long is it since Ludmilla died? Two years? And a few days after Ludmilla was taken, there was…

I don't like the way Boglárka watches you, she had said to Zsófia a lifetime ago. There are informers everywhere.

And there she was… in the exercise yard, not long after Ludmilla was taken away… Selene stumbling along the wall before falling — rain — thick globules of icy rain — glancing upwards, seeing… Boglárka? Did she say the name out loud? Hands hauling her out of the yard where women shambled, one foot, the next…

And there was Boglárka again… thrust into her cell later that day.

They stand looking at one another for a long time or perhaps only for minutes that stretch in their minds.

Boglárka, the other woman offers eventually. It's Selene, isn't it?

Selene nods.

We were at…

The National Institute of Oncology, Selene finishes for her.

Boglárka nods. You were friends with Zsófia Lenárt.

viroký Tiborné Lenárt Zsófia, Selene corrects. She married Tibor before she died.

Boglárka nods again. I'm sorry. I mean, I'm sorry she died.

Are you?

I'm not what you think, Selene…

You're not? And what do I think?

I'm not an informer, though it was partly true in the past, but not… I was an activist like Zsófia. I was going to marry my boyfriend, Lázár Tóth, but he was arrested. There are only three sorts of Hungarians, after all…

…those who've been to jail, those in jail and those who will be in jail, Selene interrupts.

Quite.

But you…

You and Zsófia were right to suspect me. I wasn't as brave as Lázár. They told me to watch people, tell them anything. They threatened me and I was terrified and stupid.

Stupid?

I was scared, but I thought I could outwit them. I was supposed to collect information on radicals and trouble causers, but I fed them rubbish, anything I thought would be misleading. I kept going to meetings… even took part in the uprising. But of course they weren't fooled… And you? Did you fight?

Selene begins to form an answer, but sits on the bench, head in her hands, looks up.

And now? Are you informing now?

As I told you — I'm not an informer now. Will you believe me?

Selene shakes her head.

Maybe you will tell them something terrible about me and then they'll… Boglárka trails away.

It's impossible, Selene says quietly. This situation is…

Quite. And…

Selene leans forward and Boglárka moves to sit on the bench nest to her.

I was always a bit jealous of you and Zsófia. Even when I had Lázár, I wished I had that sort of friendship. I was always awkward with people, never good at making friends. The two of you seemed so… it seemed easy for you… to talk, to laugh…

Selene nods. Zsófia was an easy person to be with.

And Tibor, her boyfriend… husband… you knew him too?

Not much. I saw them off on the train when they went to be married. And I met his cousin, Luca, briefly, but…

Tibor was one of the students who formed the new breakaway movement from DISZ, wasn't he? One of those that drew up the Sixteen Points. Wasn't Ludmilla one of the same group?

Ludmilla?

Yes. It's odd how we're all connected, isn't it? Small world…

And what group were you part of?

Oh me, I was never at the centre of anything. A hanger-on, I just…

…gave others away.

No. No, really, Selene. I wouldn't be here if I'd done what they wanted. Surely you can believe that at least.

So how did you know Ludmilla?

I was a watcher, I'll admit that. I had to be after Lázár was arrested. Tibor and Ludmilla belonged to the same group as Lázár. I kept attending meetings, but…

You're lying, Boglárka. Zsófia went to meetings with Tibor and she'd have trusted you if she'd seen you there.

There is silence.

I didn't always attend, I mean not regularly… I…

Tell me what Luca Široký looked like.

Luca?

Yes., Tibor's cousin. She was another member of that group. You must have met her.

I… It was a very large group… I'm not sure our paths…

Or Ludmilla?

What?

How would you describe Ludmilla? You just said you knew her from meetings.

I… I mean she was… Boglárka chokes back a sob, holds her head in her hands. Ludmilla Bíró's boyfriend was never caught, she whispers. He was involved with high-ranking dissidents. They think she must have told you…

She didn't. Selene's voice is monotone, cold.

I don't need much. Boglárka's voice changes to a insinuating wheedle. I'm asking you to help me, not to give away anything that would endanger… just enough to… If we help them, it will be better for our families, she adds.

Selene gasps. Now you're trying to scare me. In any case, you probably know more about Ludmilla's politics than I do.

Selene stands and moves away from the bench. Ludmilla didn't even tell me her boyfriend's full name, she says.

Péter Rácz, Boglárka says. He was linked to the Petőfi Circle like Tibor Široký. And Ludmilla and Zsófia might both be alive if they hadn't been taken in by those agitators…

Ludmilla and Zsófia made their own decisions, Selene snaps. We all did. Maybe not with much information, but at least with passion. It's not naïve to want freedom.

I didn't mean...

I don't care what you meant. You know more about Péter than I do, so you'll have to make something up if you want to pass on information to save your sorry self.

Budapest, Tuesday 23 November 1993

I seem to live in a permanent state of nightmare or anxiety, fearing for others. I'm sure Selene is right to distrust Boglárka, if only because Boglárka is so obviously weak. But how would I behave in such an extreme situation? Boglárka is trying to save herself, but it makes her dangerous.

And Simon... he came with me to the dinner and all was fine again, despite his certainty that no-one really likes him. But why did he dream Ben Haddaj's death? Have I filled his head with confusion? What is even more disturbing is not that he also dreamt Attila's death, but that knew that Boglárka would come back into Selene's life. He wrote her name down and I didn't see it until after the dream of her. Is that possible? But what does 'possible' mean when I'm dreaming the life of someone who had a relationship out of her own time period? Or perhaps I'm imagining all of it and I dreamt Boglárka back into the 'story' because Simon somehow influenced me to make it happen.

I don't really believe that, though. I'm convinced that the life I'm dreaming is real and I constantly feel that I am waiting for doom. Attila died horribly. I know that, but did Selene die? And Miriam? There is no news of her so far. I only have ten more days in Budapest and fear I'll never find her.

Selene Solweig

Selene wakes with Boglárka on her mind, though it's two years since she had a cellmate… She scratches the date on the wall, thinks of Simon, how he reminds her of Attila. She will make her way through another day of tedium, reach the night when she can dream Catherine's life, feel alive again — sleep to dream of…

It's extraordinary, Simon says, handing a manuscript back to Catherine.

Not quite what my editor will be expecting, though.

No, but more exciting. More…

Insane?

Only if you tell them the whole backstory. He grins. Never tell anyone the whole story.

Really? So what haven't you told me?

Lots, but mostly because we're still…

New?

He nods. What do you want to know?

Have you always suffered with depression?

He pauses. Bites his lower lip. No. No, I haven't. I would say I was quite a cheery kid, really.

So what changed?

I'm not sure I know 'what', but I know when. There was a day when I had this overwhelming sense of bleakness. I was alone and I sat on my sofa and started to cry, no — howl. I howled until I was exhausted and had no more tears in me and my throat was raw. And then I curled up on the floor and stayed there for hours, thinking that something had ended, something huge that I couldn't grasp was over, and nothing would ever be the same again.

And you don't know what caused it?

No.

But you remember the date?

Oh yes, it's inscribed in me. September 13, 1989.

It was a Wednesday, Catherine says.

Wow! That's impressive. How…?

It was the day Miriam died.

Miriam? You mean your friend…?

Catherine nods.

That's… I feel a bit…

...cold, Catherine says, I feel freezing cold, like someone...

...just died, Simon finishes for her.

They fall silent.

I think I need to go and write, Simon ventures when their silence begins to prickle.

Catherine nods. Me too.

He gets up to go to his desk in the bedroom.

Simon...

He turns towards her.

I... I'm not sure really, just... I love you.

He smiles. I'm beginning to believe that, he says, and leaves the room.

Can I read you something? Simon asks, emerging from the bedroom four hours later.

Of course.

He begins a passage about ritual magic in Prague, densely layered, mesmeric, the images looping into themselves so that the prose is rhythmic, almost incantatory.

I think I'm almost pleased with that, he says, when he finishes. And I've got this other piece about time, how it's not linear, how the perception of time makes it amorphous and strange.

He reads again, flushed and earnest.

Am I mad to think this is going somewhere? he asks, when he finishes the next piece.

Definitely not mad. It's astonishing. It's like Schulz and Quin, but it's also like neither — it's you — rich and utterly individual.

We...ell, I'm not sure I'd say that... You really think...?

I do. I wish my writing was like that. Mine's so... so plain by comparison.

Honed, not plain. You pare down to the essentials. No clutter. Mine's shit, actually, isn't it?

What do you meant, it's shit?

My writing. It's all fireworks and strutting and no substance, isn't it?

No, why would you say that? I love it. I just said how impressed I am, jealous even. It's sumptuous and layered and strange — it's enchanting — not in a sentimental way, but in how it fascinates and draws the hearer in.

You're very kind, but...

Simon, you're a fantastic writer. But you've just written for four hours straight and you're too close to see it. Let's have coffee before we get ready for dinner.

Oh... I don't think I can go out tonight...

Ah.

I'm sorry. I know you prefer me to be there, but it's just Margit and András tonight, isn't it? Will they mind too much? I don't mean to keep letting you down.

They'll miss you, but they'll be fine about it and you're not letting me down. It's not that at all. But I'm worried about you. Shall I cancel?

No. You go.

I'll be fretting about you all evening.

I'll be fine. He smiles weakly. Really. Go.

Simon, Catherine calls quietly, when she returns, bursting with the things people have said at dinner, snippets she wants to share. Simon!

Catherine pushes open the bedroom door. Are you asleep? She whispers.

There's a small noise in the darkness.

Simon?

Another sound, a whimper.

Catherine flicks on a small bedside lamp.

Simon, are you ill?

No, no, I'm… I'm sorry… ignore me… I…

What is it?

Me. I'm the matter. I'm shit. The writing's shit. Everything I do is shit. You'd be better off with András.

András? What are you talking about? Simon, I'm with you. I want to be with you. I'm going to make coffee and we're going to talk. All night if that's what it takes.

I had another dream, he says, following her into the kitchen.

She fills the Bialetti moka pot with coffee and turns on the stove. About?

Attila, he says. Or not so much 'about' Attila, more dreaming his life...

The way I do with Selene?

Apparently.

And? She takes Simon's hand and leads him to the table, pulls out a chair, sits next to him.

He went looking for Miriam.

His daughter?

Yes, he didn't find her. But, it's more than that. I don't think we will find Miriam either.

What do you mean?

I'm not sure, exactly. I just have this strong sense that... I don't she's dead, but I have this feeling something strange happened to her, that she's no longer in Budapest.

They sit listening to the coffee spurting on the stovetop. Why? Catherine asks, eventually.

I... I sense it... that's all I can say...

Catherine

Catherine doesn't sleep that night... There is no dream of Selene, no cell, no date on the wall.

Catherine dozes in the early morning, wakes anxious and unsettled.

I'll make coffee, Simon offers. I shouldn't have kept you awake all night.

I'm glad we talked, Catherine returns. I'm just feeling a bit wrecked and... it's so odd... I've dreamt a day in her life every night for nearly three weeks, but it feels much longer than that.

I suppose you've lived a lot more of her life than three weeks' worth in that time, Simon muses.

Yes. I feel... uneasy, not knowing... I don't know... not knowing whatever I would have known if I'd slept last night. No, it's worse than that... it's like I've lost her. In the day, usually I feel her presence... I'm aware that she's dreaming my life — sometimes she even seems to take over parts of it, like finding my way round Paris or speaking fluent French or walking to the flat on Wesselényi utca without realising where I was going. But today I can't feel her. Selene's gone and I'm frightened... I feel physically afraid that I may not get her back again.

Simon strokes a hand across her face and moves to hold her.

Catherine laughs softly. It's mad, isn't it? I've been terrified of losing my identity, of getting lost in Selene's life, and now I feel bereft and anxious after one night not dreaming of her... Do you think this will be the end of it?

Simon shrugs. We can't know until you next sleep I suppose.

The thought of her in that cell, Simon... and not knowing...

Shh, he soothes, stroking her face. I'm going to make that coffee I promised you.

She paces the flat as he fills the moka pot, wrinkles her nose when he finally offers her the small cup of dark liquid.

I don't think I can manage coffee. My head's starting to ache.

Simon looks anxious. Dry toast?

She shakes her head.

Hot milk?

Oh, God, no. I'd heave. I'll be fine. Maybe just some water.

She begins pacing again, stops abruptly.

Catherine?

Dizzy, she mutters. Bit sick.

She heads for the bathroom and vomits a thin trickle of mucous. Standing, she is aware of the stark whiteness of the porcelain sink, the loudness of the water as she rinses her hands. She turns towards the door, but it has disappeared, only a black blankness exists on the left side of her vision. She turns her head cautiously, reaches for the door-handle, winces at the noise of the draft excluder against the tiles as the door opens. She feels edgy, her skin prickles as she walks and there is an overwhelming smell of fruit and rotting lilies, fleshy decay tinged with acrid smoke… she heaves again, falters towards the bedroom door.

Catherine? Simon hovers anxiously by the bed.

Migraine, she whispers. Haven't had one for ages.

Simon pulls the curtains closed, tiptoes out, returns with a lavender compress. Try this, he says, easing it against her forehead. She half-sits, begins to retch.

Oh, God, I'm sorry.

Bathroom…

He helps her up, guides her to the corridor. The vomit, a gush of bile that wrenches her gut, doesn't quite make it into the toilet bowl. She is sick for a long time, sits on the flushed and doused toilet lid while Simon eases off her nightdress, gently passes a damp flannel over her too-sensitive skin, slides a fresh nightdress over her head, helps her to shuffle back to the bedroom where she collapses into bed.

In the haze of pain, jolts of light and half-sleep, she is not herself, but every nightmare of Selene's life is an event already experienced. She is not living through Selene's next day. Selene has gone, she tells herself over and over, until she sleeps, deeply, dreamlessly. And when she wakes, the day is almost over.

Budapest, Wednesday 24 November 1993

Day of migraine after a night without sleep. Simon talked endlessly last night and at least I think he now believes me when I say I want him in my life. I feel shaky and hollowed out, but the blackness that blots out everything on the left of my vision has gone and the vomiting has stopped. Amazing and painful to throw up so much from an empty stomach. Simon has been very kind and is obviously worried about me. He wants to make me soup or mint tea, but the smallest decision feels too much for me at the moment.

Mint tea — that's what Miriam made me in Toledo. Though, of course, she couldn't have been there. I went to Toledo to find Casilda, to find traces of Casilda, the year after Miriam died. It was the second day visiting Mezquita Bab al-Mardum, the little Mosque that Casilda might once have visited, the air cool, sky bright azure, almost white, and I thought I heard a rustle of silk. When I looked up, the left of my vision was clotted dark, shadows congealing beneath the vaulted arches. There was a scent of smoke and flowers, the sound of water against stone and a whisper, *Casilda*.

I felt dizzy, saw lights pulsing at the edge of the darkness, felt a heavy clot of blood slip between my legs. I hardly remember how I made it back to the apartment through the steep, narrow streets, cobbles jarring, abdomen aching, the urge to vomit. But Miriam was beside me. Inside the apartment, I stood on the cool cobalt tiles of the bathroom, let water scald and saturate every sense, blood flooding the drain crimson and the tang of iron on my tongue. Afterwards, Miriam wrapped me in a white towel. I slid between white cotton sheets, drowsed, and when I woke, the sky was dark, sharp stars dazzling through the open shutters. On the dark wood bedside table was a silk cord of palest blue, strung with a tiny hamsa: the hand of Miriam in damascene black, silver, gold that I wear always, the same one that Selene appears to carry with her. And beside it, a turquoise glass of mint tea.

Migraines and blood. The first migraine came after my miscarriage five years ago and now I seem to get them only with heavy periods. There is something about intense physical experience, even when it is pain, that takes us to the edge of the ineffable. Miriam always felt that about epilepsy, as did Dostoevsky.

Catherine spreads the palm of her hand across her abdomen, remembers feeling the clot slip between her legs, thick and gelatinous, how her friends, Zoë and Alex, had wrapped her in a blanket, taken her to hospital. Where was Liam?

I went to bed on a hot day in June, 1988, slept all day, all night, woke exhausted, pain searing through my head, half of my vision in darkness, lights flashing across the other eye, the smell of fruit, rotting lilies and smoke clinging to me. I vomited, then slept and slept and slept... through what seemed like most of the next year, hiding away with my mother in Redcar until I found the cottage in Wales not long before I last saw Miriam...

'...to write,' de Beauvoir said in *The Prime of Life*, 'something has to go adrift in life, we have to no longer be able to take reality for granted.'

How much has to go adrift? How often? I lost Miriam. I lost a baby. Now I seem to have lost Selene... And today? Is it happening again?... I can't bear to think that I might be losing...

Belief is your gift, Miriam used to tell me, but belief has mutated over the years — my simplistic view of God slowly metamorphosed into a more amorphous sense of the spiritual, one less susceptible to institutions. Selene is from a Jewish family, but seems to have no sense of faith. Did she ever? Or was it too eroded by too much loss?

Selene Solweig

Selene hunches on the bench. She stares at the wall — dates scratched to keep track of the years, runs her finger over the faint marks written to help Catherine find her in the Motherbook: 'Born Monday April 11, 1927, Wesselényi utca, 41, Budapest VII', traces the even the fainter lines she could not have written — 'Catherine Anne McManus, born August 15, 1961, Parkside Hospital, Middlesbrough, Teesside.'

She is alone. For the first time in… how many days? Catherine is not with her, is not dreaming her. Is this the end of the story? She thinks of her cellmates — Ludmilla, who she loved, Boglárka, who had tried so hard to convince her that she was trustworthy…

You said Péter Rácz's name in your sleep, Boglárka tells her.

Selene sucks in her lips, perplexed. Why would I do that? I only heard his full name from you a few days ago.

Ludmilla must have mentioned it, surely? Must have told you something…

I've told you. I've got no information to give you and I wouldn't anyway.

Make it up, Boglárka whispers, almost inaudible.

What? Selene's voice sounds louder than she had intended.

Shh. They… Boglárka's whisper drops further. They're always listening. If you tell me something, anything… rubbish… just make it up… make it easier for both of us… for our families…

No!

Boglárka begins to whimper, then sob. Just give me something. Her pleading is shrill. There is a rap on the cell door and Boglárka begins to howl. For God's sake give me something. You don't know what they'll do if…

The heavy door scrapes against the concrete floor as it is flung open. Two guards stride across the narrow space to where Boglárka, on her knees, implores Selene, keens. One grabs her hair. The other wrenches her arm backwards so that she yelps like an injured dog.

You were right, Boglárka says, as they pull her towards the door, her voice suddenly calm, though her skin looks like sweating porcelain and she shakes as the guards haul her away. You were right. I was always working for them. And look where it got me….

And then Boglárka is gone.

Selene had been moved to this cell with the dates scratched on the wall a few days later. There were no more cell mates. Only empty days for two years until Catherine began to dream her life, and she Catherine's. And now? She is alone again. There is no sense of Catherine.

O, God, this is the end of the story, I can't go on, she says to the evening.

She sleeps and dreams of...

It's definitely weird, Simon says, but not so sure I'd describe it as occult.

Hmm, Catherine agrees.

Simon studies her. You're sure you're up to this? You don't have to trail round museums with me, you know.

I'm fine. And I wanted to get out of the apartment today.

Even in this cold?

Yes.

Even to visit the strangest pharmacy ever?

Yes. She leans into him.

Look, powdered mummy.

Beneath a row of hanging bats and crocodiles, a wizened head sits on top of a wooden box.

They really ground up mummies for use in medicines?

They did indeed. Simpler times, eh? Catherine?

Sorry, feeling a bit queasy.

The mummy?

No. No, I don't think so, not that I don't have issues with disinterring other people's dead and digesting their ground-up corpses, but I don't think it's that. I'm just feeling a bit dizzy.

Migraine?

No. It's definitely gone. I'm probably just a bit scooped out after it. Maybe we could get a snack after... Oh!

Simon clutches her arm. What? Is it pain? Are you?

My hand of Miriam. I haven't got my necklace.

And you had it on when we left the flat?

She clutches the space where the tiny hamsa normally hangs. I always have it on.

Okay. Well, let's go back through the museum the way we came. Maybe it's fallen somewhere in here? You couldn't have snagged it on something?

They inch through the strange rooms of glass bottles, ceramic jars, reach the door without finding the talisman.

I've had it since Toledo, Catherine says. I... Oh! She doubles into herself, crouches, holding her abdomen.

Oh, God, what is it?

A heavy clot of blood slides between her thighs.

Oh, Simon. She begins to weep.

Catherine, what is it? What can I do? I...

She looks up, sees his panic, the way he begins to pace near her. I think I'm pregnant, Simon. And I think I might be losing the baby.

Baby? You…

It's early days — well, weeks — but… She scrunches against the pain and whimpers. A trickle of blood oozes onto the floor of the Golden Eagle Pharmacy Museum. The attendant, she says weakly. Ask them to phone… She pauses to let a wave of pain shudder through her… an ambulance, Margit… I don't know…

She's dozing, Margit says, laying a hand on Simon's arm.

I didn't know, he offers.

I know. She wanted to be sure it was alright before… She told me she lost a baby before. I'm so sorry.

Simon nods. Probably wouldn't be much of a father, anyway, but… Catherine… I think she really… wanted this and I…

It's okay, Simon. It's okay to be overwhelmed.

He looks up. At the hospital they wouldn't let me… and I don't know… I mean, was it a boy or girl or…

I'm not sure if they'd know.

Is it too much? I mean, if you have two miscarriages can you…

Yes. Yes, she can still have a healthy baby. But right now we need a healthy Catherine. It's horrible to have this happen so far from home, but you're here for her. And I'm here for both of you.

Thank you. It means a lot. What can I do for her?

Little things. Run her a bath. Make drinks. Sit with her.

Simon smiles. Yes. Even I can manage that.

Catherine wakes late in the evening. Beside the bed, mint tea is cooling. Her hand reaches for the blue silk cord around her neck, where the tiny damascene hand of Miriam normally hangs, but it is not there.

Catherine

Catherine wakes sobbing for the baby that is lost. She drifts back to sleep, wakes in Selene's cell, the date scratched on the wall...

Under the date, 'Wednesday 25 November, 1959' is scratched:

'I am sorry for the loss of your baby'.

Catherine gets up from the bench, but...

Selene falls to the floor, begins to retch.

When the guard brings food, Selene is huddled on the floor, mucous smeared across her face, dry-heaving.

Fuck! The guard offers. What the fuck?

The stench rises to assault them both.

Fucking animal! He asserts.

Selene looks down at the floor where her bowels have oozed a foul-smelling trail of fluids.

The fat guard pulls her to her feet, throws her towards the bench, where she huddles, feverish.

Fucking bitch, he says, over and over. Fucking rancid bitch.

Selene wakes wet and shivering.

Had to hose you down, the guard says, looming over her.

She shifts on the bench.

At least you're still alive. Lucky. He turns to leave. Pulls an envelope from inside his uniform pocket. Suppose you're too sick to be reading letters.

Selene tries to move from the bench, to stand, but falls onto the floor.

He walks back towards her, waves the letter in the air. Of course, if you want it... He grins, the letter waving above her.

Selene grabs at the bench, pulls herself up, teeters, tries to reach for the fluttering envelope.

His smile widens as she lurches, misses, almost loses her balance again.

Selene stands still, watches the path of the letter in the air, just out of reach. She breathes in deeply, pulls herself up, ignoring the pain, lunges, catches a corner, that rips slightly.

Ha! The guards eyes are the most alive she's ever seen as she relieves his boredom... reaches again, missing. You're right, he says. In your state, the whole thing would be too much.

He steps away from her so that on her next lunge she over-reaches, falls to the floor again.

Maybe just a bit of it. After all, you don't want to have to read too much misery, do you?

He pulls the letter from the envelope, scans it theatrically and tears it in two. He holds out half and she looks up from the floor, levers herself upright again, the pain screaming through every muscle. She puts out a hand and he lets her take the torn remnant of the letter.

Thank you, she mumbles, eyes down.

Yeah, sow like you doesn't deserve privileges. But I'm a generous man, he says, laughing. He turns and leaves.

There is no address, no date on the fragment. The ripped paper wavers through the middle of what must be her mother's final paragraph. Selene recognises her mother's delicate, rounded hand, a couple of lines and blank paper beneath:

...there is little improvement and I live in a state of unremitting fear, but I will not give up hope for her.

I think constantly of how things might have been different. If your father had nor insisted on returning to this god-forsaken country, if you had not become involved with affairs you had no power to affect, if we were not surrounded by such filthy people — gypsies and prostitutes. But it is too late for such thoughts. We can only hope.

I will write again with more news as soon as possible.

Your mother,
Marie.

Selene stares at the ragged bit of paper, reads it again... and again. No improvement? She asks the empty cell. What does she mean, 'I will not give up hope for her'? She winces at her mother's remarks about gypsies. After all they and we have suffered, she thinks. The area must have changed in the time she has been imprisoned, but what exactly is it that her mother lives in fear of?

She pulls herself back onto the bench, reads the lines again, falls into a daze between pain and agony trying to tease out what her mother might mean…

Budapest, Thursday 25 November 1993

It seems that, after all, I have not lost Selene. But I am afraid that she is dying in her cell — she is clearly starving — and now suffering from diarrhoea and sickness, no longer in control of her bodily functions. How long can someone live like this? And this letter — to receive the last couple of lines without any context, and no previous letters in the time I've been dreaming about her — it's clearly another way of tormenting her. What did Marie mean when she said there was no improvement? Do they have money for food? Are they being harassed for being the family of a convicted prisoner?

I feel so anxious for Marie, for Miriam and for Selene, but my concern for Selene, which has consumed so much of my thought, seems suddenly overshadowed by the loss of my baby. How shallow is that? Selene may be dying, yet all I can think of is — will I ever be able to carry a baby to term? And how will this horrific loss affect my relationship with Simon? In so many ways he is a stranger to me. I don't understand what matters to him; have no idea whether being a father terrifies or delights him… Attila so much wanted to be a father, and never was, or at least that is what history tells us…

But I'm not writing a history. I never was, but the novel is less and less 'conventional', despite all my research into

Attila's life, it is nothing like I expected and I'm concerned it will make no sense to my editor and publishers. Despite which, *A Remedy for All Things* is the only book I can write with any integrity.

What would Miriam say?

Till death it's all life, Cassie.

Attila died tragically. Now Selene appears to be dying. I have lost both of my babies — as though nothing can grow inside me... There's a remedy for all things except death, Quixote said, but even after death we can remember people, keep something alive...

Selene Solweig

Selene wakes clammy and shaking, her mind drifting to Miriam.

She says Miriam's name out loud, a hoarse supplication to a blank wall.

I'm still here, Selene whispers to her daughter, or to herself, sinking into a state between sleep and unconsciousness —

slipping into another body that moves through an era that has not yet been, sensing the day as if she is a woman whose name has mutated across thirty-two years: Cassie, Kat, Casilda, Kitty, Catherine; a woman writing a book about Selene's lover, Attila, who lived in another time; a time she has slid into at unexpected moments over the last seven years. But she has not seen Attila for almost a year, not since December 1 1958. And this woman, whose skin she wears, who she aches to be, lies in bed, clammy and shaking…

I'll pour you a bath, Simon offers, hovering at the bedroom door.

Catherine wonders if it's wise to bathe so soon after the miscarriage, but she aches and wants the soothing water and, in any case, the only shower in the apartment is from the hose that has to be fixed to the bath taps. She nods, smiles weakly. Thank you.

Mint tea?

She smiles again. You're very kind.

She leans out of bed to pick up a dressing gown fallen onto the floor.

My hand of Miriam!

What?

It's here. It's under the bed. I didn't lose it.

She holds out the tiny damascene talisman on its pale blue thread of silk.

Selene has one just like it, she says to Simon, her voice distant.

Really?

Identical, she says, though it's on a chain, not a silk thread, silver so thin I'm surprised it has lasted at all. She has it hidden under her clothes. Though she must have had to move it sometimes to keep it hidden all those years.

Simon nods. Yes. I imagine… I'm so glad you've found it.

In the bath, the traces of bleeding seem to abate. Catherine swirls the warm fluid, remembering the flow of blood, the clots, plum-coloured penny pieces, dense and viscous… drifts

260

into dreams and memories as the hot water soothes pain…

Dropping her off at the House, where Zoë and Alex were also staying, Liam backed the car into the gate before she was through it. She beat on the reversing vehicle, squeezed between car and wrought iron.

The baby stopped moving.

Nothing I can do, the locum GP told Zoë. Call me when she starts to lose it.

It was Zoë and Alex who took her to hospital. She felt a clot slip between her legs, blood thick, gelatinous, oozed through layers of clothing, the blanket they'd wrapped her in, seeped onto the slippery car seat. She thought of Casilda's Berber mother, haemorrhaging after giving birth to her fragile daughter, and, later, Casilda bleeding without respite.

Later, a friend found Liam with Lorraine, told him the news…

When she emerges from the bath, Simon has cooked breakfast — sausages and eggs, tomatoes and mushrooms.

Catherine sits at the dining table, shaky and uncertain, but suddenly hungry.

She's with me again, she says. Selene I mean.

Simon smiles. Good.

You think? I mean — I felt bereft when I thought I'd lost her, but now… I think she's dying, Simon, and I feel so futile.

Maybe she knows you're with her, knows you care… Perhaps.

261

He pauses. I'm sure she realises you care, but right now I think you need to eat and sleep, Catherine...

You believe all of it, don't you? Catherine asks, back in the bedroom after breakfast.

Simon nods as he tucks her into bed, a bowl of mint tea cooling on the bedside table.

Read me one of your stories, Catherine says, sleepily, something romantic, something that takes me to another world... one of those stories that transforms reality...

Simon laughs. No pressure there then... How about 'The Third Face of Virgo' if you're looking for a parallel existence?

Perfect — it's such a rich narrative...

Simon begins reading —

As I look back, I believe there was a moment when I almost stayed in my lodgings; an instant, eternal at the time, when I hesitated to retrace the steps he had taken such a short while before. I stood beside the window, tears not yet dry, and tried to convince myself all this was what I wanted. Had he not been impossible, demanding too much? Oui, absolument... Then why tears, convulsions that twisted me so tightly and yet left a hollowness beneath my breast?

I looked down at the narrow alley below and told myself it was better that he was not there, not waiting against my leaving. The window was open a little, the city's bustle seeming distant nevertheless. There was a hint of something on the air — lavender, perhaps — as the afternoon began gathering shadows about itself like an old woman burrowing deeper into her sickbed. My forehead touched the glass.

Movement: someone standing just out of sight at the foot of the house.

I flinched back, all other thought buried under a resolution to stay hidden.

Another drift of air, cool and northerly but now bearing a hint of cedar. And something sweeter. Chrysanthemum, just like the first time we walked together.

It was not him outside. Footsteps hollow against the walls, a woman's step receding until it was hidden amongst the clatter of electric trams and horse carriages, the clock on the Grossmünster striking the hour.

The curtains felt rough as I hid my face amongst them, a handful of material in each fist. Memories crowded as fast then as they do now, each overlaying the next like sheets of tracing paper until a composite image formed through them: sunlight on the side of my face; the same light reflecting from M. Joyce's spectacles; almost a dozen writers and artists crammed around a pair of tables; the interior of the Odeon seeming small and close.

Seeing him for the first time…

Zurich, 1917: neutral while the rest of Europe tore itself apart. It was a city where many streams flowed side-by-side and the Café Odeon a confluence where unusual currents met and mingled. The Dada movement had practically been born there, Mata Hari once danced upstairs; up until a few months before, Lenin had nightly held court around its tables.

It was late August, noonlight liming the coils of tobacco smoke overhead. We were crammed around a window table inside. A customarily mixed group, including M. Joyce, who was listening politely as Tzara, poet and Dadaist firebrand, held forth on the need for constant change. Convinced, at that time, I knew all, ordinarily I would have tried to correct him. Yet the weather that day had turned unusually cool and dry and, although it appeared settled on the surface, the air felt oddly restless. Something of that restlessness had infected me, so I never noticed him come in until Countess Ilona appeared at our table.

'Lieblinge, you simply must meet this wonderful young man. He's destined to be another great Irish writer like you James, Liebster.'

He stepped forward at her urging, a little abashed by Ilona's praise. I saw a man in his early twenties, just a little older than I. Dark hair combed with no attempt to hide the scars on his forehead and left temple; neither seemed more than a year old. I wondered afterwards if he had recently come from the War. Then, I thought only of his eyes. A bright cerulean they were, as if the sky had lodged itself inside him.

'Friends, this is Lawrence Sheridan Donnelly.' He offered a grin and a short bow as Countess Ilona made introductions around the table. 'And this is Mlle Benoit. Don't be fooled by her youth, Sheridan, our Sylvie is quite one of the sharpest in our little community of misfits and nonconformists.'

'And she is also in danger of being late for work.' I stood, shouldering my satchel with awkward haste. 'Please, M. Donnelly, have my chair. No, everyone, I know I have plenty of time but I really must be getting back to the gallery. Excuse me mes chéris, au revoir.'

'I'm having a gathering tonight, Sylvie, Schatzi,' Ilona called after me, 'you will come, won't you?'

I waved, hardly daring to glance back. Even so, it felt as though his blue eyes remained on me even as I hurried around the corner and up Rämistraße...

Catherine falls asleep dreaming of Zurich, a place she has never visited... she should go there with Simon... perhaps tomorrow she will suggest...

Catherine

…in the dream Catherine is crossing the bridge that she heard about in Simon's story, bleeding, sobbing… she wakes weeping. It is 2 a.m. the green clock-face tells her. She edges out of the bed to go to the bathroom, drinks water from the tap, splashes her face.

Back in bed, Simon turns and reaches a hand towards her. She drifts towards sleep, wakes in Selene's cell, the date scratched on the wall…

Under the thinly scratched words: 'I am sorry for the loss of your baby', Catherine scrapes into the wall: 'Thank you. I'm worried about you.'

She tries to get up from the bench, but…

Selene falls back, too weak to stand, begins retching, but there is nothing to vomit. Feverish, she hears a distant train sound… Attila! She closes her eyes, opens them expecting to find herself in Attila's time, but finds herself instead…

The door of her parent's gallery opens and…

The young man who enters smiles at her nervously.

This is my daughter, Selene, Marie says, scooping Selene into her arms.

What a beautiful name, the young man says. And how old are you, Selene?

She's just had her first birthday, Marie answers for her. And already walking. And talking — well lots of words, anyway — new ones every day. We're insanely doting, I'm afraid.

The young man nods eagerly. You'll grow up to be as beautiful as your mama, he says. I'm Attila, he adds, my name's Attila. Remember me, Selene.

Selene falls back onto the bench, skin oozing a film of clammy sweat. She breathes in shallow gasps, eyelids flickering.

The cell door grinds open and food is left on the floor, the guard sneering as he roughly deposits the bowl so that thin liquid splashes onto the rough concrete, dribbles down the sides of the bowl. Selene sniffs the air… faint scent of fat… but the bowl is so far away… unreachable… she leans back, falls into semi-consciousness…

Selene runs into the living room excited with her news about the part she will dance in the winter show of the ballet school in just under three weeks time. When she enters the living room above her parent's gallery a group of guests is talking in low voices.

So sad, a young woman says, the others nodding. The woman, in her early twenties, Selene thinks, has short hair and a wide, kind mouth. A Hungarian accent. She leans into a man a little older than the woman, but younger than Mama, dark straight hair tucked behind his ears, touching his collar.

I met him at the Hatvany's a couple of summers ago, says another man Selene doesn't recognise. Another Hungarian accent and Jewish, like her own family. He has a broad face and deep-set eyes, a way of looking intently at others. Irén was very taken with him and she is never wrong about talent, he says. There is another murmur of approval and the man continues. She's played hostess to so many great writers and artists. Endre Ady, Sándor Bródy, Sándor Hunyady, and Márk Modok.

Ödön Szmrecsányi, someone else adds.

Of course, the man adds. And Anna Lesznai, a relative of hers, actually.

And I heard Thomas Mann modelled the figure of Madame de Tolna on her too.

Quite, says the man. It's a terrible loss, but of course he was very unstable for some time…

Ah, Selene, Papa says, noticing her standing in the doorway. Come and meet our guests. Papa beckons her forward. May I introduce my daughter, Selene? Papa says proudly. Selene, this is Monsieur Czóbel…

Monsieur Czóbel turns and smiles. It's a pleasure to meet you, young lady, he says.

Papa smiles. And this is Imre Ámos and his wife Margit Anna, both artists from home. They had the honour of meeting Chagall recently, Papa adds.

We were talking about a poet we'll all miss, Monsieur Czóbel puts in, including her in the conversation.

Attila József, Mama says quietly. We…

… we met him, Selene says. He visited when I was small and told me I had a beautiful name. Why will we miss him?

But Selene… Mama begins, as Papa says… I'm afraid he died, darling — last Friday… rather tragically.

But he can't have, Selene blurts. We're going to meet again, I'm sure we are. He told me to remember him.

Mama puts a hand on her arm. I've no idea how you can remember, minette, you were a baby when he visited here… hardly talking…

But I do remember, Selene says. And don't call me 'kitten', she adds. I'm ten! She turns to Monsieur Czóbel. Are you sure he died?

I'm afraid so, my dear.

Excuse me, she says, and leaves the room…

Budapest, Friday 26 November 1993

What does 'loss' mean? I have lost two babies. I lost Miriam. I lost Liam. And soon, I fear, I will lose Selene. But none of these losses are analogous… each is unique.

The art of losing… it seems to me, is much harder to master than Bishop imagined.

And what of finding? Amongst all these losses, I've found Simon, who is endlessly patient and supportive, not to mention extraordinarily talented, way beyond his own estimation. But he is also fragile, which makes me anxious for him. He has lost this baby too and I have no idea what that might mean to him.

The list of 'lost and found' goes on... Amongst my finds are the dates I discovered in the Motherbook, Sándor's sketchbook, clues to extraordinary links between the Virágs and Attila, a book owned by Selene that was not published until 1951 and yet was found by Zsuzsanna under her uncle's pillow in 1937... And my hand of Miriam, apparently lost at the pharmacy museum before I began to bleed our baby away and yet... found again in this bedroom... the tiny damascene hamsa that appears to be identical to the one that Selene secretly conceals...

I really am terribly afraid for Selene... she can hardly move from the bench and in her delirium is going back to childhood memories — one of Attila, whom she seems to have met when she was a toddler — another of a group of artists at her parents' home above the little gallery they ran. Béla Czóbel, Imre Ámos and Margit Anna. All Hungarian Jewish artists who were in Paris not long before the War. It must have been 1937, a couple of days after Attila had killed himself, because they were talking about it when she came into the room. It seems that she remembered the meeting with Attila, even though she barely had language at the time, and she was convinced, as a ten-year-old girl, that she would meet him again. Could that really have been a memory or was it the dream of someone inventing memories?

I am less and less able to make sense of anything in her life or in my own...

Selene Solweig

Selene wakes shivering, her skin sticky, the smell of faeces and vomit making her retch. I'm still here, she whispers to Miriam, or to herself, curling, foetal, on the bench. Half-conscious, she dreams of —

Catherine hunches into a ball beneath the bedcovers, pulling them higher against the day.

Are you sure I can't get you anything? Simon asks.

No, she says, not emerging. No, I just want to sleep. You go and write…

Simon moves from foot to foot, then turns, leaving the door slightly open as he goes to the desk in the spare bedroom, sets out manuscripts and notebooks. He stares at his notes for a long while, writes a line, crosses it out, gets up to fetch water. On his way back, he stands at the bedroom door. The air is beginning to smell stale, there's a metallic tang over the sweet smell of something rotting. He can hear, from Catherine's breathing, that she is asleep. He backs away to return to his writing. Sitting at his desk, he downs a large water glass in one long gulp.

It's eleven o'clock when he looks up, startled by the doorbell.

He buzzes in Margit and she enters laden with flowers and food.

I won't stay long, she says, packing food into the fridge and cupboards, but I'll be back later to cook. In the meantime, try to get her to have some soup. She empties a large container into a saucepan. There's bread if she will have it, but at least the soup. Okay, Simon?

He nods. Yes. Yes, I'll try.

She hands him a bouquet of six tall red amaryllis. They need water — a long vase if you can find one. Right, I'll let you get lunch ready. Tell Catherine I'll be back at five and dinner is at six. András is bringing drinks.

András?

Yes, and don't worry. She grins and winks — Of course, he's in love with her, who isn't? But not in any way that threatens you.

Oh. I didn't mean…

Margit waves away his protest. Anyway, he'll be here later and so will Zsuzsanna. I know Catherine's had a terrible time, but she still has to eat and company will do her good. And you too. You're looking very pale.

It's good, Catherine agrees, smiling as she spoons Margit's chicken soup into her mouth. Lots of paprika.

Simon sits beside her on the bed and dips bread into his bowl. Good. Margit will skin me if I don't get you to eat.

They eat in silence for several minutes, begin to talk at once, almost laugh and tell each other to go first.

Nothing momentous, Simon says, I just wanted to check you're really okay with everyone visiting this evening.

Catherine nods. Margit's right. I need to talk, not fester away thinking of what might have been…

I've never…

Yes?

Nothing. Doesn't matter…

Go on, please…

I only meant to say — I've never imagined being a father before, but I… I mean, if you wanted… again… It seems — possible, exciting even — when you're ready, I mean — or if…

Catherine reaches for his hand. Yes. Losing the first baby was terrible, but everyone tells you that it happens to a lot of first pregnancies, that it doesn't mean anything for the future. It's not much comfort at the time, but it becomes a mantra. I'm not so sure now — what it means for future pregnancies, I mean — but I want to be a mother.

You will be, he says.

We don't know that.

Simon squeezes her hand. I do. You will be. A wonderful mother, too.

He is lost in the trance of his writing when Catherine comes into the spare room that has become his study. She is dressed in a loose indigo skirt and pale blue linen top.

You're up?

She smiles. I thought I'd better look presentable for our guests. The bath was wonderful and I've opened all the windows in the bedroom, despite the cold. It was starting to smell. She wrinkles her nose.

You look beautiful. He walks over and puts his arms round her loosely, touches the tiny hand of Miriam at her throat. So glad you found it.

Me too.

I'd better freshen up too.

András is the first to arrive, armed with two bottles that proclaim the legend 'Pamid', a small coin-shaped green bottle labelled Unicom Zwack, adorned with a gold cross against a red label, making it look like strong cough medicine, a plump bottle of honey-coloured tokaji and a long-necked, painted carafe of pale pálinka.

You're planning to fell us all? Simon asks, grinning.

She needs to relax. It will help her talk, András replies, And I'm under orders from Margit.

Ah. Well, there's no arguing with that.

Quite. András smiles and holds eye contact. And you too. I'm sorry for your loss.

Thank you. Thank you, András. Simon holds out a hand and they shake with vigour for the first time since they've met, less

273

than a week ago, yet it seems... András pulls Simon towards him and throws an arm around his shoulder, pats his back before stepping back again.

The buzzer emits its hoarse cry and Simon presses the button to allow Margit into the building as Catherine enters the living room.

András hugs her tightly. I was telling Simon how sorry I am for your loss.

Thank you, András.

You're up, Margit says, entering with more flowers.

Peonies! They're gorgeous Catherine says.

And you look lovely, my dear. Now, sit down. I've got nibbles while I cook. András, open the Unicom please. Simon, glasses and cutlery on the table and some side plates too. Thank you.

Zsuzsanna arrives as András is pouring the tiny glasses of Unicum She sets ribboned cake boxes on the kitchen surface and bends to hug Catherine, then Simon.

To the future, she says, when the glasses are full and raised.

Catherine and Simon splutter simultaneously at the first taste of Unicum.

What's in this stuff? Simon asks.

Herbs, András says, refilling the glasses. Very good for you.

Hmm, jury's out on that, András, Catherine says, sniffing the bitter liquor.

A secret blend of over forty herbs, András reassures. The story goes that it was first given to Kaiser Joseph II of Austria by the Zwack family. He declared 'Das ist ein Unikum!' — 'This is unique!' and that's how it got its name.

Later, while Zsuzsanna serves cakes, Catherine makes her way gingerly to the bathroom, hoping she is not noticeably unsteady. She sits for a while before splashing her face with cold water, steels herself to re-enter the fray of conversation, which has turned to Attila József's last day.

No, there are still no leads on Miriam Virág, Simon is saying as she returns to the table.

András pours the tokaji and nods. I'm still not sure I understand what the connection is, he says. He sips the sweet wine. Nectar, he says. Try it, Catherine. This one I promise you will like.

Catherine told you all this before, Margit says to András in mock-exasperation. Zsuzsanna put her onto it when she mentioned that Attila had a friend he met in Paris — Sándor Virág.

Did I? Zsuzsanna asks. I don't remember. I remember Selene's name, of course, though… Zsuzsanna pours more tokaji into her glass.

So you heard this name Selene Virág from Zsuzsanna? András asks, frowning. But I'm sure you mentioned having strange dreams about her before you met Zsuzsanna. And I'm still missing the connection to József. In any case, what could Selene's daughter know about any of it? András gazes into his empty glass. Time for pálinka?

Margit gets up to fetch the tiny shot glasses and Catherine shakes her head as they are set out Sándor Virág's daughter. Attila knew him in Paris, so perhaps her daughter might have heard stories of how they met, how they were connected. It's

275

a bit more research for my novel. I've already found out more about Selene. She was Selene Solweig Virág, from a Jewish family who'd changed their name from Haas when her father's family came from Austria. She was born on the same date as your uncle, but in 1927, she adds, nodding towards Zsuzsanna. And yes, the dreams came before Zsuzsanna mentioned her. I've been dreaming of her every night since I got here — sad dreams, mostly — I think she may have been imprisoned after the uprising, perhaps even killed, but in some of the dreams I see her with Attila, perhaps because I'm spending so much time researching him and thinking about him.

Zsuzsanna sits very still for a while, silent. She reaches into her bag and brings out a book, holds it carefully, looking across the table at Catherine.

But the dreams? András voice is slurred. Where do dreams fit in? You must have read something before they started. He pauses, takes a mouthful of pálinka If you've found real evidence of her then it can't have begun in dreams...

Don't badger her, András, Margit warns.

Zsuzsanna pauses. I think a carafe of water would be good, she says, standing. And maybe a pot of coffee?

Margit nods.

Coffee sounds good, Simon agrees.

While I make it, have a look at this, Zsuzsanna says. She reaches across the table and hands András the book, beautiful hand-drawn slab serif font in grey and white on the paper dust jacket, the only illustration an illuminated Paris-style street lamp at the top left hand corner.

András opens *The Ballad of the Sad Café* carefully, reads the finely inked hand-writing on the half title page: Selene Solweig

Virág.

Catherine gazes at Zsuzsanna, then at András, feels her pulse race.

It was under my uncle's pillow, Zsuzsanna says. I found it the night he died. She sets the coffee pot down and Margit adds cups to the table.

But… András turns the book over in his hands, looks up, his frown deepening.

After the railway worker left. After all the crying and commotion… I crawled into Uncle Attila's bed and wept into his pillow. The scent of him was still there and I reached under the pillow while I was sobbing, trying to quiet myself, so as not to wake the others, who had already cried themselves to sleep, and there was this book.

But… András rubs his head and gulps coffee, pours another cup.

But it was 1937, Margit finishes for him, tracing the small, looped hand-writing.

Yes, Zsuzsanna agrees. It was.

But it wasn't published… I don't understand…

No-one does, Zsuzsanna says. She picks up the empty coffee pot. Perhaps I should make more?

Yes. Catherine passes a hand over the book as András sets it on the table. I can't explain it either, or how Selene got into my dreams about Attila.

But there has to be an explanation… Books can't just appear before they're published, inscribed by people who… It's…

it's…

…fascinating, Margit offers.

No, it's insane…

The unreason of the world is more insane than any fiction, Catherine says quietly.

Zsuzsanna turns from making coffee. I showed it to Catherine not long after we first met and was struck by what she said — how Uncle Attila and Selene must both have been people who lived life in a vision. We know he met her father in Paris. The rest is conjecture, insanity perhaps, but look at the world, András. Plenty of insane things are true.

Catherine stands, walks slowly to the bedroom and returns with Sándor's sketchbook. This is Selene when she was a girl, just before they left Paris. I think she ended up in prison for years after the Uprising. How insane is that? I want her daughter to have it if we can find her.

András nods. Yes, he says. Yes, political madness is always with us. I understand that. But this… He fingers the Carson McCullers novel, shakes his head. I can make no sense of this.

When the guests have left, András looking grey and shaky, Zsuzsanna flushed and emotional, Margit repeating that all this is fascinating and that she hopes to continue the discussion when she's sober, Simon pours hot water into the bath and scents it with lemon oil, helping Catherine in, enveloping her in a huge white towel as she gets out, drying her and shepherding her to bed.

Catherine curls on her side, falls asleep quickly and deeply and…

Catherine

...wakes on Selene's bench.

On the wall, Selene has begun to scratch the date, thin marks trailing away.

Catherine does not try to move in Selene's body. Its weakness flows through her. She feels herself flushed, dehydrated, every limb burning, heavy... She falls into a dazed reverie, lights floating above her. She wills herself to hear the sound of a train whistling far off... nearer... to find herself on a platform gazing towards Attila, but the cell remains, only partly blotted from her sight by the dark void on the left of her vision. She closes her eyes, lets the nausea wash over her... drifts into the pain remembering a day two years ago... the sound of a train whistling far off... nearer... to find herself on a platform gazing towards Attila.

He rushes towards her. Selene! Five whole days without you! Oh, but you look... pale. He puts a hand to her head. You are hot. You are not well.

I feel better here, she says. And it is true, as though she can feel Catherine, who is with her again, lending her strength...

But you were arrested. That has been rectified?

Selene shakes her head.

A whole year?

Don't worry about me. I'm fine. It's so good to see you, to be with you again.

His expression changes, his smile widening. The lake? You like it by the lake, yes?

She nods and he winds a long arm around her, begins to walk with her towards the lake. Through here, he says, pointing towards a short cut between stationary trains on the sidings.

Selene pulls back.

It's fine, he reassures. They're parked. They won't move.

They might, she says quietly. We could go around. You should always take the long way round.

He grins. Is that a metaphor?

No, it's just. I don't like to think of you walking between the trains. Look at them, like giants. If one were to roll loose...

Well, we'll be Quixote and his Sancho, taking on the giants. Fearless. He pulls on her hand and dodges her around the towering rolling stock. *Just then they came in sight of thirty or forty windmills that rose from the plain...* Attila quotes, laughing. And see, we only have three or four giants.

They make their way across the tracks, Selene flinching at every turn, and come towards a ramp, emerging in another station… Selene breathes in sharply. Attila rubs his broad forehead, gazing around…

Keleti?

Selene nods. Yes, but it's not 1937.

Attila looks around slowly, raises his eyebrows.

It must be 1957, Selene says with certainty. Our meetings have always a year apart for me, but this time it's different.

Attila leans forward but says nothing, waiting; his attentiveness a mixture of concentration and simply being a taller man who must stoop to listen.

Each time we've met it has been a date in the next year, a date in November a few days after the previous one. I can remember all our meetings from 1952 up to 1958, but I have no memory of a meeting in 1957.

Is '58 the last time we met?

So far, Selene says, but anything after today in 1959 would be in my future too, so it's not strange that I don't have memories of those. This was the one missing day. I'm experiencing a day in 1957 while in 1959. It doesn't make sense, does it?

Attila shrugs his shoulders and raises his palms to the sky. None of this makes sense, Selene. I'm probably more delusional than I've ever feared, and yet…

You're not delusional, Attila, really you're not. But today is particularly odd — you are out of your own time, which has never happened before and I'm… Less than half an hour ago I was in 1959, not '57. And on this day in the 1957 I was in prison and didn't meet you. My cellmate, Ludmilla had been taken away a few days earlier. I'm certain they killed her. And I had a new cellmate, someone I'd known before and knew not to trust. Her name was Boglárka. So we have this day not as I lived it, but as though I had a different past, one in which I was free. It makes less sense than any of our encounters, but I'm glad of it.

Attila's expression turns from puzzled concentration to delight. Miriam! He declares. You are in 1957 and not in prison. I'm here with you. I can meet my daughter. This has happened so I can meet my daughter.

He hugs her to him on the platform at Keleti station, like a lover who has arrived from some far-flung place, and she feels the energy in him escalating.

Where does she live? He tugs her towards the station exit.

Népszinház utca, 19, Selene says, beginning to catch the excitement. Today she will see Miriam, not as the little girl she must be in 1959, but as a toddler. How will she explain to her mother that she is not in prison, but cannot stay? How will she explain Attila to her mother? Surely Marie will recognise him, though perhaps seeing someone out of his own time will makes him less recognisable.

By the time they reach Marie's flat, only fifteen minutes later, Selene is breathless, but as elated as Attila, who talks constantly as he strides along, Selene almost running to keep up with him, amazed that she has not fainted from the effort. At the heavy wooden doors, Selene presses the buzzer to her mother's apartment.

Mama! She sings, Mama, it's Selene.

Who? I know no one of that name.

The intercom falls silent.

Selene rings again. Mama?

I've told you — leave me alone. The voice is rough and loud.

Please, there's a mistake. Could you...

The intercom falls silent again, but after a long pause the heavy wood of the door scrapes across the entrance. A thickset woman in a lumpy grey wool dress stands blocking the doorway.

Who are you looking for? She spits out the words and avoids eye contact.

My mother, Selene says quietly. Marie Spire.

The woman hoiks spittle into her throat and it lands at Selene's feet. She feels Attila lurch forward, but puts out her hand to hold him back.

Never heard of her. All I know is the last woman here was a filthy Jew. Her whelp was a traitor and a whore, apparently. Woman like her had no right to a place like this. And I don't know and don't care where she's gone.

Attila begins to remonstrate as the woman scrapes the door closed, but Selene pulls him away. It is only when they are alone on the street that she falls into his arms and weeps, clinging to him, until she feels the hard bench under her, her body burning and sodden, a guard banging on the cell door, cursing her as she sobs, calling for Attila, for Miriam, for her mother.

Budapest, Saturday 27 November 1993

I can't stop thinking about the conversation with Margit, András and Zsuzsanna. Can others possibly believe that Attila and Selene knew one another in some way? I think it might all have been too much for András, especially when he woke up this morning without the aid of alcohol, but for the others perhaps the unreason of the world really is more insane than any fiction.

Another meeting between Attila and Selene today. She slipped from 1959 to 1957 and he with her. It was the oddest of all the encounters. Selene seemed to rally while they were together, but her health is clearly failing and I'm terrified that she will die in that cell. I am also concerned about what might have happened to Marie and Miriam, anxious that there will never be any leads from the newspaper appeals after learning that they were turned out of even the shabby home on Népszinház utca. Of course, it might be that Marie found a way to get back to Paris. How ironic if I brought the sketch book back only to find that Miriam is living there now.

The bleeding is a little less today, and I don't feel so drained and hollow. Knowing that Simon wants a baby is enormously comforting, even if my body is determined to betray me, even if it might never happen. Just writing that makes me shudder. The desire to be a mother is urgent and visceral. I want a baby. I want to will my body not to bleed life away.

Selene Solweig

Delirious, Selene chants, Attila, Miriam, Attila, Miriam, Attila, Attila, Attila, Miriam...

Between the repeated names she mouths fragments of Attila's poetry, barely audible, until she...

...sits at Catherine's desk, early in the morning, making notes on Attila's poems.

Simon brings in mint tea and places it carefully on the desk

Thank you, Attila.

Attila? He smiles.

Sorry, lost in my notes.

Simon puts a small box on the desk.

What's this?

Our first anniversary, he says.

Oh, God, no! Oh, Simon, I'm so sorry. I...

It's fine. You've had too much…

No, it's not fine. Let me take you out for lunch. Actually, I've got a better idea. We'll go to Szentendre.

But isn't the train famously uncomfortable? You're not well enough, you…

I'll be fine. I've been meaning to go and we won't have many more chances. We can catch the HEV train from Batthyani tér. It's only one stop away on the number 2 metro and Szentendre is only fifteen kilometres. How uncomfortable can it be?

Simon wrinkles his nose. Cramped, old and bumpy.

I'll take a shawl to sit on. The town's supposed to be delightful and there's a gallery of work by Margit Anna and Imre Ámos that I've been wanting to see and the Czóbel museum too. Selene met them all at her parents' gallery in Paris a couple of years before they left. Actually, only days after Attila died and they were talking about it when Selene came in. Selene was about nine and she insisted that she remembered meeting Attila when she was a toddler, that he'd told her to remember him, and that she was certain they would meet again.

Extraordinary, Simon assents.

So we really should go to Szentendre.

You look like a child pleading to go to the circus, Simon says, and laughs.

I'll take that as a yes. We could even come back on the boat. It's only an hour, because the river flows faster in the direction of Budapest, and it's supposed to be beautiful.

Okay, I'm sold, Simon agrees. I'll get my camera.

On their way out of the building, Simon checks the metal pigeonhole etched with the number of their flat: FE 6.

There's never anything in it now you're here and not sending letters, Catherine remarks.

And yet today... Simon says, pulling out an envelope. He peers at it. It's for me. English postmark, but I don't recognise the handwriting. He peers more closely. Nottingham, he says, but it's not Nathan's...

He tears open the letter.

Ha!

What is it?

Bloody Nathan. It's from Eliška. He's proposed to her. Didn't know he had it in him. Not that he could be bothered to write to me himself, of course.

That's wonderful. So I'll definitely get to know her.

Seems so. Well, life's full of surprises, isn't it?

And hope, Catherine adds.

Simon smiles, hugs her to him.

Tell me more about these painters, Simon says, when they are ensconced on the narrow bench seat in the rickety train carriage.

I don't know a lot, but Margit is a fan of Anna and Ámos. I don't know if they ever met Attila, but Czóbel did, not in Paris, but at the mansion of the Hatvany family. They hosted lots of writers and artists.

You know this from the dreams?

Catherine nods.

And they all met at the Virág's gallery when Selene was a girl. I suppose they were all ex-pats in difficult times. Ámos died in a concentration camp — disappeared without trace and Margit Anna began painting puppets in her work to signify how vulnerable we are to the events of history. Then she stopped painting altogether for a long time. When she resumed, she kept using puppets to symbolise tragedy. I think her work got more surreal and sounds fascinating. And his was extraordinary, or what I've seen from the book Margit showed me. Visionary and disturbing and he kept sending his work back to her while he was in the forced labour service — twice before the final death camp.

Simon nods. And is she still painting?

She died two years ago, but I think most of her work was done before the Seventies.

At the gallery, Catherine stands a long time in front of each picture. She reads about Anna and Ámos's meetings with Chagall, how deeply he influenced their early work. She recalls her trip to Nice last winter after commissioning Fabio's short story collection in Turin. It had been a treat to travel to Nice, to meet Fabio and have time to visit the Chagall museum...

She sat in front of 'Moses with the Burning Bush', felt herself falling:

...*numinous burning, red and yellow against blue-blue-blue. Moses on his knees, transfigured — and I am transformed with him — the power of being: I will be who I will be. Raw energy.*
288

To be, to be new, to go on being, not to expire — to have a future — burning, always, not consumed. I was. I am. I will be. Will I?

She'd brushed away a stray tear, moved on to 'Noah's Ark':

...blue-blue waters rising, a bird here, goat there. And the people, waiting in the wings of apocalypse, huddled. Who will make it? There are mothers holding children, families clustered, a man on his knees, behind him a woman stands, head bent to his, arms wrapping him. Will they make it?

How many can an Ark hold? And the covenant, what is that? The rainbow promise of no more destruction? No one can make that promise, not even God, she thought, remembering a time when she believed, a time before she lost the baby, that savage flow of blood.

Again and again, the earth is wiped out. Tribulation. A people who are persecuted, and now? She tried to think of what Miriam would say about the images; whether the story and the facts would match.

...blue tribulation. Jacob meets the love of his life at the well and how does that go? Fourteen years before they are together. And his beloved child, his son — all that love come to tears, blood, betrayal, loss. And in the middle of this Jacob meets what? Who? Does he fight the ground of being for a place to stand? Jacob — violet on blue, struggling, changed —

Catherine conjured their first meeting — Your real name is... It had taken her years to realise that Miriam had loved her. Yet, despite that love, even Miriam had seen only the Cassie she had made up: Casilda. Catherine had believed all of it and none of it. And now? The Chagall haunted her:

...so we fight with being itself to discover who we are; limp on, walking out of a past of victories and defeats and into a future of

unimagined losses, fears and hopes; wounded and blessed.

In the room of *Le Cantique des Cantiques* the canvasses were red.

Catherine had begun to weep, clutching her stomach.

Madame? The attendant reached out a hand tentatively, but pulled it back as Catherine looked up. *Madame? Vous êtes…*

Catherine shook her head, stood. I'm fine. She'd brushed a hand ineffectually across her face, smiled weakly. It's just the pictures… they're very moving.

The attendant nodded, moved away, glancing back at her.

A woman hovered nearby and Catherine had smiled at her. A slight smile. Catherine, she offered.

Miriam, she replied.

Catherine startled, her hand going to the pendant around her neck, a tiny hand. I had a friend called Miriam, but she died. This hand of Miriam was a gift from her.

My grandmother had one, Miriam replied. She died two days ago. I'm here to visit her grave.

Now, standing in front of a large canvas by Margit Anna, Catherine sinks to the floor, losing consciousness.

Simon, really! Margit chides, when she arrives with a car to take them home. You shouldn't have let her go out so soon. At least not more than a little walk.

It's my fault, Catherine insists. I talked him into it. It's the first anniversary of our being together and I wanted to do something special…

Margit grimaces. Even so…

Back at the flat, Simon pours Catherine a bath, makes hot chocolate. She sips the thick, comforting liquid. Read some more of the story, she says, slipping further under the covers, Simon's voice permeating the space between waking and dreaming…

'In —' Ilona paused, one hand raised to stem the flow of good-natured banter from across our usual corner of the Odeon. 'In Atalanta's Key, Valentinus writes —'

Tzara made a rasping sound between the curled fingers of one hand.

'Writes —'

His fellow Dadaists chimed in with their own scepticism towards Ilona's recent-found passion for the Occult. Ignoring them, she looked only at me. I pretended to spill my drink, breaking eye contact. Not wanting attention then any more than during the afternoon. I had left the gallery early, making promises to myself that I would catch up on all the work left undone from the morning's trip to the lake. Yet, when I reached my lodgings in Spiegelstraße, concentration proved impossible.

Ilona gave me a knowing smile, glanced to my right, and began again.

'Valentinus writes that love is the highest and yet most fundamental working. The forging of a perfect amalgam…'

I only half-listened, thinking of the afternoon. Footsteps had sounded constantly in the alley below my window. First an old woman, judging from the tapping of a walking-stick on the cobbles. Moments later, the boot heels and measured gait of a somewhat younger woman. And that followed by steps lighter and younger still, which themselves merged with the sound of an elderly woman's tread. I peered down, seeing no one. No matter. It was not truly the footsteps that had been distracting.

Our brief conversation on the lakeshore would not leave me alone.

Finally, I gave up and went out. As night fell, I turned towards the Odeon. Barely twenty minutes later, he walked in. I hid behind Tzara, who affected not to notice. Perhaps I was invisible after all, for he sat on the other side of the poet without apparently noticing me. And so a quarter hour passed in which I dangled between outrage and relief, sometimes glancing around Tzara, other times lurking in his shadow whenever the Irishman turned in our direction. Now Ilona leaned forward impishly, eyes once again darting to my right, towards the man I could not decide whether I was hiding from or not, and asked:

'What do you say, Sylvie? Can love be the perfect amalgam?'

Thinking to unpick Ilona's mischief, I sat up straighter. Only to become conscious of his presence in the corner of my eye. No reaction to my appearance out from beside Tzara, except to lean a little closer to the table himself. He knew I had been there all along and, at that thought, my mind stuttered.

'Is… isn't love a mirage?'

I had intended statement, not question. Neither had I intended to look directly at him. Before he could do anything, I stood and made my excuses.

'Schatz.'

292

'I did not realise the hour, Ilona. I have so much work to do.'

Hesitation outside the café, turning left only to about-face and walk the other way, then right again, off the Sonnenquai entirely. Narrow streets growing narrower, steeper.

Footsteps echoed off the high, flat-faced buildings. No stopping this time, nor turning around. I could guess whose tread it was.

'Is that what you think of love?' He matched pace with me. 'Is that why you're so often alone?'

'Why must everyone assume that simply because a person — Who says I am alone?'

'The Countess.'

'I wish she would not interfere.'

'Perhaps she cares about you. Is it?'

It was there again. That warmth that had bloomed inside me on the shore of the lake. In truth, it had not left me all afternoon. I tried ignoring it.

'I do not see, M. Donnelly, how any of this is —'

'Have all of your past loves been so traumatic?'

I did not answer. Could not. Because, in the space between one step and the next, there they were, stepping out of the dark spaces between the streetlamps ahead: Giles and Alfredo, Kurt and... the others. The buildings on either hand, tall to begin with, seemed to stretch, pointed roofs growing sharper as they rose and bent forward to look down at us. Giles and Alfredo... all those who had claimed to love me, and had failed me so utterly.

'Are you never going to take the chance that, maybe, next time will

be different?'

The vision evaporated at the sound of his voice. There was a softness to it that caught me unawares. Even so, I had an answer. The answer I always gave, because I knew it to be true.

'I think that —' Scheitergasse came into view, a trio of streetlamps turning its short length saffron. 'Is that someone watching us, M. Donnelly?'

'D'you mean that girl?'

'Non.' Lamplight touched a forehead, making hollows where eyes should be. Not a girl, but a woman of middle age. 'Was it not someone older? I could have sworn...' Confusion: footfalls echoing down the narrow alley yet no one in sight to make them, perfume carrying on the night breeze, several fragrances mingling as the air turned suddenly cooler and dryer.

'Is that —' I sniffed, frowning — 'chrysanthemum?'

'Lavender, I thought. No — pine?'

'Cedar. I think.' Silence.

'Are you all right?' He rested his hand on my arm, just above my elbow. Grip light, yet —

'Yes.' I was not going to say more but found myself asking: 'Would you walk with me, M. Donnelly?' before understanding quite how alone I felt.

'Gladly. But, if I do, do you think you might see your way to using my Christian name, Mlle Benoit?'

Telling myself I was not being foolish, not ignoring all that experience had taught me, I nodded....

…Catherine drifts further towards sleep as Simon reads. And, on her bench, Selene curls into herself, temperature rising, sweat and cold alternating, hearing Attila…

> *Now the train's going down the track,*
> *maybe today it'll carry me back,*
> *maybe my hot face will cool down today,*
> *maybe you'll talk to me, maybe you'll say…*

Catherine sleeps, dreams…

Catherine

And Selene wakes on the bench.

Catherine glances at the dates scratched onto the wall. Today's date is missing.

The guard arrives with a bowl of thin gruel, sets it down roughly near the door, the farthest point from the bench, but doesn't turn to leave.

He stands in the middle of the room, hands on his hips, cruel smile twitching on his lips, puffs himself up and pauses. I have to announce, he says, as though there is a large audience listening, that your daughter is extremely sick. Unlikely to survive, in fact.

He turns and makes for the door as Selene struggles to sit.

At the entrance, he turns to face her again. Of course, if she dies, you won't be a mother any longer. Just a traitorous whore, he says, laughing to himself as he leaves, kicking the gruel bowl so that most spills out.

Selene struggles up, staggers across the cell, which seems larger than she remembers, forces down the remains of the food. I'm here, Miriam, she whimpers between mouthfuls. Mama is here, stay strong, my darling.

When the guard brings a scummy bowl of beans at twilight she is waiting for him, standing shakily by the bench.

My daughter, she says quietly, eyes downcast. Is there any news of my daughter, please?

His laughter is derisive. He shoves her towards the bench and she collapses there, but when he's gone she gets up, stumbles towards the bowl and makes herself eat, choking on the scrap of bread that is so hard it will hardly soak up the thin liquid around the beans.

I'm going to live for you, Miriam, she says to the wall, when she has managed to struggle back to the bench. And you must live for me, my darling.

She slips towards sleep, shivering and burning by turn, clutching the tiny hand of Miriam she has fished from her underwear.

Budapest, Sunday 28 November 1993

In an attempt to distract myself from Selene's pain and the worry that Miriam might be dying, I've forced myself to read more of Attila's poetry and biography today, to make notes for the book that will never be the one I originally set out to write. Today, I've read 'Well in the End I have Found my Home Country' and 'I May Suddenly Disappear' over and over. Despite his melancholy, there is always an edge of joy in the poetry, a kind of raw elation, and the mixture is strangely disorienting — it is not so much that there are highs and lows at different points in the poems or pieces with different moods, but that the two are held together intensely, just as they are in him whenever he meets Selene — he has the capacity to be full of sorrow and delirious with delight all at once. His love affairs were always suffused with pain and it is no different with Selene.

I know Attila's death is coming and I believe he committed suicide, but so much about him will always be unknowable. Attila is no longer merely the person that lived, but larger than that — a symbol of the proletarian poet since the end of the Second World War, despite the fact that he had serious issues with the Communist Party; a symbol of intellectual creativity and freedom since the Sixties. We find in his complex, angst-ridden, existentialist poetry whatever we need to find, but the man, with all the nuance and mysteriousness of a human being whose life was marred by depression, is beyond our knowing, as each of us always remains essentially mysterious to others, maybe even to ourselves.

After the emotional turmoil of the last few days, I don't feel up to another shock. If Selene loses Miriam I think I might break with her, and yet a few days ago, when I thought that I would no longer know what was happening in Selene's life, I was bereft. Either way, I feel like I'm walking towards doom. Selene is so ill and now her daughter is sick too, though I have no idea what is wrong with Miriam or even whether the guard is making this up as a cruel taunt so that Selene thinks she won't have immunity from execution. And then there is Attila, moving inexorably towards a horrible death, one that Selene knows is coming, though she hasn't told him so. Will they meet again before it's December 3 for him? Only five more days.

Too many questions and I need to sleep — perhaps Simon will go on with his story...

Later. The Altstadt looked normal. Sun setting, kindling lights on every street corner. Restaurants and cafés bustling. Trams. A barrel organ. Voices. Smells of tobacco, perfume, a Bierhalle, even a hint of cedar, astringent underneath the rest.

I walked blindly.

By the time it was dark, I had crossed the Limmat unnoticed and now wandered through almost-deserted streets of stiff-necked buildings. Some watched me pass, lights half-concealed in upstairs windows. Others seemed simply to turn away. The night was beginning to feel judgemental. I tried to think but nothing clear would form. So, empty inside, I walked on.

It grew quieter. And the breeze changed, becoming drier, more northerly. I hardly noticed then. Now I remember its fragrance: lavender and chrysanthemum, that thread of cedar wound between them.

Crossing a road, heels striking the tramways, I paused. How long since I had heard a tram, or even a dog bark? Turning, I tried to work out where I was. A cobbled road. Buildings tall, pitch-roofed, their faces oddly twisted. A lone streetlamp reached crookedly from a bracket on the nearest wall, a sign beneath it.

Dreigesichterstraße.

I had never heard of it.

Walking on a little, I passed by a cross-street.

Hecatequerstraße.

Surely there was no such place.

I tried retracing my way. I remembered a straight road and a T-junction. Now it curved sharply to become a series of crossroads. Some junctions were extraordinarily broad; others so narrow I would have to walk sideways to take them. Every building bent oddly out of true. Streetlamps picked out unfamiliar names.

To be so thoroughly lost should have brought panic. I felt only mild irritation.

Another turning. A gentle hill, black but for a dowdy light at its bottom. The breeze was in my face now, cedar uppermost. I picked my way through the darkness, footfalls slapping back from otherwise unseen buildings. It was a relief to reach the streetlamp's tallow glow.

'It's a sad hour for anyone to be out on their own.'

I lurched around and saw the old woman behind me.

'My, but you're a pretty young thing, aren't you?' She was dressed in black shawl and cardigan, like the concierge of a small pension; a kindly despot and matriarch of a large family. The lamplight deepened the many lines around her face, highlighting each liver spot on her hands as she leaned on a walking stick of willow. Her eyes glinted. 'Why so sad, child? All alone?'

'Everyone is.'

'Oh my, is that what you believe?' This old woman stepped closer and peered up into my face. 'And love, do you believe in that?'

'Love is… hideous.'

'So sure.'

I bridled, although there was no criticism in her voice. Brusquely, I said, 'I am afraid I am a little lost, madame. Could you —?'

'I'm not sure I know these streets myself.'

'You must know where —'

'You must look for yourself. Look anew.' The old woman pointed behind me. 'Look!'

300

Every shadow fell back, lamplight surging and changing, recasting the road in tints of sapphire and lilac. Flaxen light spilled across the pavement from a window ahead. My forehead and eyes grew tight, relaxing as every building roused itself and subsided into a new position. The breeze flexed, stronger then gentle again.

She was gone when I turned back. Perhaps I should have been concerned. Instead I peered through that lighted window at the people inside.

A party, although no sound came through the glass. As I turned away, familiar faces caught my eye.

Giles, who told me over and over that he loved me. Yet Giles had loved his country more, dying for it at the Second Battle of Ypres. Alberto sat beside him. My first lover, the week I reached Zürich. The affair had hardly begun before he threw me over to take up with a dancer from the Laban school. Why had I felt such shock, such remorse at what he did when it simply confirmed all that I had come to believe?

This time, they did not vanish, even when I squeezed my eyes tight shut. When I opened them again, I saw him sitting at the back of the room. Quite alone.

I ran. Through shadows of lilac and saffron.

The square opened without warning. It thronged with people. Giles and Alberto were there, as was Kurt, who had stared at me with such longing. Kurt who had decided to return to Austria the year before, leaving without saying goodbye. Another one who had lied about love.

Most of these people were strangers, faces and forms indistinct as if glimpsed in passing, say from the deck of a moving tram. Some stood in groups, others alone; many wandered, never settling. All in silence.

Here and there, there were people I recognised besides Kurt and Giles and Alberto. All of those few who had professed their love, together with that handful that might have done under different circumstances. Keeping my distance, I walked through the crowd. And, as I did so, something quiet and vulnerable opened inside me.

I continued searching. Better that distraction than letting that quiet thing find its voice.

Maman.

She was one of those who wandered. I had come to imagine her differently. Brazen or perhaps predatory. Not slack shouldered, tired of step. Filled with the pain of exile. That I had never expected, although I had seen it often enough in my friends these past years.

I looked away. Seeing him again, abandoned on the edge of the crowd.

Papa.

My fault. All — Oh, not my mother's infidelity, father's suicide, perhaps. But Giles had enlisted because, feeling the strength of his love, something in me needed to test that love. So I plagued him with talk of his patriotic duty until he volunteered. I pushed him away in the hope that he would not go. And Alberto… the same. From the first I tested him, allowing him close only to thrust him away. Away into the arms of someone else…

I needed something. The unthinking emptiness of earlier would have done. Better still, cynicism or anger to pull about myself like a comforter. Anything to separate myself from all this. I could find nothing.

Only running.

Away. Always away.

Nothing seemed far enough. So I ran on until my footfalls turned hollow.

'Mon Dieu. You did give me a fright, mademoiselle. Whatever can be chasing you?'

She was leaning on the wrought iron guard rail, back now to whatever she had been looking at over the bridge.

'Pardon, madame.'

'Good heavens, you look all in. Please, mademoiselle, stand a while and catch your breath.' She patted the guard-rail. Her hands, although large and chapped, seemed gentle. Caring. 'I come here every morning. It might sound silly, but I love standing on bridges, held up in the air. I imagine it must be like being in an aeroplane. Don't you think?'

I did. Being on a bridge was to be suspended, caught between two places and belonging to neither.

Numbly, I leaned on the balustrade and looked over. It was utterly dark, not a glint of water.

'Is it love?' The hairs escaping her scarf were old gold turning to steel, lavender-water hanging between us like a memory. Just for a moment there was something familiar about her — around her eyes; her features, lined but not yet deeply so — and then it was gone.

'It often is,' she continued. 'That or a lack of it.'

'Do you think then that there are people who are unable to love? Or, only to bring sorrow should they do so?'

'Oh my, what questions!' She smiled. 'You know, mademoiselle,

you remind me of my daughter. She's just a snip younger and full of questions: 'Maman, why this? Maman, why that?' I try to answer as best I can, of course, but sometimes…'

'And when you have no answer?'

'It depends. Sometimes, I say: 'Petite, what does your heart to tell you?''

'Oh.' Had I really expected something more? 'Doing that, truly understanding your mind, is not an easy thing to do.'

'My daughter is the same. Scared to look.'

'I did not say scared —'

'I say to her: 'Petite, why be afraid? Look. Who's to judge?''

'Your daughter. If what she finds, what she believes…'

'Can it be so bad to look, whatever you find? So disappointing? Ma petite, it sometimes takes more courage to admit a mistake than to punish yourself for it. And all the more to let go of guilts, real or imagined, pick yourself up, and go on afterwards.'

Selene Solweig

Delirious, Selene chants Attila, Miriam, Attila, Miriam, Attila, Attila, Attila, Miriam...

Between the repeated names she mouths fragments of Attila's poetry, barely audible, until...

She sits at Catherine's desk in the early morning, making notes on Attila's poems, glances up. Another half hour and she will wake Simon with coffee, give him the antique pen she managed to buy in Szentendre while he was across the square taking photographs — a late present for their first anniversary. She settles to work, loses track of time... until Simon comes into the room and stands behind the desk, hovers there for a moment, turns to leave, turns back again.

Simon?

Sorry, he says, beginning to leave the room.

What is it?

Catherine gets up from the desk littered with notes.

I'm not sure. I've been up for a while, but I can't settle to anything today.

We could go for a walk, Catherine offers. I'll be fine. We don't need to go far.

I'm not sure... I... No, I shouldn't be disturbing you... you were working... I'm just being...

It's fine. I could do with a break. We could go for a coffee.

No really, you get on with your work. He attempts a smile and moves to go back to the little bedroom, set up as his writing room.

Oh, I nearly forgot — I got you an anniversary present in Szentendre.

Catherine offers him the box and he unwraps it carefully.

It's beautiful, it's...

...old and a bit fragile, Catherine says, but it works.

He hugs her. Right, I should shake myself up and get writing with this fine instrument. He fingers the elegant tapering, the dark burgundy-brown of the barrel. Thank you, he says. His smile is tight and she can feel the tension in him, but he hugs her again. Thank you, I love it.

It's dark when Catherine next looks up, feeling a presence behind her. Simon is standing, head down. He looks smaller, ill at ease.

I didn't see you there, I...

No, you were completely in the flow. It's going well?

I probably won't know till I read it all back. It could be rubbish, but at least it's something to get it onto the page. Much more fictional than I'd planned, even for a novel, but I've made my peace with that. She pauses. You don't look well, Simon.

No, I'm feeling a bit… I don't know… just low I suppose. You should ignore me. I'm being stupid.

Why is it stupid? You've been supporting me for days. That must be exhausting enough at any time, but I'm not the only one who lost a baby. I do realise that, you know.

I don't even know if that's what it is, he returns. I keep thinking about András. He is definitely in love with you, and why wouldn't he be? I know he wouldn't make a move or anything, but you'd be better off with him. Look at him — older, established, intelligent, charming… What have I got to offer? Morose, second-rate writer with…

Stop it, Simon. That's rubbish. We've been through this and I thought we'd finished with it. András wouldn't make a move because even if he wanted to he'd have no chance whatsoever. And you're not a second-rate writer.

Just morose?

No, that's not what I meant. You get depressed sometimes. I know that and it doesn't stop me loving you.

Perhaps it should. Or perhaps I can't cope with dragging your life down with mine.

Simon! Stop it, please. You're not dragging me anywhere. She takes a deep breath. This is going in circles. Let's go for a walk, go for a drink, anything you like… Or I'll pour you a bath, cook something — tell me what will help.

Nothing.

They stand facing each other, silence tautening the space between them.

Eventually he says, I don't think I could take another miscarriage. I'm not even capable of being there for you...

But you...

I know. Sometimes I think I can hold it all together, but I'm kidding myself. I'm scum. András...

That's enough! Catherine winces at how loud her voice is. I'm not interested in András, she says more quietly, but slowly.

Well maybe you should be. Or interested in anyone but me. I'm...

Are you saying it's over?

I don't know what I'm saying. Or maybe I'm saying I'm not good enough... I'll only...

I'm not listening to this!

Catherine dashes for the door, grabs her thick wool coat that hangs near the entrance, bolts from the flat, running towards the stairs.

Outside the cold is brutal. Margit has warned her to stay indoors this weekend, that it will be as low as minus eight today. She looks up, towards the flat, wondering if Simon will be at the window, but there is no sign of him. She thinks of going back in, but her exhaustion is heavier than the cold gnawing at her. She hunches into the coat and wraps her scarf around her ears and face, fishing in her pockets for gloves, begins walking briskly, not caring where she is going, losing herself in grim thoughts as she walks and walks...

There was an incident so slight, so small, so brutal that she could not go on.

Liam held her down in the bed by the throat and told her not to be stupid. But it wasn't true that she could not go on...

There was a night when she sat on the bedroom floor shivering. Her clothes stuck to her, rain-sodden, icy. She couldn't remember how the argument had started or what it had been about; couldn't piece together why she'd left the house on a wet December night, walked into the darkness; rain and wind harrying her. She waited to be told how ridiculous she was, began peeling off wet layers.

It's okay, Kitty, we can work this out. Have a bath, get some sleep. We'll talk. We'll talk properly. It's going to be okay, Kitty. We can do this. It's okay.

She had waited for him to start the conversation. How it would be okay, how years could be re-invented — narrative working backwards and forwards to make all things well.

She walked to the lake, sat on a wall, watched clouds scudding over the hills, iced peaks reaching into the sky, remembered when the sky was simple; a light-blue crystal. She waited.

It was two weeks before she asked: This conversation — is it ever going to happen? Can we make it okay?

His look veered from surprise to disdain.

Ridiculous. No one but you would take that seriously. Fucking hell, Kitty, what was I supposed to say?

She had been hysterical, running out into the rain, into the night, surely she must have realised he was only trying to calm her down.

I said what you wanted to hear, anyone would, the state you were in. Anyway, you don't want to talk. Not really. You never wanted to give it a chance.

This is the end of the story, Catherine says to herself softly, her breath pluming ice. She stops, tries to get a sense of where she is. Not far from the river. She can walk towards the water and back-track to the flat. This will not be the end of the story. There will be another chance, there has to be another chance...

Catherine

Selene paces her cell, counting steps, changing the rhythm constantly. Her body aches, trembles with every movement, but she persists — five to the left, four to the right. I'm here for you, Miriam, she says with determination. Mama's here. Stay alive, my darling.

Catherine wills Selene's body to keep going. She tries to focus on a patch of sky barely visible through the high-set bars and filthy glass, tries to recite poetry, collapses...

In the dream Selene is a child, learning great Hungarian poetry by heart — she repeats a muddle of lines, lines from Attila József mixed with others from Ady, Arany.... She sees herself in the apartment in Montmartre...

Mama, I have it!

Have what, minette?

Selene sighs, but does not tell her mother not to call her 'kitten'.

The poem Papa was teaching me. I have it by heart.

Excellent. Can I hear it? Or do you want to wait for him to return?

Selene considers. I'll try it on you now. To make sure.

Marie smiles and nods. And who is it by?

Sándor Petőfi. It's called 'The Tree'.

Selene takes in a deep breath and stands as she would if she were about to dance.

> *I'll be a tree, if you are its flower,*
> *Or a flower, if you are the dew—*
> *I'll be the dew, if you are the sunbeam,*
> *Only to be united with you.*
>
> *My lovely girl, if you are the Heaven,*
> *I shall be a star above on high;*
> *My darling, if you are hell-fire,*
> *To unite us, damned I shall die.*

It's very sad, Marie notes, but beautiful. And you recite it very well.

Selene smiles, hears a step on the stairs that lead up from the gallery below.

Papa! Papa, I have the poem by heart...

When she comes round, she is mumbling a line... *My lovely girl, if you are the Heaven...*

On the floor of the cell, there is a bowl of scummy beans, cold and congealing. It will be another night before she can beg the
312

guard for news of Miriam.

Tomorrow, Selene promises the empty cell. I won't miss the guard tomorrow. She begins to weep.

Tomorrow, she whispers, after eating the clotted beans and stumbling back to the bench. Tomorrow I'll have more news of you and you will be doing better. She huddles under the tattered blanket, shivering, too weak to weep, though a stray tear slides down her face as she drifts into unconsciousness... dreams that she is...

...eating dinner at the table in the Paris apartment...

Stunning work, Charles says, helping himself to a spoon of green beans.

Mama and Papa nod together.

Yes, so alive. I can see why Brassaï has taken an interest in him, Marie adds.

What's his name? Selene asks. Will he come here?

Ervin Marton, Sándor tells her. Sadly, another one of my countrymen who has moved to Paris to avoid the antisemitism that prevails at home. And yes, you will meet him. We're privileged to have his work here to sell. Your mama is extremely talented to sign such a fine photographer.

She is, Charles agrees, passing a platter of chicken to Selene. And not only did your clever mama snap up the Marton pictures, but also a number of fine paintings by two other Hungarians, newly arrived here.

Sándor nods. In the studio downstairs. I'll show you after dinner.

Marie smiles broadly. We were lucky to get them before the big dealers like Bölöni or even Weill realised what they're missing. I don't suppose we'll keep them long, but in the meantime...

Mama looks radiant, Selene thinks, so beautiful. Papa and Charles are obviously full of admiration for her too. What are the new couple called? Selene asks.

Sándor Józsa and Ilona Fiszl, Papa tells her.

This is a good time to grow up in Paris, Mama says.

There is a moment of silence. Papa and Charles begin to talk at the same moment, then stop...

France won't become like Hungary, Mama says, waving a hand across the table, as though someone had already argued with her.

Let us hope not, Charles says quietly.

We have to be vigilant wherever we are, Papa adds. The new laws limiting who can practise art then medicine, and now commerce...

Charles nods. And politicians like Marin and Laurent are worrying. I fear for the future if a man like Darquier de Pellepoix is elected to the Municipal Council.

Quite — he's been posturing since he got himself injured at the Place de Concorde riot. And he's got bolder in his pronouncements too.

We must, with all urgency, resolve the Jewish problem, whether by expulsion, or massacre, Charles quotes.

Marie stands up abruptly. Charles! Sándor! My daughter is listening to this... this scaremongering. Please!

Charles colours and stands too. I'm so sorry, Marie. Selene, ignore me. Too much of your papa's good red wine... I'm mortified.

Papa looks down at the table and shakes his head. Ah, well, let us hope, he says. Let us hope.

Selene turns on the bench, half-wakes, moans... drifts into another dream of...

Selene Solweig

…Catherine weeping…

Catherine wakes sobbing. She looks around, disoriented, wondering where she is, why she is in a strange bed.

She moves towards the door as Margit bustles in with a laden tray — coffee, sweet buns, eggs.

Into bed with you, Margit insists. You need to eat before anything else.

But Simon?

You can phone him when you've had breakfast.

Catherine remembers the evening before — her determined march back to the flat through the bitter cold. But she hadn't taken a key when she'd run out, and he didn't answer the bell when she pressed repeatedly. She barely remembers walking to Margit's — the long tramp through icy air, her feet becoming slow in the cold, breath painful even through the scarf wrapped across her face, but she had no money with her, no purse with her monthly travel pass, so she'd kept on… wind icing her lungs, the skin of her face burning cold, muscles trembling with effort. The walk had become a shamble, but she staggered on — one foot, the next, any bleak wall grasped for balance. Don't cry. Don't fall. Chant in her head: right foot, left foot, right… Falling — snow — falling, one flake, another, soft as she finally reached Margit's door, frozen flakes caressing her neck, wet, shivering, crying.

When she phones Simon, there is no answer. She tries several times before Margit says she will take her back to the flat. Margit has the spare key. It will be alright. It will not be the end of the story.

Inside the silent apartment, a note on her desk reads: *Sorry for everything. All my fault. Love you always. Goodbye, my darling. Simon.*

Catherine begins to howl.

Sit down, Margit says, ushering her onto a dining chair.

Margit marches to the phone, begins dialling.

I appreciate that, Margit says, her voice stiff and clipped. But we are fearful for him. We're concerned he's not in his right… Yes, I realise he's an adult…. No, he's not registered as a mental health patient with… All I am asking is… Right. Well thank you for nothing, she finally says, slamming down the receiver.

I'm going to phone András, Margit says. Police are never any help. But András will find him. He's bound to be in a café or bookshop… I'll call András, then get you something to drink. Try not to worry.

Catherine smiles weakly and nods, fear congealing in her throat and stomach.

Each time András phones, Catherine's body surges with hope that soon becomes disappointment, more fear.

What if he's...

Don't even think it, Margit cautions.

Later, when Margit can no longer quell Catherine's keening, she phones a doctor, who arrives with sedatives.

Catherine drifts into drugged sleep, remembering...

How Miriam is death speaking...

I will never leave this room, she says, voice thinner than the light edging round the curtains.

The room smells of night-sweats, sweet decay, oranges... oranges clotting Catherine's throat.

Do you remember...

No, Miriam says. No, I hardly remember anything now.

Silence gnaws into the afternoon.

Outside the bedroom, Judith puts a hand to her throat, fingers the gold and silver damascene hand of Miriam that rested there.

She was in the street... raving... about illness and dreaming... Judith tells Catherine.

In my illness I had such strange dreams... Oh, such dreams... I dare not tell you in case you think I'm mad, Catherine had supplied for her.

318

Yes, that's it. You were very close, weren't you? I shouldn't have…

Catherine puts a hand on Judith's arm…

They would have committed her, Cass… I'm sorry — I know it's Catherine now.

It doesn't matter.

A thin smile.

They wanted to lock her away, but her neurologist was very good. So here she is, determined to die. You will come again?

Yes.

Thank you, Catherine.

Who are you? Miriam asks when Catherine visits again.

Cassie, Catherine says. It's Cassie.

I'm sorry, I don't know anyone of that name, Miriam says.

Casilda, Catherine tries. I'm Casilda.

No. I've never known a Casilda. I've been ill. I am confused by shadows. Perhaps I knew you once, I don't remember.

Once you found a girl and called her Casilda, Catherine continues.

I don't remember, Miriam insists, voice brittle.

Miriam!

The trace of a shudder. There is a moment of sadness, opaque dark that drops and is gone. Miriam is transfigured: dazzling, serene; the beatific smile an instant before the unbearable — the uneven jerk of her limbs, the hum rising to a howl, the sound that marks the margin between ecstasy and unconsciousness, the stare signalling her absence.

The grey September afternoon falls away and there is only the story that Miriam told: belief is your gift. For one aching second Miriam is still in the room... then Judith is howling beside her daughter's body...

God, this is the end of the story. I can't go on, Catherine whispers to no one.

When she wakes, Simon is standing by the bed, pale, shaken, but he holds out a hand before throwing his arms around her and they weep together, clinging to one another.

When they finally move a little apart, Catherine fingers the hamsa at her throat. It was Judith's, she says. My hand of Miriam belonged to Miriam's mother. So how did Selene get it? Or rather, how did Judith get it from Selene?

Perhaps they're just similar, Simon ventures, kneeling beside the bed.

No, they're the same, Catherine insists, one and the same.

When Simon eventually falls asleep, Catherine sits in bed fingering the little talisman, begins to write...

Catherine

Catherine wakes in a cell. Selene no longer scratches dates on the wall, letting one feverish day drift into another as she waits for news of her child... drifts into a fever of hopeless sleep...

Selene does not stir when the guard clangs open the door.

Get up! He shouts across the narrow space of the cell.

Selene jerks awake, stands unsteadily.

The guard approaches and pulls at the thin cloth of Selene's tunic, pushes her ahead of him, goads her into the corridor, where another guard stands, smirking.

They march her along labyrinthine passages. Every step, she thinks, will be her last — she will fall and not be able to stand and they will... Miriam has died, she thinks. They are taking me to be executed. Yet she continues to put one foot in front of the other until they finally shove her through another door, this cell even smaller, danker than the last. There is no tiny patch of high-up window-light and she blinks, makes out the form of another young woman, standing with her back to the cold wall.

The door slams shut, resounding in the stale, still air.

Kati, the woman says, inching towards Selene.

Selene, she replies uncertainly, before falling to her knees on the cold, hard floor.

Kati moves next to her, lifts a thin blanket from her shoulders and places it on Selene. Let me help you to the bench, she says.

Budapest, Tuesday 30 November 1993

I am no longer fearful of Selene 'taking me over'. I was more afraid when I thought I would stop dreaming about her, but now I fear for her health, for her life. The sense of her presence has shifted. She is with me, but I'm also aware that it is me, living my own life with Selene 'on my shoulder', rather than the creeping feeling that she was assuming my identity. Is this because she is so much weaker? What does the move to the new cell mean, if anything? Selene was certain she was being taken to her death, but there is no news of Miriam. She has another cellmate, but why? The encounter with Kati was brief, but my instinct is that she is not like Boglárka. I suppose someone who wanted to take Selene into their confidence, even as a pretence, would offer her help and a blanket, but my gut tells me that Kati is genuinely kind and I am going to believe that until proved otherwise.

I am also worried about Simon. His emotional fragility outstrips my own and I'm feeling increasingly uncertain of myself since the miscarriage — brittle and liable to become weepy at any moment. I sometimes feel I'm not strong enough for both of us, yet I never shake the feeling that he is who I am 'meant' to be with — he is my Attila... Perhaps he is also my Miriam, my Ben Haddaj...

'I'm your Ben Haddaj,' Miriam said to me the night after the incident on the beach at Nairn. 'I'm supposed to save you, my enchanted girl.'

I never saw the enchantment, only story and facts aligned. Miriam was my Ben Haddaj. I was Casilda. I was not Cassie (Catherine Anne McManus) from the Lawn's Estate. Miriam was so certain that in this lifetime Ben Haddaj would save me and that we would be together forever. And I clung to her until an incident so small, so brutal, sent my world spinning apart. And then I rationalised it all away... I survived Liam and the first miscarriage, convinced myself that life was beginning to make sense. And it was, even through the shock of Miriam's death, even through the strange experiences in Toledo — the sense of Casilda with me at the tiny mosque, the inexplicable certainty of Miriam comforting me after the sudden flow of blood, the mint tea that I found, cooling by my bedside when I woke, and the hamsa that I wear always, that Selene also carries, and that I now remember seeing Judith wearing the last time I saw her...

I have lived without the facts and the story conforming to one another for years. I have learnt the art of ambiguity, but the intrusion of this other reality, this fragmented sense of identity and perception, is straining my ability to function, more so since losing the baby, and even more so with the knowledge that Simon is so close to breaking.

It feels as though it is not in my power to make sense of life at the moment, only to wrestle with dreams, images and overwhelming feelings, my own and Selene's... My internal experiences of Selene's life are as real to me as the feelings of aura when I have a migraine, the perception of blueness when I look at the sky...

Perhaps one thing that might be in my power is to find out more about this tiny hand of Miriam that I wear. Tomorrow I will phone...

Selene Solweig

Selene wakes in Catherine's bed, the covers churned around her. On the floor notebooks and pens in several colours are strewn, the purple pen lidless. One notebook, beautifully bound and with a poem by Charles Bukowski lettered in glitter-red Italian on the front cover, the legend *'Bottega Fagnola — Torino'* in the same cursive script on the back cover, lies splayed on the bed, as though Catherine had fallen asleep over it, mid-sentence, the previous night.

Catherine gathers the books and takes them to her desk in the main room.

Morning, Simon calls, emerging from the other bedroom. You seemed deeply asleep, so I thought it best to leave you.

Is it late?

Just after ten. Shall I make breakfast? I've got croissants and eggs. Sit down and I'll bring coffee. You can drink while I cook.

She smiles. Thank you, she says, piling the notebooks on her writing desk. I was up late journalling. She flicks through one of the sheaves of notes on Attila's last days. I think I need to call Judith, she says.

Judith?

Miriam's mother. My Miriam.

Simon tilts his head to one side.

I'm sure she will know where my hand of Miriam came from.

I'm not even going to ask how you're going to manage that conversation, he returns, but smiles. But for now, breakfast.

Yes, Catherine agrees.

Simon sets the table carefully, makes coffee and places it in front of her. She cups the satisfying roundness of white ceramic, savours the warmth, sips slowly.

I think my editor will be convinced I've lost my way with the novel.

Well, you of all people must know how to handle editors, he quips.

Perhaps. In any case the book I'm writing is the one I have to write. If they don't want it, that's fine.

Well, it's not like it was ever meant to be a biography. It was always fiction.

Yes, it's just rather off piste in this case.

There should be much more freedom in fiction than our narrowing conventions allow, I always think, Simon asserts. More fiction filled with deeper truth. Facts are slippery devils. In my not very humble opinion, we need to invent a great deal more in order to tell real truths, to make any kind of significant narrative in a meaningless universe.

I'll remember that at the editorial meeting. Catherine says.

And anyway, what you're writing says something vital about the boundaries between fact and fiction. You can't know whether or not Selene and Attila met as adults, even though their meeting seems contrary to other things we think we know about what is possible. Fiction that moves beyond linear time-lines seems the pre-eminent way to go in the circumstances.

He sets down two white plates, each traced with a thin line of silver at the rim.

Your eggs, madame. More coffee, madame? He asks theatrically.

Thank you, yes. You seem to be feeling better this morning?

Well, I'm trying to stay out of my own way at least. He pours fresh coffee, dark and fragrant, and sits opposite her. After all, I've got a lot to be positive about if I can just allow myself to see it.

Hello? Hello? Judith's voice sounds older, though it's only four years since Catherine last saw her at Miriam's funeral.

Hello, Judith. It's Catherine… Cassie.

Cassie? There is a pause. Cassie. Sorry, it's Catherine now, isn't it?

Catherine smiles down the blind receiver. Yes. How are you?

I'm old, Cass…Catherine.

Old? You're only in your sixties, Judith. That's young these
326

days.

It doesn't feel young. I lost Sol last year. With Miriam gone too…

Oh, I'm so sorry. How's Sarah and…

Oh, they keep in touch, but none of them live nearby and they have their own lives to lead. Sarah phones every day. She's always been good, but the days… Anyway, you didn't call to hear me whining. What can I do for you, Catherine?

It's an odd question, but I remember noticing once… I think the last time I visited Miriam… you wore a hamsa, a little…

Hand of Miriam.

Yes.

Yes, it was my aunt's. I'm afraid I lost it about three years ago. Tiny little thing. I still sometimes wonder if it will just turn up. It was terrible to lose something that had survived so long…

Right. I… I found one when I was in Toledo. That would have been about three years ago too. It looked… well, very like the one I remembered you wearing and… I wondered how old it might be, if it's as similar…

Hmm. That is a co-incidence, but then Toledo is the home of damascene, so perhaps not so odd… Aunt Marie got hers when she went on a family trip to Toledo. It was a gift for her twenty-first birthday. That would have been… oh, must have been 1924. My mother would have been nineteen, I suppose.

Aunt Marie?

Yes, my mum's older sister, Marie Spire.

They were French?

Yes. They both met partners from other places and left Paris. Mum came to England, Aunt Marie went to Hungary, to Budapest. Terrible life she had. Lost everyone...

Your aunt was Marie Spire?

Yes, you've heard of her? I can't think how...

I'm in Hungary doing research for a book. Her name came up when I was researching people who met the poet Attila József. I think they first met in Paris.

I see. Well that's a real co-incidence. Yes. They had a wonderful life in Paris. We visited when I was nine. Selene — my cousin — was only a couple of months older than me, but she seemed so elegant, so much more confident and grown-up. I adored her. They ran an art gallery, had interesting friends... but of course the Nazis put an end to all that.

So your aunt left the hamsa to you?

No, she gave it to her Selene, on her twenty-first birthday. But after... Well, that's a long and terrible story, but it eventually went back to Aunt Marie after she lost Selene. Judith pauses... Anyway, you don't want to hear all the details, but I named Miriam after my cousin's little girl... Aunt Marie left the pendant to Mum and she left it to me. I lost Mum in '88, the year before Miriam...

There is a sound of a sob being swallowed.

I see, Catherine says softly. I'm sorry to...

No, it's good to remember them, Judith says, her voice brisk again. So that's a very convoluted way of saying that the one you have is probably from the early Twenties.

Yes. Thank you.

You didn't wonder about its age when you first bought it? Judith asks.

I... well, I idly wondered I suppose, but I'm writing a novel and wanted to use one like it in the story and I couldn't seem to find out anything about how to date it.

Ah.

Catherine is not sure that Judith's sharp mind hasn't sensed that there is more to the story, but she can't think of a way to say that Miriam passed on the family heirloom a year after dying.

I'd like to imagine it's the same one, Judith says. Silly, I know, but mine would have gone to Miriam and I'm sure she'd have wanted it to go to you.

Catherine's voice catches in her throat. Thank you. Thank you, Judith. Take care. And give my love to Sarah.

I will, Catherine. And you take care too.

The line goes dead and Catherine stands holding the receiver, tears falling silently down her face.

Catherine

Catherine wakes in Selene's new cell, the bench as hard and narrow as the last one.

Kati stands close by, looking concerned.

Oh, you're awake, Kati says. I was so worried. I thought you might… but you're awake. I saved you some water.

Selene edges herself into a sitting position and retches, but there is nothing to vomit.

You were feverish all night, Kati says. I tried to give you water then, but it just bubbled back and I didn't want to waste it. Can you drink?

Selene nods and Kati helps her to sip. Each mouthful burns her throat as she swallows, but Kati is patient, talking to her as she tips the water drop by drop.

You called out the same names over and over in your sleep. Miriam and Attila. And you mumbled lines too — poetry, I think. Are you a poet?

Not mine, Selene's voice rasps and sounds strange to her. Attila

József.

Ah. He is the Attila you called for? But he…?

I love his poetry, Selene says.

Of course. And Miriam?

Selene pauses.

Sorry. I shouldn't ask so many questions. I'm so glad to see you awake.

Selene smiles. It's fine. Miriam is my daughter. She's four and a half. They told me she was very sick, but now they won't tell me anything.

Oh! God, that's terrible. Bastards!

Yes, Selene agrees.

When the gruel arrives, Kati spoons it slowly into Selene.

You must have some too, Selene insists.

I had last night's beans. I couldn't wake you. I hope I made the right decision. They'd have taken away what was left if…

Of course. But you must still be hungry. These are hardly portions for two.

No, but you are ill. I'll be fine.

You remind me of Ludmilla, Selene says. A friend I had in here once.

Dead?

I think so.

Kati nods. Bastards, she says again.

After the effort of swallowing the thin gruel, Selene slides back into sleep, dreams of this day a year ago — December 1 1958, a day of tedium like so many others…

She had been in the last cell alone since Boglárka had been taken away — her routine of pacing different steps each day, making her body stretch, forcing down the wretched food. She'd paced in the afternoon, reciting Attila's poetry and…

pacing…

…had found herself walking by the shore of lake Balaton, where Attila was pacing, his face clouded with anxiety, brows knit tightly together, head down, stooping, muttering to no one.

Attila!

Selene! The change of expression is instant. He lopes towards her, arms outstretched. Only four days! Selene! He hugs her so tightly she thinks she might bruise.

But you are so thin! God, I should feed you, but… I have hardly any money with me and the house is bursting with people. What shall we do? You need to eat.

Shh, she soothes. I'm much better for seeing you. Let's walk. Tell me how you are doing. I… I worry about you.

As they walk, his melancholy descends again.

332

I feel my best work is behind me, Selene, he says, after they have walked in silence for several minutes. Last year 'By the Danube' appeared in *Beautiful Word*. I thought it was the best thing I'd written, but it hardly got noticed.

It will, Selene says. It will be recognised in Hungary and all over Europe.

A prophet in his own life time, eh?

Quite, but the recognition will come.

Last year was not so bad. I suppose. I met Bartók, you know. Just before Christmas. And Thomas Mann a little after. And many interesting artists at a huge house owned by... But you know all this, don't you?

Some of it. Selene smiles. They're just facts in books, though, or connections I've put together. I met Imre Ámos and his wife Margit Anna when I was a child in Paris, and Béla Czóbel too. Those were the interesting artists you meant?

Amazing, he says.

But knowing people in common is not like really knowing you, like this.

He grins again for a moment, before a look of anguish overtakes him.

But this year has not been so good. The sanatorium and now being ostracised in Balatonszárszó with sisters who want to know my every move.

They care about you, Attila.

I know. I'm an ungrateful wretch. You must think so.

No, I...

But tomorrow will be better.

Of course.

No, really. Tomorrow I have visitors. People with minds. My co-editors of the *Szép Szó*. I even have a plan of escape.

Oh!

Selene what is it?

She wipes her hand across her face, breathes deeply. I... I can't...

You know something about tomorrow, something terrible and you can't tell me. I'm not going to die, surely? I'm planning to hitch a lift back to Budapest. I need to work again, to be useful. Tell me I'm not going to die tomorrow... at least if it's true.

You won't die tomorrow, Attila. I'm sorry. I'm so caught up in myself. You will have a wonderful day with your colleagues. I promise.

He lifts his head higher, smiles, takes her in his arms again.

You do me so much good, Selene Solweig Virág. His face melts into sadness again. And I can't even buy you a meal.

I'm fine. Really. She slips her hand into his. Let's walk faster. It's cold standing still, but a beautiful day.

He sets off at a pace she can barely match and as they walk...

Selene paces her cell.

She stops. Dissolves into tears trying to weep silently.

Oh Attila, I never even said goodbye, she says to the empty cell. There are only two more days, Attila and I may never see you again.

Selene wakes on the bench in 1959.

Kati is standing over her looking anxious. She shakes herself — a whole year since she last saw Attila so briefly, his mood so volatile.

Selene, are you alright?

She nods.

You were talking in your sleep again, something about not saying goodbye... Kati puts a hand to Selene's damp forehead. And you are so hot.

Sorry I scared you, Selene manages. It was only dreams. I'll be fine.

The guard stands at the door, smug, triumphant. Letter for you, sow, he says, waving an envelope. Selene tries to pull herself from the bench, but falls back... He waves it again. Want to take it to your friend? He waves the letter towards Kati, who approaches slowly, stops just out of arm's reach, looks at the floor of the cell and holds out a hand...

He drops the letter and she catches it as it flutters towards the ground.

Thank you, she says, amazed, as he turns and slams the door.

Budapest, Wednesday 1 December 1993

I have been making notes on Attila's last days. If that car had not been full on December 2, he would have gone back to Budapest. How long might he have lived after that? Our destinies turn on such tiny events — a full car, a small and brutal moment, a slip in time...

Like Selene, I fear that this might have been her last meeting with Attila. It's a depressing thought, but there are two more days so it's not impossible that she will get to say goodbye. But how would she do that? She can hardly tell Attila when he will die, surely?

I can only wait. In the meantime, Simon is right about fact and fiction and I am right to go on with the novel as it is developing, however strange, and whatever my editor's reaction.

And today — an extraordinary turn of events — Selene has been given a letter. The first time (apart from the torn fragment) in all the time she's been in prison — at least to my knowledge. I have no idea what it portends, but can only hope that it isn't bad news...

I've also been thinking about my conversation with Judith yesterday. I was so focussed on finding out more about the hamsa that when I discovered that Judith was Selene's cousin it didn't occur to me to tell her about her uncle's sketchbook. I haven't been able find Miriam, but Judith might know where she is, and if not, she should have it anyway. All this time I've been telling people I'm looking for Miriam on behalf of friends of mine who are relatives, and it turns out to be true. If I don't find Miriam in the next two days, I'll phone Judith again when I get back home and send her the sketchbook.

Selene Solweig

Selene wakes with Kati knelt beside her, soothing her.

Go back to sleep, Kati says softly. I'll wake you when the gruel comes.

She tries to sit, but can hardly move her head and lights swim in front of her eyes, piercing lights that jab with pain....

Shh, lie down, Simon soothes.

Catherine weeps softly. I'm sorry, she whispers. I'm sorry I lost the baby.

Shh, he says again. You can't blame yourself for that. There'll be a baby. I know there will. Is the pain very bad?

Yes. And nausea.

You don't normally get migraines so close together, do you?

No, but...

It's been a lot to take, I know. Lie back.

He moves away to get a flannel and walks into the dark spot of her vision where nothing exists. She feels the world tilt and spin and closes her eyes.

In the state between migraine and sleep, caught in the miasma of lights, scent of oranges, clot of darkness blotting out half of the room, Catherine hears a voice calling...

Catherine...

She tries to sit, heaves a thin trickle of bile over the side of the bed, the room spinning...

Catherine, please help me... The voice is insistent, disorienting...

She falls back against the pillow, feels the closeness of Selene... the strangeness of knowing Selene's life, not by night, but in her daytime...

Please, Catherine... the letter... tell me it's not real... that it can't be...

Catherine struggles to sit up, reaches for a notebook, a pen. The pain across her temples is dizzying, but she forces herself to sit, as Selene writes out the letter...

Monday 30 November 1959
Magdolna utca, 25, Budapest VIII

Dear Selene

I have to let you know that Miriam died this evening. As I told you in my letter of November 24, she had scarlet fever. The doctor gave me medicine for her, but she was too sick. She was such a brave little girl, but her throat and whole body burned and even though I made broths to nourish her, she could hardly swallow and often vomited. Her head hurt terribly and the chills and aches that wracked her tiny body were agonising to see. And then the rash came, red and itchy, the awful bumps merging till her whole body and even her tongue was covered and her stomach cramped so that she cried, even in her sleep.

Yesterday her skin began to peel, rough like sandpaper, and she began to complain of earache. All her glands were inflamed and I could only hold her and bring cool compresses and watch as the fever got worse and worse. By the afternoon she could hardly breathe, but the doctor wouldn't come to her. He sent a message that the fever would soon break but it didn't happen. If you had been here, with your nursing skills, perhaps you might have saved her. A mother should be with her child, Selene. I know you will grieve for her. I know you loved her, but you should not have become involved with those people when you had a child to consider and now I must do this.

I had hoped they would let you attend her funeral, which will be tomorrow. The Rabbi wrote to the authorities to ask that you be present, but could give them only a day to decide, so as not to humiliate the dead, and he says they will not allow it. But the Chevra Kaddisha have prepared her poor little body so you can be sure that she is honoured as the dead should be. She will be laid to rest in the Kozma Street cemetery.

I am sorry. There is no life for me here and now I will be allowed to return to Paris.

Baruch dayan emet.

In love and sorrow,
Your mother,
Marie

Catherine begins to sob… and Selene writes —

There is something not right about this letter. The handwriting is… it is like my mother's, but not quite as I remember it, smaller … as though … I cannot say what it is exactly, only that it is not right. How can she return to Paris when no-one is able to leave the country without the approval of the government? And there are phrases *'I must do this'* and her apology, there is something in them making me sense that there is something is odd here. I can't say how I know this, but this letter is not what it seems… please help me, if you can…

Catherine collapses back onto the bed, the pain unbearable, her vision a swarm of light and darkness, the scent of rotting lilies and fruit making her heave. Even lying back, the room spins and spins and she feels herself being whirled… until…

When she wakes the day has almost gone.

There's more chicken soup from Margit, Simon tells her. Can you eat?

Not yet, but a bath maybe?

Simon nods. I'll pour one. Do you want to sleep some more after the bath or…

Simon, she interrupts… Selene was with me when the migraine was unbearable… she wrote in my journal…

She holds out the notebook and Simon takes it and reads.

That's… I hardly know what to say. I guess we won't be hearing from Miriam, he says disconsolately.

But what if she's right? What if the letter… I don't even know what she thinks is wrong with it, but…

Well, it has an address for Miriam and a date of death, so at least we have something to go on…

Yes, Catherine says, realising he's right. Yes. We can ask Margit to help, but in the meantime, I'm never going to sleep tonight — do you think, after the bath perhaps, you could finish reading your story?

I thought of Sheridan, what he had said to me before I sent him away, and shook my head, whether to dismiss the memory or what this woman was saying I am not sure.

'Oh my, just like my daughter.' Only sympathy in her voice, nothing more. 'Think about it, at least, mademoiselle, while you walk.'

'I've walked enough, madame, I want only to go home.'

'The only way back into the city is that way. It might not be too far. Look.'

I squinted towards the end of the bridge. It was far, very far, and for the first time fear quickened within me.

Of course, she was gone when I turned back.

Reluctantly, I made myself walk. What else could I do?

The end drew no closer. A hundred paces made no difference; nor did a second hundred. My starting point, however, was now horribly distant, growing further still when I took a step towards it.

I was caught, between one side and the other, and belonging to neither.

If I could have stopped where I was I would have. Quite what made me turn again, I did not know at the time. I let fear close my eyes but nothing more. In small, trembling steps, I pushed on in the direction the woman had pointed.

Slowly, the perfume of chrysanthemum grew, cedar and lavender shading the breeze. When it was too strong to ignore, I opened my eyes again.

She was dressed in a navy pinafore dress, hair the colour of corn. We were the same height, almost the same age. But she carried no regret, no guilt, no lines of judgement around her deep, sapphire eyes.

So young.

She smiled, saying nothing.

I could think of nothing, could not speak in any case. I could only look at her. It was clearer now, the resemblance. She might have been daughter and granddaughter. Or she may have been the child who would grow to become first one, and then the other woman.

So virginal.

But not naive. Openness yes, but not naiveté. How can I explain this? This young woman had the confidence of youth, yes, with no trace of its arrogance. Instead, there was that quality so easily lost when we become marred by disappointment, when others or ourselves fail to meet whatever standards we choose to set. It was courage. The courage to look without fear of what may be found. Look without judgement.

She cupped my face. I did not flinch as she slowly brushed her thumbs over my closed eyes. Once, twice. I no longer felt I was standing on a bridge. It felt like a mountain, anchored deeply into the earth with me anchored to it. No longer caught between two places.

After the third and last touch, she gently pushed against my eyelids. I opened my eyes.

The sun was beginning to rise over the mountains. It was the last day of Virgo. My birthday.

I was not truly surprised. It took so long to be calm enough to begin to think, to choose to act. So it was no surprise to find Sheridan gone. Apparently, he had left at around the time I stumbled along Spiegelgasse towards my lodging-house.

My friends could see that something had happened. There was speculation and gossip aplenty. I was too preoccupied to notice.

Tzara maintains links throughout Europe. Despite his carefully nurtured pose of Dadaist contempt, he was eager to help. It will take a while but he assured me he should find some hint of my mother's whereabouts in the end.

Ilona, not surprisingly, was anxious for explanations, detail. She relented with bad grace, and then only after extracting my solemn promise to tell her everything some day. Regardless of her disappointment, she was tireless and what she achieved seemed utterly miraculous. Perhaps because it was easier to comprehend.

And now, thanks to Ilona, I sit and reflect on these instants which seemed eternal but lasted… only a handful of weeks. Can I trust myself to truly fathom what happened? Perhaps not, yet I think I feel the first stir of understanding. Lisbon is cold today, the Atlantic cut from flint and seemingly endless. But it is only miles. Just a handful of miles before New York.

Catherine

Catherine wakes in the cell with Kati.

Selene inches onto her side, slides into a sitting position.

Do you think you might ever have lived before? Selene asks Kati.

Kati considers, as though this is an ordinary question. No, she says at last. I don't think I have. I'm not sure what I think about reincarnation. Everyone who believes in it seems to have been someone famous. They're all Napoleons or Catherine the Great.

Selene laughs. Yes, I take your point. But sometimes I think I feel another presence…

Ghosts perhaps, Kati offers. I carry mine with me. I often feel my husband is very close.

He died?

Kati nods. During the Uprising, but he is with me all the time. Sometimes I think I hear his voice, but he never says anything profound. Just small things. Things that keep me going.

Selene waits.

Like — Don't give in to the bastards, Kati. Remember Lilla.

Lilla?

My daughter. She's with Benedek's parents.

I'm so sorry. I didn't know. I mean, you've been so kind about Miriam and all the time...

You've been very sick, Kati says. Lilla is seven. I hate that she won't know me if... if I die. Though she may have forgotten me even if I ever get out of here.

I'm sure her grandparents will tell her lots about you. I'm hoping my mother does that for Miriam.

Yes. They are good people.

And your parents?

They did not approve of Benedek — wrong class, wrong politics...

Ah.

Do you think your 'presence' might be a ghost? Kati looks genuinely interested and Selene has lost the will to obfuscate.

The odd thing is, it's not people from the past so much as people from the future — or rather one particular person. I have dreams in which I'm living another life in the future — an English woman called Catherine, but she's here in Budapest. It's a good life. Even Budapest is better. No more terror. And in the daytime I have this strange sense that she's with me — as though it's night for her and she is dreaming my life. Yesterday... when... when the guard brought that letter, I... Well, sometimes I seem able to leave messages in her time... And sometimes she's left them for me. I wrote out the letter for her, asked her to find out if it's true... I've probably gone mad in here.

Kati shrugs. It sounds... unaccountable... but not mad. I don't think you're crazy even if I don't know what it means. Do you think they would really lie about something like that? She hardly pauses before answering her own question... Yes, they'd do anything for the sheer hell of it, I suppose... the cruelty here is so random...

When the guard brings the meagre food, he pauses at the door, a smug smile on his jowly face.

You'd better enjoy it. Might be your last meal, after all.

Despite her weakness, Selene lurches towards him, grabs his arm. Please tell me the truth. My daughter! Is she...

He strikes her hard, sending her reeling into the wall. Selene crumples, beginning to howl.

You read the letter, sow. He turns towards Kati. Make her shut up or we'll see that she does, he says. He spits in Selene's direction, leaves.

Shh, Selene, Shh. Kati kneels next to her, tries to rock her. Don't give them the satisfaction, she says. And don't believe him. We don't know yet. Your 'presence'... What was her name?

Catherine, Selene whispers, nodding, but her tears keep flowing, quietly now, choked down as Kati goes on comforting her.

Let me help you to the bench, Kati says when the soft guttural sobs subside into sporadic breathless waves of distress. You have to keep hoping, perhaps Catherine will discover...

Selene leans into Kati and hobbles towards the bench. She can feel bruising on her jaw from the blow and along her right arm where she slammed into the wall.

When the beans arrive later, it is another guard, taller, sharp-featured and dead-eyed.

Can you tell me if my daughter is... ? Selene begins, eyes down, her voice quiet.

We've already told you, bitch, he says. You're no longer a mother. He grins, relishing her pain. The whelp's dead. Dead and buried by now, I should think.

Selene begins to wail, the sound turning to an eerie keening...

The guard ignores her, but as he leaves he glares at Kati. Tell the whore to shut her filthy mouth or someone will shut it for her and it will be worse for you if you can't make her stop.

Kati strokes Selene's forehead. Shh, she says, shh, don't let them hurt you any more than...

Budapest, Thursday 2 December 1993

It seems now that I will never hear from Miriam Virág. The letter says that she died on November 30, 1959. If it was right, she would have been buried on December 2. I have no idea how Selene can live with so much loss, but I'm equally terrified that if she is no longer a mother, as the guard told her with such spite and glee, then they might execute her.

And yet, during my migraine yesterday, perhaps the worst I've ever had, Selene was with me and asked for help. She is sure that there is something wrong with the letter, something that doesn't quite add up. A mother's desperate refusal to believe that her child is dead — or genuine intuition? Judith said that her Aunt Marie's family had 'a long and terrible story', but that doesn't begin to describe so much anguish.

How many letters had Marie sent to Selene in prison? In the one about Miriam's death she mentions two previous letters, but Selene only ever had one fragment, not enough to warn her that anything was wrong with her little girl. And the first time a guard mentioned the illness to Selene was November 28. Such heartlessness is unfathomable. If Selene had got the earlier letters, then she would have known that her mother and Miriam were at a new address — and she and Attila could have visited them last Saturday instead of going to somewhere they'd already been turned out of. It would have been appalling to Attila to meet his child when she was sick and for Selene to see her so ill after such a long separation, but at least they could have said goodbye.

But would it have been goodbye? I can't imagine why they would give Selene a fake letter or why Marie would co-operate with such a thing, but Selene is adamant that there is something amiss, even if the handwriting is her mother's. I'm not sure what I can do, but I will ask Margit to help me investigate... again. If we can find the death certificate then at least Selene will know for certain...

Selene Solweig

Catherine wakes screaming.

It is Selene screaming, but the howl has filled her, inhabited her and together they howl for their lost children as...

Simon pulls Catherine to him saying her name over and over.

The wailing subsides to sobs that wrack her body. Selene sinks into Catherine's day as....

Simon clings tightly to her until the howls become intermittent judders, until Catherine is calm. He wipes her face with a clean handkerchief from his pocket.

I'm so afraid that Miriam is dead, she says. I keep trying to think that the letter was a lie... invented to torment Selene, but...

The tears start again, but briefly.

I know, he says. It's all too horrible to take in.

Oh, God! Catherine says, suddenly lurching out of bed.

Sick?

No, sorry. I forgot. I promised Margit I'd meet her at the university this morning.

I'll phone her, Simon says. I'm sure she'll come here. She knows how hard it's been and she'll want you to be well enough for the meal tonight.

You think?

Of course.

Thank you. I don't feel like going out, but now I'm up, a bath would be good.

Go and get one. I'll phone.

Waiting for Margit, Catherine paces anxiously.

I need to do more research into the Motherbook, she says eventually. I have to see if Miriam's death is recorded.

Well, at least you have an address now, Simon says.

Catherine nods, sits down at her desk and writes:

Miriam Marie Virág, born July 7, 1955, Népszinház utca, 19, Budapest VIII. Died November 30, 1959, Magdolna utca, 25, Budapest VIII.

Simon stands behind her and begins to rub her shoulders.

I hate to believe it, but if Marie's letter was real and Miriam died, that would explain why we've had no response to the adverts. But, if that's the case, I have to see the record for myself. Does that make any sense?

Simon nods, smiles. I don't think any of this is about sense, but of course you need to check.

You realise it's a different registration district, Margit points out when she arrives. I'm not sure we should be leaning on the services of the lovely Hanna Farkas to go outside her own district yet again, and not all officials are so accommodating.

I know, Catherine agrees, but I have to see the record before I leave Budapest.

Margit spreads her hands. Of course. I knew you would say that. I'll make some calls.

Right, Margit says when she returns from phoning. Our friend Hanna will indeed help us once again and András will deal with picking up the paperwork. I don't want you trailing around the streets today.

András?

Yes, of course. He thinks we are losing touch with reality, but he's a good friend, a loyal man.

Thank you, Margit.

Now, Margit says briskly. I will cook and you will eat. Both of you. This is my condition.

Fair enough, Catherine consents.

They are eating goulash soup when András arrives.

I'm afraid there's nothing, he says. You are certain of the details?

Yes, Catherine says. Absolutely. Miriam Marie Virág, born July 7 1955, Népszinház utca, 19, Budapest VIII. Died November 30 1959, Magdolna utca, 25, Budapest VIII.

The birth, as you know, is in the records. But the death… it's not there, Catherine.

Is she alive? Catherine ask, her voice almost inaudible.

That we don't know, András points out. It may mean many things — that she moved district, or left the country, or that she died, but at another address or another date… I'm sorry, Catherine…

So I might never be able to hand on Sándor's sketchbook, Catherine says and begins to cry, apologising as she does so.

No, no apologies, Margit says firmly. But you must finish the soup and then you must rest. It's important you make it to the farewell meal. Everyone from the university will be there to say goodbye. Viktor Kovács. is bringing his new girlfriend, so we're all curious, and of course Zsuzsanna Makai and György Kalmár want to say goodbye to you too, not to mention the endlessly helpful Hanna Farkas.

Catherine looks anxiously at Simon.

Of course we'll be there, he says. It's important for us too, isn't it, Catherine?

Yes, she says. Yes. There have to be proper goodbyes.

352

Margit quickly wipes a hand across her face. I'm going to miss you both so much, she says.

We all will, András adds. We'll miss you both. You have to promise to come back to visit us. But for now, we should go and let you rest. It will be a big meal tonight and a big day tomorrow — your last in Budapest. He pauses. And Attila's last day, he says quietly. He pauses again. Tonight we must drink to many things.

When they are alone, Catherine turns to Simon. Could she be alive?

I really don't know, Simon says, but Selene has never been wrong before — all the details she has given you have turned up in official records — all except this one, the one she said had something not right about it, the one she asked you to help her disprove...

Quite. Do you think I could phone Judith again? I mean, I don't want to dredge up terrible memories, but...

What would you say?

I'm not quite sure, but she seems like our only hope...

Perhaps, but Margit and András are right about how important tonight is. All these people have done so much for us here — it would be terrible if you got another migraine and couldn't make it...

I know, but I think I have to do this, even if it means rather fudging the details to make up a story... And then I will sleep and be ready for this evening... I promise. I'll make it to tonight's dinner, whatever I learn.

Catherine?

Sorry to ring again so soon, Catherine begins…

No, no, it's good to hear from you. Is there something else I can help you with?

It's going to sound rather odd, Catherine says, but… I mentioned I'd read something about your aunt meeting Attila József in Paris. Well, I visited recently and went to what would have been their gallery. I met a lovely man, Marcel Delval, whose father, Charles, had worked with Marie and Sándor. I told him I was researching in Budapest and he asked me if I might try to find the daughter, Selene, or some other relative. He had a sketchbook that belonged to Sándor and wanted the family to have it. His father was ill and had kept it for them for years…

Catherine pauses, wondering if any of this sounds convincing, before going on — Anyway, I asked my contacts at the university here to do some research, but we haven't been able to find anything… And then, after I spoke to you… I mean, I hadn't realised you had a family connection — it's so extraordinary — but you mentioned that Selene, Marie's daughter had died… so maybe I could bring you the sketchbook when I get back to…

Well, it should go to Miriam really, Judith says.

Miriam?

Yes, Selene's daughter.

She's alive? But why didn't Marie leave the hamsa to her?

She'd disappeared, Judith says.

Disappeared?

354

They were terrible times in Hungary, Catherine. Selene was in prison and Marie could hardly feed herself and the little girl. They lost their apartment and ended up in a terrible place. Aunt Marie was afraid to go out of the flat to get food. And then Miriam got sick, almost died, though it was rare to die of scarlet fever, even in those days. But the families of prisoners had terrible lives and living in a street full of prostitutes and criminals... Well, anyway... The doctor who'd seen Miriam while she was ill had a son who worked for the prison services. He suggested that he could help Marie get out of the country with the little girl, that she could get to Paris, give the child a proper home. Apparently he told her that as a foreign national she would be allowed to leave, but that he could only get papers for her grandchild if she had been officially wiped from the records so they could give her a new identity. So Marie went along with a terrible plan to tell Selene that Miriam had died of fever in order to get a fake death certificate and be able to take Miriam with her. Of course, he didn't tell Marie what would happen to Selene. He told her that his son would let Selene know that her mother and daughter were safe as soon as they left.

Judith pauses. It's a terribly convoluted tale, Catherine. Do you want to hear all of this?

Yes, Catherine says, go on.

So Marie wrote the letter and... Well, she did get to Paris with Miriam, but Selene...

Oh!

She was never certain what happened. I mean, not so many women were executed... she might have lingered in prison... might have died much later, but afterwards, Marie heard that only mothers were exempted from execution... and she was never able to find Selene... so naturally she thought... She always blamed herself.

And Miriam?

Marie told her the whole story when she was eighteen. On her birthday... and Miriam left — walked out taking nothing. Marie never heard from her again. The hamsa was among the gifts she was going to give her that day, but of course...

So she might be alive?

Yes, there's no reason to think otherwise. She'd be only thirty-eight.

Thank you, Catherine says. Thank you so much.

Catherine

Catherine wakes in a cell.

There is no writing on the wall, only Kati and Selene.

Catherine forces Selene's body to sit, writes on the wall — 'Miriam did not die in 1959'.

Later, Kati rouses Selene gently. It is dark, long before dawn. Try to drink, Kati coaxes. You're so hot.

Selene feels herself drift towards some dark pit where confused memories swirl and ebb like the spectres of dreams that disappear as soon as they are observed.

She sees a yard, walls rising, blind, mute, slabbing out sky. Her guts twist. Air ices lungs, skin burns cold, muscles tremble in unfamiliar shuffle. Don't look back. Stagger on — one foot, the next, bleak wall grasped for balance. Don't cry. Don't fall. Don't piss. Chant in her head: right foot, left foot, right... Falling — snow — falling, one flake...

a train sounds in the distance…

You look pale, Zsófia says.

I thought I heard a train and all the blood in me ran cold,
Selene tells her.

She turns down a corridor, hears another train… is by a lake…
and there is…

Selene, Kati calls softly. Selene, try to wake up. Just a mouthful
of water, then you can sleep till morning. Look, Selene,
Kati's voice strains with tears. There's writing on the wall
— Catherine must have written it for you.

Selene moans, turns away, not seeing…

…watches Attila walk towards the village, retraces her steps
telling herself the shaking is simply the cold November air…
hears a distant train, the click of her feet on the new green
linoleum.

…hears another train… I didn't think I'd see you again, he says
— or at least I thought — I supposed that I'd imagined you,
that perhaps I was getting worse —

At the restaurant he buys her porcini soup and pork mignon.
She drinks pálinka with relish. Maybe he will live, she thinks
to herself. Maybe I'll wake up in 1953 and there will be a new
collection published by the great Attila József…

Please Selene. Kati struggles to lift her, to coax her to sit up,
tries to drip water into her mouth, but Selene chokes and
coughs, rolls towards the wall…

In the bathroom Selene looks at her face in the pitted mirror. Her skin is grey. I'm an old twenty-seven, she says to her reflection, peering closer, closer, so the face dissolves into shapes — into forms melting — into reflections on the face of a lake —

Selene! Attila runs towards her as she turns to his voice, scoops her into his arms, lifts her in the air laughing.

At his sister's house, everyone out for the day, she cooks for him, leaves him her precious copy of *The Ballad of the Sad Café*. When they make love they are each a surprise to the other.

Just some water, Kati tries again, but Selene only whimpers softly and huddles into herself. She feels Kati dabbing at her forehead with a corner of the blanket that she has dampened, drifts into...

...the station, where Tibor tugs Zsófia further into the train as it pulls out and they run along the corridor waving to Selene until they run out of train and she stands, waving into the smoke.

Selene stands on a platform, another train pulling away in front of her, smoke clearing.

Selene! Attila runs towards her...

I had a baby, Miriam, Selene tells him at last. She was born on July 27, nine months after we —

A train sounds behind her and she turns, dizzy — falls into the arms of —

Attila, catches her on the platform, smiles.

But another train sounds far off… and the guard spits at her feet. Keep moving, bitch, and keep in line.

Kati struggles to move her again, saying something about water, about Miriam… She feels herself flushed, dehydrated, every limb burning, heavy… falls into a dazed reverie…

…hears the sound of a train whistling far off… nearer… finds herself on a platform gazing towards Attila.

He rushes towards her. Selene! Just five days. Oh, but you look… he puts a hand to her forehead. You're hot, very hot…

Through here, Attila says, pointing towards a short cut between stationary trains on the sidings.

Selene pulls back.

We'll be Quixote and his Sancho, taking on the giants. Fearless. He pulls on her hand and dodges her around the towering rolling stock.

Just then they came in sight of thirty or forty windmills that rose from the plain… Attila quotes, laughing. And see we only have three or four giants.

…Mama! She sings into the intercom outside her mother's apartment. Mama, it's Selene.

…Last woman here was a filthy Jew., a hoarse voice says. Heard her only whelp was a little Jewess traitor and whore…. And no, I don't know where the filthy old bag and her bastard grandchild have gone.

Please wake up, Selene, please don't die…

You won't die tomorrow, Attila, she tells him, not mentioning the day after that.

He lifts his head higher, smiles, takes her in his arms again....

Selene wakes, dazed, strains to hear a train, wills herself to be in 1937, but to no effect. Kati drips water into her parched mouth and she manages to swallow before dozing again, hot and restless...

When she wakes, Kati is kneeling at her side. Selene, look, Kati says.

Selene gazes at the wall, trying to make sense... Miriam?

It was a lie, Kati says, the letter was a lie. Your 'presence' must have left this for you.

Selene breathes deeply, almost smiles. She lets Kati drip water into her, but chokes on it, coughing. She falls back onto the bench, whispers Miriam's name as she loses consciousness...

When the guards arrive, Kati has fallen asleep on the floor next to Selene's bench. She rouses Selene as gently as possible, stands by the bench.

The tall one leans on the doorjamb, brash and vindictive, joking with the stocky, jowly guard about how the Jewish sow is no longer a mother.

Maybe you'd like a chance to try for another child? The lanky guard calls across the cell.

The other laughs roughly, moves across the space and prods Selene off the bench. She wavers, standing, teetering, but doesn't fall.

Where are you… Kati begins, but the dumpy guard raises his arm and Kati cowers away, slides down the wall, head in her hands. But she is a mother, she whispers.

What was that? the guard growls, spitting towards her.

Kati begins to weep.

They goad Selene along faceless corridors, into an enclosed, dank courtyard, the sky just beginning to lighten as the sun's angle shifts towards day. She falls as they reach the open air, cold, the sky tingeing with winter dawn. She struggles to her feet, sees the pole ahead, three men standing by it, waiting for her… she stumbles again, feels uneven grit and wood beneath her, looks down at train tracks… disoriented, she looks up at the station near Lake Balaton….

Selene, I'm sorry! Attila calls down the tracks.

She turns as he runs towards her.

Don't be sad. His voice sounds further away than it is…

Just then they came in sight of thirty or forty windmills that rose from the plain…

Get off the tracks, Attila calls, waving his arms. Be safe, Selene. Goodbye!

He moves towards her along the track, gesturing to her, and she sees a wagon begin to move behind him.

Attila! She shouts. Attila! Attila! No! Her screams are swallowed in the cold air, not dawn, but twilight, the outline of the train visible against the darkening sky…

In the dimming light, Selene thinks he shakes his head. I can't be with you, Selene, he calls. And Flóra... Flóra will never marry me... Don't be sad, Selene...

She shouts again, moves towards him... stumbles, lurches and trips, gesturing wildly towards the rumble of the wagon barrelling towards him, but he does not try to move out of its way, half turns towards it, places an arm on the track.

Attila! No!... Selene closes her eyes as his arm is crushed... as he twists towards the wagon and...

She pitches forward, retching, dazed... she is in the yard, the executioner and his assistants waiting by the pole, rope swaying, steps to climb...

Catherine wakes screaming, Simon beside her, holding her and stroking her forehead, saying her name over and over.

The clock says 5 a.m.

She's gone, Catherine tells Simon. They're both gone. Selene saw Attila on the tracks, saw the wagon hit... and then, she chokes, breathes deeply... they hung her. Attila saw her fall as she was taken into the yard to be... murdered...

Simon holds her tightly, rocks her, says nothing.

He killed himself, Simon, but he wanted her to be safe... wanted to save her. They died together, separated by twenty-two years... but together.

It's all we have sometimes, Simon says quietly. We can't always save each other, not always, but we can love, we can bear witness.

Did any of it happen? I mean...

Is that what matters? A poet desperate for love, yearning for life to be other than it was, ended his life on a railway track. Selene, or people like her, died in the aftermath of an uprising meant to make the world better. Do the story and the facts have to match?

Catherine smiles. No. No, they don't, but I'll write the story anyway. Since he was a child Attila was haunted by witnessing a suicide at a station. He told his family it felt like someone had died in his place. I wonder how those who witnessed his death felt afterwards. I understand what Margit and András mean about suicide being the only possible way Attila's life could end now — it wasn't simply foreshadowed, but somehow integral, not just to him as a person, but to his ideas, to his moment.

Yes, Simon says. But, if we can bear it, we have to stay alive for each other for as long as possible.

Yes, Catherine agrees. We have to stay alive and Miriam's still out there somewhere... we might find her yet. *For hope is always born at the same time as love.* And they had so much love.

Yes, an extraordinary love, Simon says, wrapping his arms around her. Like ours.

Catherine smiles. Yes, so let's stay alive, for them and for us. There's a remedy for all things except death.

Acknowledgments

The following books, websites and interviews were valuable background reading:

Bahun, Sanja & Haynes, John Cinema, *State Socialism and Society in the Soviet Union and Eastern Europe*

Caron, Vicki, *The Path to Vichy: antisemitism in France in the 1930s*, The United States Holocaust Memorial Museum 2005 @ https://www.ushmm.org/m/pdfs/Publication_OP_2005-07-02.pdf

Esbenshade, Richard S, *Symbolic Geographies and the Politics of Hungarian Identity in the 'Populist-Urbanist Debate,' 1925-44*

Farkas, Tamás, *Jewish Name Magyarization in Hungary*, PhD thesis: Eötvös Loránd University @ http://www.academia.edu/2766198/Jewish_Name_Magyarization_in_Hungary

József, Etelka, TV interview @ http://holnapmagazin.hu/articles.php?article_id=2296

Kabdebo, Thomas, *Attila József, Can you take on this awesome life?* Cardinal Press 1997

Makai, Zsuzsannam Obituary @ http://www.jatarsasag.hu/2015/02/bucsu-makai-zsuzsannatol-19292015.html

Marsh, Norman S, *Justice in Hungary Today: Third Report of the International Commission of Jurists on the Hungarian Situation and the Rule of Law* @ http://icj.wpengine.netdna-cdn.com/wp-content/uploads/1958/01/Hungary-justice-thematic-report-1958-eng.pdf

Murray Davis, Robert, 'Desperate, but not serious: the situation of Hungarian Literature in the Nineties', in *World Literature Today*, January 2000.

https://www.thefreelibrary.com/Desperate+but+Not+Serious%3A+The+Situation+of+Hungarian+Literature+in...-a062655948

Sebestyen, Victor, *Twelve Days, Revolution 1956*, Orion Books, 1988

The following are quoted from or alluded to in the novel:

Ady, Endre, poems: 'Because you love me' & 'I should love to be loved'

Biblical quotations are from Psalm 91 and Deuteronomy 6:4-5. New Revised Standard Version Bible, copyright © 1989 the Division of Christian Education of the National Council of the Churches of Christ in the United States of America. Used by permission. All rights reserved.

Cervantes, Miguel, *Don Quixote*, Gutenberg Project edition, translated by John Ormsby.

Craig, Adam, 'The Third Face of Virgo' (used as the story told by Simon) & taken from the short story collection, *High City Walk*, Cinnamon Press, 2017.

Eliot, George, *Middlemarch*

Forster, E M, *A Room with a View* ch 3 & *Howard's End* c.22

József, Attila, poems: 'Ode'; 'Only You Should Read My Poems' & 'Transparent lion'

Petöfi, Sándor, poem: 'The Tree'.

The characters in this novel are fictional except where the book intersects with the history of Hungary and well-known historical figures are mentioned. Attila József is a historic figure and one of the twentieth centuries greatest poets, who committed suicide on December 3, 1937. I researched his life as background for this novel, but his meetings with Selene and his words in the novel are purely my creation. Similarly, whilst his family were real people and I have read interviews with them and articles about them, particularly in the cases of Etelka József and Zsuzsanna Makai, their portrayals here are heavily fictionalised. Catherine and Selene are entirely fictional creations, though young women like Selene did take part in the 1956 Uprising, and were imprisoned and, in some cases, executed by hanging, for example the 25 year-old medical student, Ilona Tóth.